WALKING MOUNTAIN

Joan Lennon lives in the Kingdom of Fife, in a tall house overlooking the River Tay. She writes about Victorian detectives, a miner boy on a forgotten planet, short Vikings, medieval orphans, talking gargoyles, a ferret princess and the occasional flying horse. In her most recent novel, *Silver Skin*, which was shortlisted for the Scottish Teenage Book Prize 2017, sci-fi meets prehistory when a time traveller from the far future accidentally ends up in ancient Scotland. To find out more about Joan's books, visit her website:

www.joanlennon.co.uk

Walking Mountain

JOAN LENNON

BC

First published in 2017 by
BC Books, an imprint of
Birlinn Limited
West Newington House
10 Newington Road
Edinburgh
EH9 1QS
www.bcbooksforkids.co.uk

ISBN 978 1 78027 456 0

British Library Cataloguing-in-Publication Data
A catalogue record for this book is available from the British Library

Designed by James Hutcheson
Typeset by Initial Typesetting Services, Edinburgh

Printed and bound by Grafica Veneta, Italy

This book is dedicated with thanks to the original members of
Team Walking Mountain:
Lindsey Fraser, Callum Heitler, Maureen Lennon
and Jamie Zeppa

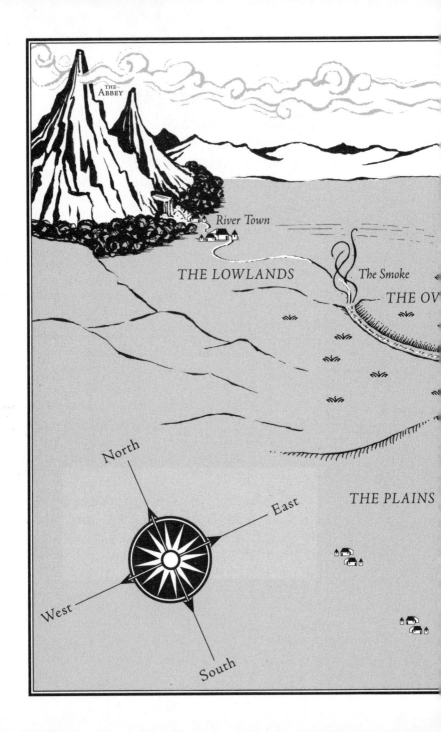

BOOK ONE

Look to the Mountain

Thanks be to Mother Mountain. She is the arrow of light and the giver of life. The rain-clouds are her skirts: she wraps her shoulders in the deep snow; her head brushes the sky. She is the eater of death and her footprint is the world. Thanks be to Mother Mountain.

(High Land Prayer)

CHAPTER ONE

The Rogue

It shouldn't have happened.

There were strict rules about leaving the herd to its own devices.

That close to a busy solar system, the Drivers should have been on constant high alert. They were experienced. They understood the dangers. But it had been so long since they'd had a party, and the herd of meteors had seemed so peaceful, grazing contentedly on the outer asteroid belt. There had been no hint of trouble, and the Drivers had let down their guard. They tethered their comets in a circle and mingled and danced and shared stories and jokes and laughter.

After the party, when they counted the herd in preparation for setting off once again, no one could believe it at first. They checked, and checked again. But there was no denying the stark fact. The count was one short.

One of the meteors had escaped. And not just a small one. A huge bull meteor.

The Drivers looked at each other. Waiting.

Who will go after it?

There was a pause, and then . . .

I will.

I will.

I . . . will.

And so it was decided. The herd must move on. The

Drivers knew that if they stayed they'd over-graze the belt. The three volunteer Drivers would go into the solar system, find the rogue meteor and bring it away again before it could do any harm. Then they would do their best to catch up with the rest of the herd.

If not, we will meet at Harvest, said one of the volunteers.

At Harvest? Surely long before that! squeaked the youngest.

Of course. Of course, they reassured.

There was no time to lose. Three by three, the Drivers turned their comets and began to manipulate the magnetic field around the edges of the herd, gently detaching the meteors from the asteroids and nudging them back into the depths of space. Back onto the Great Circuit.

The route was unimaginably old and long. Beings shorter-lived than Drivers would never survive long enough to complete the great elliptical way. Even Drivers themselves rarely volunteered for the trip more than once. But it was known as *the* great adventure. To gather a herd, gradually adding to it, visiting grazing grounds among the asteroid belts of the universe, drawing feral meteors in by the strength of the others' magnetic field, increasing the bulk of the individuals. Always moving on, round the great loop of the Circuit, back to the Drivers' Homeworld and the Harvest, where minerals in the meteors would be processed into a silvery nutrient dust to feed everyone.

That was the reason for the Circuit.

To feed the Driver world – but, in the process, *to do no harm*. Driver philosophy had few tenets and this was the chief of them. *Do no harm.* Something a rogue meteor from a herd could do a lot of.

The three Drivers in search of the missing meteor moved anxiously inwards towards the system's central star. They checked each moon and planet they passed for any sign of recent impact. They lost precious time at an inner asteroid belt, looking for any indication that the rogue was somewhere near, accruing yet more mass.

We should have found it by now, the youngest of the three wittered nervously. *We should have found it.*

The others said nothing, but urged their comet forward at ever greater speed.

And then they did find it. They spotted their rogue in time to see the blue-green planet it was streaking towards, but too late to adjust its path. All the herding skills the Drivers had amassed were of no use. It was too late to send all those tons of accelerating rock off the collision course, send the meteor safely past the planet, back towards clear space.

There was nothing they could do.

In silent horror, the Drivers watched the sudden flare as the rogue screamed through the blue-green planet's atmosphere, trailing a tail of flame. They watched the sickening judder of the world as it hit, the giant circle of the meteor's impact growing outwards at ferocious speed. They watched the dust and ash from a hundred triggered volcanoes begin to rise up, a hundred plumes that caught on the winds and melded into one great towering canopy, till the entire planet was wrapped in a blanket of grey.

The Drivers knew what the greyness meant.

They knew what they had to do.

CHAPTER TWO

The Aeons Passed, Until . . .

'Wadipa, you bake-brained, stiff-backed, stubborn old groat, you're not *listening* to me! After all the years we've known each other, do you seriously think I'd make something like that *up*? And if I *did*, would I climb all the way to the top of the world just to tell *you* about it? Put some more logs on that fire, for the sake of Snow – I'm freezing to death!'

Outside, Pema paused, surprised. They hardly ever had visitors. Even their nearest neighbours were a day's climb away. Besides, who would think of this balmy spring morning as *cold*? He shoved open the cottage door with his shoulder – his hands were full of the last of the lichen his grandmother wanted for her end-of-winter tonic – and managed to bang his head, yet again, on the lintel.

Snows! When would he get used to this latest growth spurt?

He tried to rub his head with his arm and dropped half the lichen onto the floor.

'Pema,' sighed his grandmother.

'Sorry, Dawa.' He bent to pick up the mess while still holding on to the rest, before his grandmother took it all from him and shooed him out of the way, tsk-ing. She went to the window, where the light was better, to clean any twigs and dirt out of the lichen. The other ingredients were already bubbling in a pot on the fire.

'Pema! Hello, lad!' bellowed their visitor. Then, in a

loud whisper, he added to Wadipa, 'That's *Pema*? What have you been feeding him?' It was Zeppa, all the way from Jungle Head. So that was why the room was so hot. Zeppa was a short, blustery man, an old friend of Pema's grandparents. He lived in the settlement right at the bottom of the Mountain, where it met the green Jungle. He was a sort of unofficial headman down there, in charge of the trading post where the High Land people brought their cheeses and wool and leather to exchange for weird and exotic goods like celeriac and botatoes brought up from the Low Lands, and even the occasional oil-powered gadget all the way from Elysia, the City by the Sea. Zeppa was born for the job, right at the heart of everything, knowing everybody, and everybody's business. Pema had last been to Zeppa's shop with his grandfather the summer before. He hated Jungle Head – the heat, the humidity, the way the air seemed too thick to breathe.

'Holy Mother Mountain, can you not shut the door? I'm perishing here.'

Pema grinned as he pushed the door to.

'You talk to this mad man, boy, before he melts my brain with his craziness and his jungle blood,' Wadipa grunted, wiping the sweat from his face.

Zeppa glared at his old friend and huddled himself tighter inside his coat.

'Why, what's happened?' asked Pema. What in the name of Snow was so important it had made their visitor drag himself all this way up the Mountain? 'Oh!' He squatted down beside Zeppa's chair. 'I didn't know you had a dugg!'

Zeppa grunted. 'I didn't, but someone had to take the poor brute in. Hey, careful!' he warned as Pema reached out a hand. 'He's a biter!'

'Don't worry,' said Wadipa. 'The lad's got a way with beasts.'

'He'll need more than a way with this one,' grunted the shopkeeper, but he moved aside to let Pema get near.

The dugg was pressed against the wall, its lips pulled back in a silent snarl. Pema hunkered down, crooning low in his throat, not staring. He sent calming, you-can-trust-me thoughts to the animal. The snarl became a whimper and, after a while, the dugg crawled over to lean up against him. Pema gently stroked the dugg's chest and under its chin, then ran his hands over its sides and back. He could feel the ribs starkly under the rough coat.

It didn't take special gifts to recognise the animal had been abused.

'How'd he get in such a state?' Pema demanded through gritted teeth. 'I'd like to get my hands on whoever did this!'

Zeppa made a warning gesture and shook his head. 'Best not speak ill of the dead, boy.'

'What?'

'It's what I've been trying to tell your grandparents. About the Mountain. You know it's been getting worse – the lurchings and the judderings, the splits and the chasms coming out of nowhere, the avalanches … Well, I don't need to tell you about that.' Zeppa nodded to Dawa, and reached out a hand and awkwardly patted Wadipa on the knee. Their son and daughter-in-law, Pema's parents, had been killed in an avalanche the year Pema was born.

The shopkeeper cleared his throat. 'We've all had to learn to live with the Mountain's moods. It's the price we pay for the new strip of land that she leaves us every year, as she walks north. But trust me, *all that's changed.*'

Even in the heat of the room, Pema felt a sudden chill. Zeppa noticed him shudder and shook his head.

'None of us wants to believe it,' he said. 'That poor beast's owner, for one. As bad-tempered an old ... Well, as I say, best not to malign the dead. He refused to believe that he was in danger. He thought we were trying to trick him or steal from him when all we were trying to do was *warn* him – get him to leave – for his own safety! "Get off my land or I'll set the dugg on you!" was all he said, and since everyone knew he kept the poor thing half-starved and crazy, no one wanted to tangle with it. And the next morning it was too late. When we went back, we found that in the night the Mountain had done more than just shudder or shake. It had walked ... *backwards.* There was nothing left of the old man or his house. Only the dog, whimpering at the full stretch of its chain, the Mountain's edge only inches from its nose.'

Pema stared, horrified.

It was no secret that the Mountain walked. It had been moving north at a steady pace for as long as anyone could remember, and who knew how long before that. Every year, the story was the same: when the winter rains ended, another new strip of bare ground was revealed at the base of the Mountain, ready for the Jungle to creep out its green fingers and claim it. That was the way it was. That was the way it had always been.

9

'What are you saying?' said Wadipa.

Zeppa slammed his fists into the arms of the chair. 'I've *said* what I'm saying! How many times do you need told? It's turned around! *The Mountain's walking south!*'

The dugg whimpered, unhappy with the raised voices. Pema soothed its ears absently, comforting himself as much as the animal. His mind struggled to take in what Zeppa had just told them.

In the silence, the quiet shuffling sounds of Dawa's fingers sorting the lichen eased the tightness in his chest. Very few things agitated his grandmother.

'And they all expect you to fix it,' she said to the shop-keeper, her voice amused.

Zeppa turned to her, wringing his hands. 'That's been the worst of it, Dawa. They *do* expect me to fix it! Me! Stop the *Mountain!*' His voice dropped to a hoarse whisper. 'I don't know what to do.'

'Well, of course you don't,' said Dawa calmly. She washed her hands and dried them on her apron. 'How in the world could you? No, the Mountain is the Sisters' responsibility. Always has been.'

Zeppa looked doubtful. 'The old Abbess' door was always open, true enough. But this new one, well, you know how people like to gossip and I've heard—'

'We don't want to know,' said Dawa firmly. 'Going to the Abbey is what needs to happen. But not you. By the time you got there, you'd be too ill to speak – it's far too high for you. You can't deny you've got a killing headache already, and we're but halfway to the Abbey. The sooner you go back down to Jungle level, where you belong, the better.'

Wadipa stirred, but she turned on him before he could speak.

'No, you're not going either. I need help with the cheeses and the gows, and I'm not having you crippling yourself with a two-day climb. We're sending Pema to the Sisters, just as soon as he's changed his shirt.'

Pema's hand froze on the dugg's head.

What?

Wadipa and Zeppa started to protest at the same time.

'He's just a boy!'

'It's my responsibility!'

Dawa ignored them both. She turned to where her grandson squatted on the floor. 'No time to waste. Close your mouth, boy! What are you waiting for?'

Well, for one thing, Pema had to wait for Zeppa and Wadipa to argue with Dawa some more. And then he had to wait while Dawa considered which of the winter cheeses was the best to send to the Sisters, and then she fussed over the fact that because Pema had grown again his best shirt was getting short in the arms (if the world turned upside down she'd be as cool as dew, but a too-short sleeve on public display threw her into a tizzy). And then he had to wait for Wadipa to wonder whether the bothy Pema would be spending the first night of his journey in would still have a roof after such a hard winter as they'd just had, and *then* to tell him in painstaking detail what the best way up the Mountain to the Abbey was, and then the second-best way, in case there'd been slippages since the autumn, and then the third best, in case of, well, just in case.

It was too much, too fast! His head was spinning. When

he'd got out of bed this morning, Pema's biggest worry had been how to get through the day without knocking himself out on doors. Now he was being told that the Mountain had turned in its tracks and was starting to eat the world and kill people, and somehow now it was his job to climb up to the White Women and get them to do something about it.

He'd never been to the Abbey. *I'll knock something over! I won't know what to say! Dawa would know. Why doesn't she go?* But he knew why. His grandparents were old, though he rarely thought about that. He looked at them suddenly, as if for the first time.

'Will you be all right without me?' he whispered to Dawa, as Zeppa and his grandfather argued about something manly on the other side of the room. She just patted his cheek. She had to reach up to do it, which made Pema feel even more wobbly inside.

'Take the marmole,' she told him. 'He'll fret if you leave him behind.'

With a dry tongue, Pema clucked to his pet. Jeffrey, a friendly rodent the size of a kitten, trundled over, climbed his trouser leg and settled into his coat pocket . . .

And then, suddenly, there was nothing left to wait for, and he was on his way, alone (except for Jeffrey), head buzzing, on the long climb to the Abbey of the Sisters of the Snow.

CHAPTER THREE

The White Women

The Sisters were an ancient order. No one knew where the first of them came from, or what had possessed them to set up their community amongst the Mountain's frozen rocks and perpetual ice. The Abbey buildings clung to narrow ledges and crags not far below the very summit of the Mountain, and were as often as not hidden from sight by banks of cloud or mist. But on a clear day, the home of the White Women could be seen for great distances, glinting like ice in the sun, looking almost as if it had grown there naturally.

Everyone regarded the White Women with great respect, even awe. They knew about things that were important but, well, ferly. Out of the ordinary. They studied ancient writings, practised powerful medicine, helped the High Land people when they struggled with questions about life and death. They taught the people their prayers. And they looked after the Mountain. Everybody knew that was the way it was. And, as far as Pema was concerned, the way it was was fine.

Everything had always just made sense to Pema. Life in the High Lands might be dangerous but they were all *known* dangers – avalanches, wulfs, the slip of a foot on the edge of a chasm. The rest of the world, though – that was another thing altogether. Pema had listened with horrified fascination to the stories and rumours from beyond the

Jungle that trickled up even as far as his grandparents' cottage: tales of harsh, strange religions; of more people stuffed into the towns and countryside than there were snowflakes in a storm, each one desperate to outwit the others; of men called Protectors who stole children for their chain gangs; of soulless metal machines. Sometimes Pema would stare into mid-air, imagining an evil-hearted Low Lander watching him from behind a tree, or what it would feel like being kidnapped and enslaved, while a vicious Enforcer shouted at him from the back of an oil-fired metal beast, *Faster! FASTER!*

But then a gow would try to put her foot in the milk bucket, or Dawa would call for help with turning the cheeses, or he'd spot some delicious-looking mushrooms sprouting by a log. And he'd give himself a shake and be grateful he was a gowboy who need never worry about the monstrousness of the great wide world.

But if Zeppa was right and the Mountain had suddenly decided to go crazy, maybe the monstrousness was coming *here*. Maybe there were dangers he hadn't even imagined . . .

But that's the Sisters' problem, he reminded himself. *My job's to tell them what Zeppa told us. They'll know what to do. Dawa said so.*

Meantime, now that he was on his way, it did feel good to be out in the clear spring air, stretching his legs to their full, new length. Jeffrey the marmole was a reassuring weight in his pocket, his head and front paws sticking out as he watched the world go by, making chirruping comments. They made the halfway bothy in good time. There wasn't a lot of comfort in the hut but, in spite of Dawa's worry, its roof had survived the winter intact. Pema cut some fresh heather for a bed and he and Jeffrey slept surprisingly well.

The next day started well too, and by noon he'd reached the snow line. The sun glinted off the whiteness and the mica in the exposed rock glittered. Pema was glad of his quilted coat and hat, glad of being out in the high, thin air – glad just generally – and then, all of a sudden, the path swung round an icy boulder and he let out a strangled gasp.

There it was: the Abbey of the Sisters of the Snow, clinging to the mountainside above like a vision in a dream. It was so ... white. And majestic and impossible and awe-inspiring.

All his doubts returned in a rush. What was he doing here? He was the last person they should have sent!

'I could do with a break,' he muttered to Jeffrey. 'Let's finish the breadcake.'

A marmole never says no to a snack.

So Pema set them up a little picnic there beside the path, and Jeffrey was chirpy and cheerful, snitching more of the food than was his share and then dancing away with it across the rocks until he was just out of reach.

'You filcher! That was *mine*!'

Jeffrey made a rude comment in marmole. Pema, laughing, turned away for one moment. The next, there was a horrible scream and a fierce rush of wind that made him cower and cover his head with his arms. It was only for an instant. But when Pema looked again, there was ...

... nothing.

'JEFFREY!'

Pema leapt up, staring wildly from side to side, but

there was no sign of the marmole or whatever had taken him. Rabbid? Fur snake? Dentrice? No predator he could think of could disappear like that. Then his eye caught the drift of a falling feather and he looked up.

An ice eagle.

'Jeffrey,' he whispered in despair. And then he saw the marmole move in the grey claws. Still alive!

The eagle was labouring to gain height. It had found a thermal, but the marmole's struggling kept knocking it off balance, making it lose its place in the ascending spiral. Pema yelled and began to run and almost immediately fell on the jagged ice, scraping the skin off his hands. He scrambled to his feet – he must watch the path as well as the bird.

It's my fault. It's my fault. The words kept pounding round and round in his head, keeping time with the pounding of his feet. *It's my fault.*

Twice more he slipped on the ice, sliding perilously close to a sheer drop. He cursed himself – a year ago he would never have been so clumsy. The path crawled up the mountainside in zigs and zags, while the bird had the whole clear sky to climb through. It was starting to get away from him. He had a moment of pure panic when a wisp of mist hid the eagle from sight, then a wind shredded the cloud and he saw it again.

But higher. Always higher.

Jeffrey . . .

Pema struggled on, his breath tearing in his throat. The next stretch of the path demanded his complete attention, thinning along the edge of a deadly chasm. He took it at a suicidal speed. When things levelled out again, he peered up desperately, searching the sky for the eagle and its prey, only to find that everything had changed. The bird had reached the apex of its climb and was beginning a long swoop down again.

It was going to land!

Pema plunged forward round an outcrop of rock and saw ahead of him a white wall, twice his height, with a set of tall, solid wooden doors tight shut within it. And it was clear the bird was aiming for the other side.

'No!' Pema tried to scream, but his labouring lungs could only produce a squawk. Without breaking stride he bent, scooped up a handful of jagged icy stones and began to throw.

His first shots went wide, but at least they caused the eagle to jink aside. Pema forced himself to stop running and take careful aim. He shook his head, trying to clear his vision – white spots fizzed in his eyes and every muscle quivered. Jeffrey hung from those brutal claws like a sad rag, not moving anymore. The eagle wasn't in great shape either. Its beak gaped as it gasped for breath.

One last chance . . .

The eagle was barely higher than the top of the white wall when the stone found its mark. The bird lurched silently in mid-air, too blown to cry out, and then it and the marmole plunged earthward . . . on the other side of the wall.

Pema staggered forward and fell against the gate, pounding at it with both fists, half-shouting, half-sobbing, 'Let me in! Let me in!' He kept banging and flinging himself against the wood until suddenly it gave way and he pitched forward.

'—the matter? What's wrong? Wh—'

A small door inset in the big one had opened. Pema landed in a tangle at the feet of a round woman in white clothes. He barely noticed her. All he saw was Jeffrey, pathetically small on the courtyard stones, and the eagle splayed out a few paces beyond. It must have dropped the marmole in order to try to save itself from a crash landing. Sides heaving, unable to move, the bird stared at him with its mad yellow predator's eyes.

Pema rushed over, gathered Jeffrey up and cradled him. The marmole lay limply in his arms, but he was still warm and Pema could feel the little creature's heart thumping under his fur. He staggered to his feet, turned wildly – and the courtyard exploded with noise.

A girl in dishevelled beige robes screeched down the steps from the top of the wall and thundered past Pema, practically knocking him over again. She fell on her knees by the eagle and spread out her arms as if to protect it from further attack.

'I saw you! I *saw* you!' she yelled over her shoulder at Pema. 'You threw *rocks* at him! Don't try to deny it!'

'I'm not trying to deny it!' Pema shouted back. 'Look what he's done to Jeffrey – he was killing him – *he was going to eat him!*'

The girl glanced up at the bleeding bundle of fur in Pema's hands.

'He's an eagle. What do you *want* him to eat? Grass?!'

'Not my friend! *That's* what I don't want him to eat!' yelled Pema. The girl hesitated, looking suddenly uncertain. Then Pema became aware of the flutter of white robes.

The courtyard was filling up with Sisters. He was suddenly deeply conscious that he was red-faced and sweating, clutching a bleeding marmole to his chest, and that he had just finished shouting at a White Woman. Well, a White Girl, anyway.

A voice rang out, but it wasn't Pema who was being addressed.

'Singay. I might have known.'

Pema saw a weary sort of horror dawn in the girl's eyes. A tall, gaunt Sister was looking down on them from a balcony. Her voice was chilly.

'Singay. Those animals are damaged. Take them to Sister Menpa. I will await you in my chamber. You might like to tidy yourself before then. Sister Shing, if you would be so good as to deal with that *boy*, then send him on his way. I need hardly remind you we are the *Sisters* of the Snow. I am not aware of any change in that.'

There was a chorus of dutiful tittering, which the tall woman pretended to ignore. She was already turning away when Pema, without meaning to, found himself calling out.

'Wait! I mean, stop! I mean ... I have to talk to the Abbess! It's about the Mountain.'

The tall woman froze. In the sudden silence, Pema heard the round Sister suck in her breath, and the girl Singay's eyes went wide in her sharp little face, as if she were appalled and, perhaps, also impressed. Pema could feel his face turning even redder.

'I *am* the Abbess,' said the tall woman, looking down at him over her shoulder. Her voice could have cut through stone. 'What do you have to tell me about the Mountain?'

She said the words as if what she really meant was 'What could YOU *possibly* tell ME?'

'It's turned around, ma'am,' Pema blurted. 'It's going backwards.'

And then, to his complete astonishment, the Abbess pointed at Singay and spat, '*You* put him up to this, *didn't you?*'

CHAPTER FOUR

The Way of Mother Mountain

What?

Pema stared, bewildered. The girl – Singay – hung her head wearily for a moment before scrambling to her feet and bowing to the furious Abbess. Then, awkwardly, she managed to get the eagle onto her arm.

'This way,' the girl said to him in a dull voice. 'I'll take you to Sister Menpa.'

'No ... yes, but ...' Pema hesitated, looking from her to the Abbess. *This can't be happening – I can't have bungled everything already!* Jeffrey stirred and whimpered in his hands. He didn't know where to turn, what to do. And then the round Sister – Sister Shing – took him by the elbow in a kindly way.

'The Abbess will see you, lad, don't worry,' she murmured. 'She's bound to see anyone who comes looking to be seen, whether she likes it or not. Singay'll take you to her once the beasts are tended.' Then, in such a quiet voice that he had to bend down to hear her, 'Is it true, what you just said? About the Mountain? You didn't make it up?' Pema looked into her homey round face and longed to tell her everything. But before he could speak, she glanced up at the Abbess and gave him a shove instead. 'Go on. Follow Singay,' she said, her voice loud enough now to be heard from the balcony.

Not knowing what else to do, Pema took a ragged breath and did as he was told.

'Right then, that's as much as I can do for the moment.' The marmole's wounds had been examined, cleaned, salved and bound by Sister Menpa. 'My prescription is a soft blanket and a long sleep, and my prognosis is a total recovery – in the fullness of time, lad, so you mustn't be impatient. If you go picking the animal up or jolting him about, my work will all have been for nothing.' Sister Menpa glared at Pema as fiercely as she knew how, which wasn't very, and Pema nodded earnestly. There was a wonderfully soothing quality to this Sister's voice that gave him almost as much comfort as seeing the marmole so gently cared for.

She turned to Singay. 'And what trouble have you got yourself into this time, eh?' Then she shook her head with amused resignation. 'No, don't tell me. I can guess.'

The girl! thought Pema with a start. He'd forgotten about her, but there she still was, standing to one side, waiting by the ice eagle. Someone had brought in a wooden perch and the bird was clutching it with claws still dark with Jeffrey's blood. It was breathing normally again, and taking occasional swipes at its feathers with that vicious beak to groom them.

Sister Menpa began to examine the bird, who promptly tried to eat her hand.

'Behave yourself!' she said. And it did. Without further protest, beyond some dirty looks, the eagle let the puny human extend his wings, examine his feathers, and generally poke and prod.

'Well, Singay,' Sister Menpa said at last, 'for the beasts, at least, it's been a lucky day all round. No primary feathers are broken. In fact, the bird's got no damage he won't recover from in a day or so.'

Pema could see the relief written all over the girl's pointy face.

Sister Menpa shook her head ruefully. 'All I have to do is help the animals, thanks be to the Mother. It's up to you to square things with the Abbess. I'll take the marmole to the back room and settle him where it's quiet.'

'Thank you, Sister,' said Pema.

And then there were only the two of them left in the room. Pema's arms and legs felt too long, and if he didn't concentrate he would probably trip over his own feet, but he knew he had to say *something* to her, even if it meant her yelling again.

'I – I'm really glad I didn't hurt him too much,' he said hoarsely. 'I wasn't thinking. I just . . .'

'I know.' Luckily, the girl didn't seem to have any anger left. 'And it's not that I don't like marmoles. I do. There was a burrow behind my house, where I grew up. I like . . . I used to like watching them.' She was looking anywhere but at him as she said in a rush, 'It was my fault. I thought I was ready to fly the eagle on my own. Sister Hodges said I wasn't, but I was so *sure* . . . I've been working so hard to train him. Anyway, I couldn't get him to come back. He just flew right away from me.' She lifted a finger as if to stroke the eagle's breast, but then dropped it again. 'You're not supposed to. Stroke them, I mean. It's bad for their feathers. But it's hard not to.'

Pema nodded. 'I've never been up close to one before. He's very beautiful, isn't he. I didn't know that about the feathers.'

There was a pause. Neither of them knew what to say next.

'What – still here?' It was Sister Menpa, coming back into the clinic. 'No point putting it off. Better out than in, I always say.' Here she paused. 'Though perhaps comparing an audience with the Abbess to a bout of wind is not perhaps *quite* the thing.'

Grinning feebly, Pema and Singay left.

'The Abbess' rooms are on the top floor,' the girl told him as they started up the stairs. 'Best view.'

'Look, I didn't mean to get you in trouble. It's just I've been sent . . . I'm supposed to tell—'

But Singay shook her head.

'Better not talk any more to me,' she said. 'Then you can tell the Great Gow I didn't corrupt you.'

They climbed in silence until they arrived at the Abbess' antechamber.

'You took your time!' snapped an undersized Sister with tight lips.

'Sorry, Sister Khalu,' muttered Singay.

'Well, you're here now,' said the Sister. She ushered Singay immediately in through an ornate door. The expression on her face suggested she was ushering in a grunt pat.

Sister Khalu shut the door on Pema with a bang. *I guess I'm next,* he thought. He looked around for somewhere to sit down but there were no chairs. He felt stupid standing in the middle of the room so he went and stood against the wall instead.

He didn't feel much smarter.

Even through the closed door he could hear raised voices.

What am I doing here? he wailed inside his head. *What in the name of all that's cold . . .*

Part of him – the cowardly part – hoped Singay was in for a long session, just to put off his own audience, but it seemed like no time at all before the door opened and she came out again, alone. Her face was wan and pinched. Pema could still hear the Abbess fuming – either she was so angry she hadn't noticed the door wasn't shut, or else she didn't care.

'That *girl* – she doesn't belong here! She's been nothing but trouble from the very first day. I should *never* have accepted her. If her family hadn't been so desperate to get rid of her . . .'

Pema stared in horrified embarrassment at Singay, who stared back. Neither of them seemed able to move.

'And her dreams, Abbess, *so* disruptive—'

'*Alleged* dreams, Sister. *Alleged*. We only have her word for it. What's to stop her just making them all up, eh? We can't trust a thing she says – you know that!'

Sister Khalu said something too quiet for them to hear, but the Abbess' response was clear enough.

'Well, what of it? What's to stop *all* of them just making it up? And then whispering, spreading rumours, undermining me. It's bad enough in my own Abbey but now to have ignorant gowboys breaking down the doors, daring—'

Here the Abbess' voice was drowned in a flurry of soothing murmurs, ending with, 'If you'll just see the boy, Abbess. Squelch his nonsense. And then he'll be off down the Mountain and away.'

There was nothing Pema wanted more.

The sudden appearance of Sister Khalu in the doorway broke the spell. Singay flushed red, turned on her heel and fled.

Pema stumbled forward.

'Pick up your feet, boy!' snapped the Sister, glaring up at him, and he was led into the presence of the Abbess.

It was a fine, impressive room, spacious, with wide windows that opened onto white distances and the clear blue of the sky. But Pema had little chance to admire the view. The Abbess stood, glowering, hands on her bony hips. There was the distinct sound of an impatiently tapping foot.

'So. What is your name, boy?'

'Pema. Ma'am.' Pema had no idea how to bow, but ducked his head awkwardly to show willing.

The Abbess looked at him disdainfully.

'I understand you have *concerns*. You *question* the ancient Way of Mother Mountain.'

'No! It's not . . . I just . . .'

'You just what? You just want to come to this holy place and disrupt everything? Spout wild stories? Lies? Blasphemy? Are you not *grateful* to Holy Mother Mountain? I know things were lax before I took over here, but oh, Poomba, Poomba, did no one ever teach you your *prayers?*'

'Er, it's Pema, and yes, of course, but—'

'I'm disappointed in you, Poomba. Deeply, deeply disappointed. Go home and say your prayers. Thank Mother Mountain. I have nothing more to say to you.'

'But . . .'

It was no use. Without quite knowing how it happened, Pema found himself on the other side of the Abbess' firmly closed door, dismissed in every possible way. Then, before he could even begin to worry about what in the name of Snow he was going to tell his grandparents, someone grabbed his arm so hard it made him yelp.

CHAPTER FIVE

Cracked

Her heart burning with the Abbess' words and the look of pity on the boy's face, Singay had fled. Partway down the corridor she turned and blundered into a windowed alcove. Fists clenched, she leaned her hot forehead against the cold glass and stared out at the view.

I won't cry, she thought, swallowing a sob. She scowled at the cold whiteness of the Mountain. *I won't and you can't make me. So there.* She knew she was being childish. And wrong-headed. Again.

'Why can't you be like your big sisters?' her parents would say wistfully. 'Why can't you be like your little sisters?' Out of all their large family of girls, only Singay, bang in the middle, was a worry. She was awkward. She was spiky. She was always getting into trouble, always *getting ideas*.

When she got it into her head to join the Abbey, everybody knew things would be a lot more peaceful at home, so they scraped together the dowry and said goodbye – and Singay had been so excited . . .

She'd been wrong-headed to think that anyone would ever look at her with the respect accorded a White Woman. She'd been wrong-headed to think that there was something special waiting for her, just around the next corner. She'd been looking for that something ever since she was old enough to toddle off into the garden to tame the dragons that should have been there. And then, sooner or later (but usually sooner), there would be that sick taste in her mouth as she realised she'd made a mistake. Again. Nothing ever went as she wanted it to go.

She had that sick taste in her mouth now.

That's it. Not any more. She wasn't going to feel like that another day. She'd get the evidence she needed and then she'd *make* them listen to her. The boy would be her witness. She'd take him and show him. He'd be impressed.

He'd never look at her with pity again.

She heard a door open and close and realised that the boy's interview with the Abbess must be over. Before he could get away – before she could change her mind – she rushed down the corridor and grabbed him by the arm.

He gave a satisfying yelp.

'Come with me.' Singay dragged him back to the alcove, trying to quell the doubts in her mind. What if he didn't believe her? What if he just laughed, or worse, acted sorry for her?

Eyes narrowing, looking for any sign of mockery or pity, she glared at him.

Pema tried to take a step back, but the cold window at his back stopped him short.

Now what?

It was as if she were trying to look inside his skull. Then she gave a small, fierce nod that reminded him all at once of the ice eagle.

'You'll do,' she said. 'Come on.'

'I'll do *what?*' Pema began, but she had already turned away. She didn't look back to see if he was following. For a second he considered staying put, just to spite her, but as soon as he had the thought he knew he wouldn't.

What a good little dugg I am, he thought sourly, and trotted after her. *What a nightmare this has all been.*

Then he stopped. 'The Abbess – she said you had dreams.'

The girl's back stiffened visibly but she kept on walking. 'So? What of it?'

'Well? What do you dream about?' It took only a few strides to catch her up.

'None of your business, gowboy,' she snapped, turning abruptly to face him, then bit her lip.

She'd been a fool to blab about her dreams. Her family had stopped listening to them years ago. They didn't think a little girl's made-up adventures were quite ... *proper.* But when she came to the Abbey her dreams had flared up in such a different way. They had become horrible nightmares, and they seemed so vivid, so real. Maybe if the old Abbess hadn't died ... She'd been a woman with a wise and open mind, but the new Abbess was cut from very different cloth. And Singay knew how strange her dreams sounded.

'Sorry,' she said. 'I'd rather not talk about it.' She hoped he'd be well-brought-up enough not to insist. She was right, though she might not have been so pleased if she'd known what he was thinking about her just then.

Snows, she's spiky! She's just like that gow we got cheap that year, the one who used to bite the others all the time. That was one bad-tempered gow ... Where in the name of Mother Mountain is she taking me?

The Abbey was huge, and built on no plan that Pema

could discern. He followed Singay along hallways and up spiral staircases, past doors, *through* doors, into rooms that led to more corridors. Any hopes he might have had about finding his own way back died as they scurried further and further into the maze, and then she stopped so suddenly he had to twist sideways to avoid running her over.

'This is it,' she said, reaching for the handle of a closed door. 'You need to be quiet. The birds are hooded, and tied by leads to the perches, but there's nothing wrong with their hearing. Or their claws. And their wings can give you a nasty whack if you get them agitated enough. So keep your voice down and move softly.'

'Birds?' Pema began, but Singay had already opened the door and gone in. There was nothing for it but to follow.

It was a long, low, dimly lit room. There was a row of wooden perches running down one side of it, and along the other, pegs hung with leather hawking equipment, gloves and jesses and things Pema couldn't identify. What Singay had said about the birds' keen hearing was obviously true: a dozen hooded heads had turned to stare blindly at him, and here and there bells tinkled as eagles, killstrels and hawks stirred uneasily.

'We think this is probably the oldest part of the Abbey,' said Singay, in the kind of low voice that is quieter than a whisper. 'The birds are best away from any bustle, and no one comes to this part of the buildings except me and Sister Hodges, our falconer. She's old, and very deaf, and she knows everything there is to know about raptors. The birds will do anything for her. They just tolerate me.' He thought she looked a bit bleak at that, then the moment passed. 'But I didn't bring you here to see *them*. I wanted to show you *this*.'

She led him down the length of the room to the end wall.

'There,' she said, and pointed.

Pema looked at the wall – and then realised that what he was looking at wasn't a wall at all. It was the Mountain. The original builders had simply built out from the raw rock. But it wasn't the cleverness of the joins they had made at wall and ceiling and floor that Singay was pointing out.

It was the crack.

Or rather, a series of cracks, mostly diagonally from left to right, but a few that crossed them going the other way. Cracks . . . *in the rock*.

He reached out a hand as if to touch them, then changed his mind.

'See?' said Singay. 'What you tried to tell the Abbess makes sense of a lot of things. For years, there have been walls and ceilings shifting and cracking all over the Abbey. But these cracks are in the Mountain.'

'But . . . why are you showing them to me?' asked Pema. He was suddenly horribly aware that he was a long way from home. A long way from *anyone*. Nobody knew where he was! For all anybody else at the Abbey knew, he'd walked out of the Abbess' rooms and just disappeared. What if this strange girl was cracked like the Mountain? What if she'd *kidnapped* him?

'Why have you brought me here?' He stepped back, but she wasn't even looking at him. She was staring at the fissures in the stone, as if she could read them like a book if only she looked hard enough.

Pema shifted nervously, shooting a quick glance towards the door.

'You'd never find your way back, you know,' she said meanly. Then she seemed to regret her tone. 'Look, I'm sorry. But before you decide I'm crazy, you could at least listen to me. Promise me you'll listen.'

He hesitated, and then nodded. What else could he do?

'All right,' she continued, taking a deep breath. 'It happened like this. One night I couldn't sleep and I brought my blankets up here. It's quiet, and out of the way, and sort of peaceful, and the birds don't seem to mind. Anyway, I was just dropping off when I heard it. A sound like . . . someone crying.' Her voice had dropped so low he could barely hear her. He leaned closer. She looked at him, her eyes wide. 'It was heart-breaking. I tried to get up and find whoever it was, but I got tangled in my blankets and then I banged one of the perches and the birds got upset and started screeching, and by the time I'd got them all settled and quiet again, the sound was gone. But I was sure I'd heard it. So I decided to come back another night and *not* sleep, to see if I would hear it again.'

'And did you?' said Pema.

Singay nodded. 'Yes, but not the first night, or the second. I couldn't come every night, of course, or I'd have dropped in my tracks. I had to spend some nights catching up on sleep. I grabbed naps in the day too, when I could manage without anybody noticing. But then, about a week after the first time, I heard it again.'

She looked at him with the utmost seriousness. 'I heard somebody crying,' she said, 'from *inside* the Mountain.'

Pema realised he'd been holding his breath, and let it out now in a low whistle.

'Who was it?' he whispered.

'I don't know!' Singay's voice was suddenly too loud. Down the line of perches, birds of prey clacked their beaks together and thrashed against the leads. Two ended up hanging upside down, and she had to go and rescue them. She came back to Pema licking blood off her hand.

'Sorry, that was stupid of me,' she said quietly.

'Never mind. Go on with your story!' Pema urged.

She spread her hands helplessly. 'I can't. That's it! I rushed off to tell the Abbess but of course she wouldn't listen. I tried to tell her what I heard, offered to bring her here so that she could hear it too, and all I got was "little girls shouldn't tell tales" and "you're just trying to make yourself seem special again" and "haven't we talked about that before?" She wouldn't believe me.' She gave a laugh that was close to a sob. 'Though I've had doubts too! Sometimes I can't manage to sneak up here at night, or I do manage and I don't hear anything, and then on the night when I say to myself, *This is it, this is the last time, no more,* I'll catch the faintest echo of it again.'

There was a pause. He reached out a hand and carefully touched her sleeve.

'I believe you, Sister,' he said. 'What can I do to help?'

Singay looked at him in surprise.

'Oh, I'm not a Sister. Not yet. Probably never will be,

if Abbess Great Gow has anything to say about it. No, I'm just a novice. But . . . do you mean it? You'll help?'

Pema nodded, though he gulped as well. 'What's the plan?'

'I'll tell you,' she said, with a smile that completely changed her face.

It was simple. After dark, when all the Sisters were asleep, Pema and Singay were going to return . . .

. . . and break down the side of the Mountain.

CHAPTER SIX

On the Other Side

'Be as quiet as you can,' Singay muttered tensely. 'I'll do my best to keep the birds calm, but you've seen what they're like.'

It was later that night. Fortunately the Sisters went to their beds early, and there'd been no one else staying in the guest quarters. So Singay had been able to collect Pema and lead him through the silent corridors to the mews without alerting anyone.

Then she'd shown him the hammer.

'I nicked it from Sister Loong this afternoon.'

Pema looked at the hammer doubtfully. *She says be quiet, but who ever heard of hammering quietly?*

They'd discussed exactly what bit of the wall he was to strike. There was a place low down where the cracks crossed each other, making a large, rough diamond shape. If Singay was right, and there *was* a space behind the rock, the hope was that he'd be able to loosen the block and push it through. Then all they had to do was crawl through after it . . .

'Here goes,' muttered Pema, and he grasped the wooden handle with both hands.

Fortunately, Sister Loong's tools were all well made, and the hammer had the balance of a quality instrument. Pema's aim was a little erratic, but after a number of near misses, he hit just the right spot. He felt the block shift.

'I did it!' he whispered proudly, but Singay was too busy soothing the birds to hear him. He gave the wall a few more bashes and grinned to himself. It was definitely moving!

Now that the block was loosened, Pema used the head of the hammer and all his weight to push it through to the other side. It dropped down out of sight with a satisfying thud, and then something happened that made him jerk back with a gasp, leaving the hammer sticking out of the hole.

Light flooded into the mews – from inside the Mountain!

Even through their hoods, the birds sensed something strange and instantly fell still.

Pema and Singay stared at each other, and at the light. Then Pema leaned forward cautiously and retrieved the hammer from the hole. He turned to lean it against the wall.

'I'll go first,' he began, but Singay was already halfway through the gap, blocking the light. Her kicking legs disappeared, then the strange glow poured back into the room.

'This is . . .' she said. Her voice sounded muffled and strange.

'This is *what?*' called Pema. 'What is it?'

But she didn't answer.

He waited. Nothing.

He raised his voice, even though it made the birds shift unhappily. 'Are you all right?'

Silence. The moment stretched horribly.

This is where I should go and get somebody, he thought, trying not to panic. *This is where somebody needs to be told.* Then, *Why am I here? This has nothing to do with me – I should be halfway to home again by now!* But he knew he couldn't leave. She needed to be rescued. He had to save her. He gritted his teeth and, hands sweating, he shoved himself into the gap.

'Isn't this amazing?' squeaked Singay as he landed in a heap on the other side.

She didn't need rescuing. She was fine, standing there with a great grin pasted across her face. He scrambled to his feet, all set to yell at her for scaring him like that. But then he forgot all about it.

What in the name of . . .

Instead of the cramped, little hole he'd somehow expected, he found himself in a tall, vaulted space, a wide passageway that curved away in both directions, bending out of sight at a distance that was hard to judge.

'What . . . where . . . ?'

There was a clunking sound, and Pema turned round to see Singay pushing the block of rock back into the hole.

'*What are you doing?*' he squawked.

'What does it look like?' she said, grunting with the effort.

'It looks like you're blocking up the hole!'

'Well spotted.'

'But *why?* The hammer's on the other side! How are we going to get back in?'

She straightened, dusting her hands, and looked at him as if he were an idiot.

'I'm blocking the hole because I don't want anybody following us. Not until I get this sorted. Er, I mean, not until *we* get this sorted.' She gave the rock one more shove.

'We find out what this is all about, the cracks and the crying and everything, then we just pull the stone out again – look, *I* can move it! – and go tell everybody who thinks I'm crazy that *they're* crazy!' She frowned at him. 'Why are you staring at me like that?'

Pema's brain was struggling. He was inside the Mountain in the middle of the night with nobody knowing where he was and there was something very weird about the person he was standing beside. She looked . . . not right.

And then it clicked.

'You haven't got a shadow!' he exclaimed.

Singay stared at him.

'It must be the light.' He waved his hands about vaguely. 'It's coming from . . . everywhere. So, no shadows.'

It was true. The light was coming from the walls, the ceiling and the floor with an equal, silvery luminousness.

'Snows!' exclaimed Singay, craning to see behind herself. 'You're right. Light from everywhere!' She shook her head in amazement and then, disconcertingly, started to walk away.

'Wha— wait, wait, where are you going?'

'Where do you *think* I'm going? I'm going to find the crying person. That's what we came for, isn't it?'

'Well, yes, of course. That's what we came for. But how do you know that's the right way to go?' he asked desperately.

'I don't,' said Singay. 'I *guessed*. Look, you can go the other way, if you like. Or you can wait for me here. I really don't mind.'

'What? Wait? Don't be silly. I was just . . .' He paused, afraid his voice was going to squeak. The last thing he wanted was to be left on his own. 'Of course I'm coming with you.'

'Suit yourself.' Singay hoped he couldn't tell how relieved she was.

They carried on in Singay's chosen direction. As they walked, Pema checked over his shoulder. He checked again, and again, until finally Singay turned and glared at him.

'What are you *looking* at?'

'The place where we came in. Only, I can't see it anymore. The curve of the passageway ...'

Singay stopped abruptly. 'What's that?' She sounded a little breathless.

Pema frowned. 'I said, I can't see—'

'*Shh!* Did you hear that?'

Pema shushed, and listened.

At first he heard nothing and then, there it was, coming from up ahead: soft, wordless, piercingly mournful, it was the sound of someone singing. And then the singer was not alone anymore, for other voices were joining in, in subtle, melting harmonies.

'I thought you said you heard crying,' whispered Pema.

'I did. But this isn't ... this is ...' Singay couldn't find the words. It was the saddest, most beautiful thing either of them had ever heard and it drew them on like a lure.

'There. Just ahead,' she murmured, pointing at an opening in the wall. Hearts in their mouths, they crept forward, and looked inside.

It was a high, vaulted room, lit with the same ambient light as the passageway. It was furnished with tables and cases and chests, all of luminous stone and covered in clutter of a hundred sorts. There were pieces of rock and books and small machines and a collection of timepieces and gizmos and a mishmash of other things they'd never seen before. And there, in the midst of it all, dressed in a wildly coloured, exotic robe, was a little man, so small he would barely reach Singay's shoulder. He was silver-skinned and silver-eyed, with fluttery pale hair and an odd face. He was singing to a row of rocks laid out on the table and, unlikely as it seemed, the rocks appeared to be singing back. The achingly beautiful music that had drawn Pema and Singay was coming from this impossible choir.

There was no knowing how long they might have gone on standing there, mesmerised by the strangeness of sight and sound, but then the little man, in the throes of emotion, raised his arms, lifted his head and looked straight at them. For a moment it was as if he didn't realise what his eyes were telling him, and he just went on with the performance. Then the notes trailed off, and though his mouth stayed open, nothing came out of it. Without taking his eyes off them, he reached out to the rocks, still warbling on the table. As he touched each one, its voice was cut off as if by a knife, until there was only silence, and three pairs of eyes, two sets of brown and one of silver, staring in astonishment. The silence stretched and stretched, until . . .

'Who *are* you?' exclaimed Singay.

CHAPTER SEVEN

The Little Silver Man

The little man screamed.

'This isn't happening!' he shrieked. 'I'm not here! You can't see me!' He flung himself into the corner of the room, grabbed a woven rug off the floor and dragged it over his head. 'Please don't kill me,' came his muffled voice. 'Please!'

An image leapt into Pema's mind. *He looks a little like the albino lamb Shisha the shup man showed us that time. It was scared of everything too.*

'We're not going to kill you,' he said gently.

'Why would we *want* to?' said Singay. 'What have you done?'

'What have I done? I got found out!' The rug shifted and one silver eye peeped out from its folds. 'How *did* you find me?' the little man whispered.

Pema hunkered down and spoke softly. 'Well, there were these cracks in the rock and Singay heard someone crying ...'

The rug drooped. 'That was me, I'm afraid. I've been so *lonely*! We're not meant to be alone, we really aren't.'

'We?' said Singay. 'Who's we?' She looked over her shoulder, but there was no one there.

The silver eye disappeared again. 'I shouldn't be talking to you! You're going to kill me – I know it, I know it.' The heaped-up rug trembled and whimpered.

Pema shook his head. None of this made sense. 'Will

you come out if we both absolutely *promise* not to hurt you
– any of you?'

'There's nobody here but me,' came a whispered reply.

'Then why'd you say *we?*' insisted Singay.

The voice from under the rug squeaked, 'I can't tell you
about the others. What am I saying? There *aren't* any others!'

'He's just talking nonsense!' cried Singay in frustration,
but Pema flapped a hand in her direction.

'All right, then, can you tell us who *you* are?' he said, as
gently as he could.

'Which is where this stupid conversation started,' muttered Singay. But this time it seemed that the little man
couldn't resist an answer.

'Call me Rose!' He jumped up, dropping the rug to
the floor and clasping his strange silver hands together
beseechingly. 'Oh please, *will* you call me Rose?'

'Well, yes,' said Pema, 'if you like.'

'Why *wouldn't* we call you Rose?' demanded Singay.
'Isn't that your real name?'

'Well, no,' the little man admitted reluctantly. 'We don't
really have names much. Well, not at all.'

'We? Who's we?'

'I can't tell you.'

'What are you doing in here?'

'I can't tell you.'

'Oh, for Snow's sake!'

'All right, all right!' said Pema. 'Let's all calm down. If
you can't tell us anything about the others, or about yourself, can you tell us anything about the Mountain? Can you
tell us, for example, why it's started moving backwards?'

'WHAT?' Rose shrieked, leaping back wildly and knocking a chair over with a crash. He began wringing his hands and twitching from foot to foot in agitation. 'What do you mean?' he wailed. 'About the Mountain? Did you say it was going …' He seemed unable to say the word 'backwards' out loud and only mouthed it.

'What if it is? Stop being so ridiculous,' said Singay through gritted teeth. 'Acting like it's your fault!'

Rose turned a stricken face to her. 'Of course it's my fault!' he cried. 'I'M DRIVING!'

Pema and Singay couldn't get any sense out of the strange silver man for some time after that. He dived back under the rug and they could hear him muttering wildly, 'No, no, NO! That's *terrible*! Think of the destruction! Think of … People could be *killed*!'

'Too late,' said Pema, thinking about the angry old man at Jungle Head.

Rose moaned. 'Oh no, oh no, oh no.' He burrowed deeper.

'Right,' said Singay abruptly. 'That's *it*.' She snatched the rug off Rose's head. 'You're going to tell us *exactly* what you're blithering about.' As Rose opened his mouth to answer, she loomed over him. 'And don't you *dare* say "I can't"!'

The little man stared up at her and quivered.

'I … but … I …'

'I really think you should tell us everything now,' added Pema gently. He tugged on Singay's sleeve. 'Back off – you're scaring him,' he muttered. He helped Rose off the floor, righted the toppled chair and settled him into it.

'Whenever you're ready,' he said, keeping his voice mild. He was using gow-calming techniques his grandmother had taught him. It seemed to work.

'All right. I'll try,' said the man and then, in a rush, he confessed, 'I'm a Driver.'

'And?' Pema prompted. 'What is it you drive?'

'Well, mountains, obviously. But not normally. Normally we drive meteors.'

Before Singay could say anything, Pema dug an elbow in her ribs.

'And why do you do that?' he asked Rose.

'For the Harvest ... for the Homeworld ...' Then he broke off again. 'Oh no, no, no, this is all wrong. You're not supposed to find out about us. Everyone *knows* it only leads to disaster, if people find out about us.'

Pema nodded as if he understood, though he really didn't. *The thing is to get him to talk. We can figure out what it means later.* 'Whatever you tell us will be our secret, just you, me and Singay. Just take your time ...'

And, gradually, in fits and starts, with gentle coaxing and encouraging noises from Pema, the Driver's story began to emerge.

It was strange. Unbelievable.

Beings that lived in space. Drivers, who travelled unimaginable distances in the blackness, herding meteors. Helping them grow. Avoiding collisions.

Amazing. I wanted something amazing. Singay was struggling to take in what she was hearing. *But what if he's just crazy? Just showing off? What if he's making it all up?* She gave a sour grin. *And now I sound like the Great Gow.* She

45

suddenly realised she'd been sounding like the Abbess the whole time. Because she was scared. Because Rose was different. But there was no time to think about that.

'At first,' Rose was saying, 'we were an entirely nomadic people. And then we found Homeworld. I wish I could tell you how lovely a planet Homeworld is.' There was a longing in his voice that Pema understood. He knew what it felt like to love your home. 'And it was so wonderful to have a place to come back to. After the journey.'

He explained how Drivers now travelled *with* the meteors, instead of just hoping to come across them by chance. The Drivers and the herds followed a specific route, a gigantic arc out from home, beyond the stars and back again. The Great Circuit.

'We gather more meteors as we go – we usually have herds of a thousand or more by the end of a Circuit. In some ways, a larger herd is easier to manage. We can fine-tune the magnetic fields within it to re-enforce the general direction we want them all to go in. Then it's just a question of controlling any external influences to the edges of the herd – solar systems or other sources of gravity pull, or perhaps an exploding star that might create a bit of a shove.'

The enthusiasm that had started to sparkle in the little man's eyes died away, and his voice grew sombre.

'As I said, we guide our herds from one asteroid belt to the next, so the meteors can prosper, accruing bits of rock smaller than themselves, growing big. It is our duty to keep them safely away from planets and moons. We take our responsibility very seriously. You must believe me when I say this.' His voice was desperate, pleading.

Singay could feel her heart tightening.

'It's very rare – it really is! – but sometimes, every once in a very long while, one of the meteors escapes.'

There was a pause.

'And . . .?' Pema prompted.

'And we catch up with it and steer it back to the herd. That's what's supposed to happen. But, well, sometimes, we don't reach it in time and it . . . it's out of control, and . . . and it crashes into a star or . . . a planet. Of course, not every meteor that hits a planet comes from a Driver herd,' the little man added quickly. 'There are plenty of feral ones out there, roaming about loose. But, as I say, sometimes it's one of ours.' He quavered to a stop.

'What are you trying to tell us?' Singay's voice was hoarse.

Rose closed his strange eyes for a moment. When he opened them again, he looked down at the floor.

'We had arrived at the asteroid belt that runs round the rim of your solar system. Everything seemed under control. It was my cousin's birthday and we had a party. Oh, I know, I know, it shouldn't have happened. But everything *seemed* all right . . . It was only when we were about to leave that we realised.'

'Realised what?'

'One of the meteors was missing.' Rose's voice dropped to a whisper. 'Three of us volunteered to bring it back. It takes three Drivers to control a comet. We searched the whole outer asteroid belt, hoping our meteor was still there, lurking about, getting fat too fast. But it wasn't in the belt any more. It had headed *inwards*, towards your star, right into the heart of your busy system. All we could do was check each planet and moon we came to for damage, and hope for the best. Eventually we arrived at your *inner* asteroid belt. Still no sign. We carried on. And then we came to your world. That's when we saw it. Ahead of us. But we were too late. It happened, right before our eyes.'

Pema felt a sense of dread growing in his chest.

Singay looked sick.

Rose nodded, still unable to meet their eyes.

'When a meteor above a certain size crashes into a planet, it sets off a series of events far more destructive than the impact itself. There are earthquakes and tidal waves and volcanic disturbances, but even these only do damage in the short term. What *really* devastates a world is the dust.'

'Dust?' whispered Singay.

With an effort, the little man looked up.

'When the rogue meteor hit your world, huge quantities of volcanic dust were thrown high into the air in a choking cloud. Winds took the cloud and spread it round the planet, so thickly that there was nowhere that the sun could pierce through. The green life of the land struggled in the gloom, and then it died. And, eventually, everything that depended on green things died too. There was nothing but desert left. Nothing—'

'Stop it!'

Singay's cry took the others by surprise.

'What is it?' Pema jumped up. Singay was shaking. He put his hand on her arm. 'What's wrong?'

She looked at him, her face stricken in the alien light.

'I've dreamt about this,' she whispered. 'This was in my dreams!'

48

CHAPTER EIGHT

The Long Walk of Mountains

For a long moment no one spoke. There was only the sound of Singay's ragged breathing.

'Are you trying to tell me that was *real?*' she asked at last, staring wide-eyed at the Driver. 'The things in my dreams really *happened?*'

Rose nodded. He looked at Singay with a kind of sad wonder. 'The memories are all there, of course. In the rocks. But I'd no idea anyone who wasn't a Driver would have access to them. This is most remarkable. Please, if you will, tell me what you saw, what you dreamt.'

Singay's dreams had always made people uncomfortable. They told her to 'stop showing off'. They didn't want to listen. This time it was different. This time there was someone nodding their understanding as she haltingly described the images of destruction, the darkness and the cold, the feeling of things dying all around her, out of sight. Of not *having* sight, really, but still *knowing* that the world had changed utterly. She was so busy explaining and describing that she didn't notice Pema's increasing restlessness until he couldn't contain himself any longer.

'But you're not making any *sense*, either of you,' he blurted. 'The world hasn't *been* destroyed – it's still there! It's right outside! I was there, in it, only yesterday! Unless . . .' His voice trailed off and he looked at Singay with a sudden horror. 'Unless your dreams are of the future. Is that what the Mountain is going to do to us? But that's impossible . . . isn't it?'

But Rose was shaking his head, so hard his pale hair blurred in the air. 'No, no, you don't understand. The world out there – the world you live in – is what came much, much *later*. After we'd entered your Sea, after we'd waited, after we'd rebuilt.'

'Waited for what? Rebuilt what? How?' asked Pema. It was all so much nonsense! He was talking to a man who had probably gone mad from living alone too long, and a girl who even the Sisters thought was cracked. He would not listen to another word of this craziness.

But before Pema could make a move, Rose began to tell them about the Long Walk of Mountains.

'First, once the dust in the air had started to filter out, we encouraged the rocks beneath the ocean to make this.' He waved his silver hands. 'The first Mountain. And then it was my job to drive it out of the sea. We needed to create an enclosed area of desert, enclosed by mountains I mean, and allow the normal action of the winds to produce rain which would in turn produce green things which would in turn produce the life that depends on green things. So of course *one* mountain wasn't enough. We needed a sort of V shape, so while I was driving this mountain north, the other two Drivers were building, so to speak, more – two strings of mountains, one on each side, but fanning out so that there'd be a big wedge of land between them.'

He began to speak about tectonic plate manipulation, encouraging a specific configuration by influencing mantle convection currents, utilising strong magnetic polarisation and susceptibility. The little man's eyes shone with pleasure as he talked, even though he left Pema and Singay more bewildered with every word. Finally, he noticed their faces and slowed to a halt.

Singay tried to hang on to the words she thought she understood. 'Are you saying . . . No, that's ridiculous,' she said, though her voice shook. 'Nobody can *drive* a mountain!'

Rose looked at her. 'Drivers can. It's not dissimilar to driving a comet. As long as you're not asking rocks to do anything outside their nature, it's not that hard.'

'But how could you know that it would *work?*' Pema asked. 'That making a wedge like that would make the rain and all the rest?' He stopped suddenly, appalled. *I'm talking like I believe what he's saying – at least the parts of it I understood! I'm talking like I've just accepted this whole, mad tale.*

'You know the old saying,' said Rose. '"Geography makes History". Drivers know rocks, and we found all the information we needed by listening to them. Rocks have long, *long* memories. They remember being a bit of debris in the blackness of space. They remember coming together with other rocks to form a planet. Heating to molten states, cooling, coalescing. Wearing away. And for most rocks, that's all there is. But a very few are part of a world where there has been *life*. And the rocks remember that too. If life is destroyed, the way it was on this world after the meteor struck, then the rocks' memories can be used to learn how to recreate what was lost. Make it so it can happen again. And, you know, the fascinating thing is that it happens *faster* the second time around. As if each stage of the process is able to say to itself, "Oh yes, *this* seems familiar. *This* has happened before." Accelerated Evolution, it's called.'

Singay stirred restlessly. Everything the little man was saying made her stomach hurt.

'Let me get this straight. You're telling us you're the Driver,' she asked, speaking carefully, eyes narrowed. 'You're telling us you *drove* the Mountain up out of the Sea.'

'That's right.'

'And there were others—'

'Two others, yes.'

'Two others *organising* other mountains and the land in-between them for you to, um, drag along behind you.'

'Pretty much. Yes.'

'So there are three of you, altogether.'

'There were. Three Drivers. Always three.'

'What do you mean, there *were* three?' Singay asked. Pema might scold her for not being gentle enough with Rose, but she had to know. She had to know everything. 'Aren't there three anymore? Did something happen to the others?'

Rose's eyes welled up, and a single silver tear rolled down his cheek. 'I don't know. But, for quite some time, I haven't been able to hear them.'

'*Hear* them?'

'I'm sorry – so much to explain!' He wrung his silvery hands. 'You must understand, when I say we hear each other, it isn't as if we can talk to each other, the way I'm talking to you now. But still we are *aware* – yes, that's a better way of putting it. I had an *awareness* of them. And then I started to lose it.' Rose looked bleak. 'For a long time, it was just gradual. You see, it wasn't so much that they *stopped*, but that more and more of something else *started*. My guess is that some new activity in the rocks somewhere between here and the Sea started, but I don't know what. It's like … it's like when a bird is singing, you can hear it, and you can tell where the sound's coming from, right? But if there are a hundred birds singing, you couldn't possibly pick out that one bird anymore, could you? That bird could still be singing, but you wouldn't know.' He added wistfully, 'We have beautiful birds on Homeworld. So beautiful.'

'And I guess they can't tell if *you're* there anymore, I mean, here anymore, either?' said Pema tentatively. 'I mean, Singay heard you crying, but that's a different thing?'

Rose nodded miserably, and then a strangely haunted look came over his silvery face. 'Though I don't lose hope, of course. That *would* be fatal.'

It sounded an odd thing to say, but Singay was already pursuing another thought.

'Maybe they just left,' she said bluntly. 'Drove home.'

'Singay!' Pema was shocked at her tactlessness, but Rose just shook his head.

'No,' he said. 'They haven't left.'

'I don't see why not,' Singay persisted stubbornly, though she could feel herself turning red at Pema's rebuke. 'All those years sitting at the bottom of the ocean – maybe they got fed up and flew away. I know I would. Especially if they thought you were dead. They'd be daft *not* to leave then.'

'No, you don't understand,' said Rose. 'It takes three to drive a comet. So, without me, they *couldn't* leave.'

'Oh,' said Singay.

'It was so gradual for such a long time and then, suddenly, I realised I was on my own, holding everything. On my own. I'm so sorry. For ... for everything. I ... It's the mountains. I think they're trying to revert.'

There was a horrified pause.

'What do you mean, revert?' said Pema. His mouth was suddenly dry.

'I mean go back to what they were. Where they were. Return to their original components. Their original place.'

'Under the Sea?'

Rose nodded.

'But ...' He grabbed Rose's arm. 'But if all the land goes back into the Sea everyone will die! Again!'

'Yes. I know.'

'But can't you *fix* the mountains somehow? Permanently? You're a Driver – can't you make it so they stay the way they *are*?' Pema realised he was shaking the little man, and abruptly let go.

Rose drooped. 'I can't. Not alone. If I were back with the others, the three of us would be able to ground the mountains properly, once and for all. Now, all I can do is do my best is to keep things steady. Amelia's the one who's in charge, really.'

'Amelia?'

'Such a nice name!' Rose gave a sad little smile. 'I gave us all names, you know. Amelia is the oldest. She's very wise and knows an extraordinary number of things. And then there's Trout, a lovely lad, but between you and me, ever so slightly flighty. Oh, nothing a good full Circuit won't fix, but still, he really is a bit silly, even for such a youngster. He'd be the first to admit it – it's one of the main reasons he volunteered to come with us. He thought it might steady him down a little, to commit to a reconstruction like this . . . Dear Trout.'

'Rose, there's a thing I don't understand,' began Pema.

'Oh?' muttered Singay. 'Just *one* thing?'

Pema ignored her. 'Why you haven't gone to *look* for them?'

'I should have!' Rose hung his head. 'I meant to. The plan had always been that as soon as Amelia felt we'd done enough – that the life that had been destroyed was firmly re-established – I was to leave the Mountain and head south to the Sea, carefully, quietly and as quickly as ever I could. Then, when I'd rejoined the others, we'd ground everything – readjust the magnetic fields so that the Mountain stood still and no new land moved out of the Sea. Then we'd get back on the comet, launch it from the seabed, and be off. Back into space. Back home. Oh, to be going home!'

Rose looked from Pema to Singay, his strange silver eyes so sad.

'But then I discovered something shameful about myself. I discovered that I'm a coward. I wanted to leave, I really did, but I hadn't the nerve. All I could do was stay here, alone inside my mountain until . . . I mean, well, I was trapped. Because of my own cowardice.'

'But what were you afraid of?'

'EVERYTHING!' Rose's shout made Pema and Singay both jump. Then his voice dropped to a whisper. '*Do no harm*. First and foremost that's what the Drivers who go on the Circuit have drilled into them. But if the worst happens – if harm is done and we are doing everything we can to put it right – then *don't get found out!* Everyone knows what happens if we're discovered. And outside is so big! All I could think about was how little I knew. How would I find my way? How would I know what to do? What to say? All those long leagues, on my own . . .'

'I'll take you,' said Singay suddenly. The words were out of her mouth almost before she'd even thought them, but once said, they seemed obvious. She'd take him. Of course she would.

'. . . what if they found out I was a Driver? That I was *responsible*? What if . . . *What* did you say?'

'I said I'll take you,' Singay repeated. Her heart pounded in her chest. 'I'll take you to the Sea.'

CHAPTER NINE

Singay's Plan

Rose stared. 'You *will?*' he squeaked, at exactly the same moment that Pema squawked, 'But you *can't!*'

'Why not?' Singay was pleased to hear how completely calm she sounded, even though, inside her head, everything whirled.

'Well, for one thing,' spluttered Pema, 'you don't know the way. I bet you've never been out of the High Lands in your whole life!' His hands were sweating again and he hid them behind his back.

'Don't need to know the way,' said Singay. 'Haven't you ever heard of the River?'

'There are lots of rivers. Which one do you mean?' Though he knew exactly which river – there really was only one main one.

'*The* River,' she said scornfully. 'The one that starts at Jungle Head! It goes all the way to the Sea, as *everybody* knows, so all *we* have to do is follow it till we get there. Simple.'

'Yes. All right. But that's beside the point, because they won't let you. The Sisters are never going to say yes when you tell them you're going swanning off with a – a – an *alien!*'

'Tell them? You can't *tell* them!' yelped Rose, his eyes wide. 'You can't tell *anyone!*'

'You keep saying that, but why *not?*' Pema turned to him, distracted for a moment.

'No, no, no,' said Rose, wringing his hands. 'Telling people is the *worst* thing you could do! I *told* you – the worlds that find out about Drivers always try to kill them.'

'But *why*? It makes no sense!'

Rose shivered. 'No? It was *our* meteor that hit the earth. *Our* fault. Besides, for many species – most species! – finding that they aren't who they thought they were, that their history isn't theirs alone, that they are, in some sense, the creation of *another* species – these things lead to confusion and anger, violence and killing and destruction.' He looked at them with horror in his silver eyes. '*Don't get found out!*'

'But ...' Pema couldn't picture it. 'It wouldn't be like that *here*!'

'Yes, it would,' muttered Singay. 'You're talking like a baby. That's exactly how it would be.'

Pema glared at her. 'I have no wish to offend you,' he said, turning to Rose, 'but you *have* been inside a mountain for the last whoever knows how long. You can't possibly know what we're like.'

'Oh, don't be so *stupid*!' Singay exploded. 'He knows because we're just like everybody else! We think we're special, but we're not – I'll bet we're just the same as all the other worlds.' She sounded bitter and twisted. She *felt* bitter and twisted. 'If Rose says knowing the truth makes people crazy then I've no doubt crazy is what we'll be. Maybe not everybody, maybe not everywhere, but enough to ... Oh, use your head! People would be changed. They'd have lost something. You expect them to like that?'

'Oh no,' murmured Rose in distress. 'It's already starting.'

Singay looked at the Driver and, with an effort, forced herself to smile.

'What? Oh no, no, not really. Best of friends, us, aren't we?' Singay gave Pema a shove with her shoulder that practically knocked him over.

'Ow! Right, yes, really, you don't need to worry,' he mumbled through gritted teeth. 'Nobody's going to kill *you*.'

I wouldn't mind killing that girl though, he thought, rubbing his arm.

'Absolutely,' said Singay firmly. 'Now, this is what we should do. It must be almost morning by now so I'll need to hurry. I'll go back through the hole and collect some food and clothes and my dowry – officially it's still mine until I take my vows. What else? Oh, right, leave a note saying I've left, leave a note saying Pema's left—'

'WHAT?'

'Don't start arguing again, you'll upset Rose. Look – he's half way under his rug again already.'

'But—'

'Just *think*. Imagine you go back to the Abbey and the Great Gow corners you and says, "You there, Poomba, tell me where that ingrate Singay has gone!"' Pema couldn't help a weak grin at her impersonation. 'Do you really think you'll be able to look her in the eye and lie? A nice boy like you? Come to think of it, a nice boy like you isn't going to let a mere girl and a terrified little alien head off by themselves either. You'll feel obliged, I'm sure, to escort them, for the first leg at least.' She smiled all of a sudden and Pema was struck again by how it completely changed her face. 'Won't you?'

He'd never felt so hunted in his life.

'My grandparents—'

'Won't be expecting you yet.'

'Jeffrey—'

'Can't be moved for, oh, at least a week. And he couldn't be in more caring hands. Sister Menpa is wonderful.'

'But … but …' He couldn't think of anything else to say.

'Don't worry – leave everything to me,' she said and, with a spring in her step, she was gone. He heard her footsteps echoing along the tall silver corridor, getting further and further away.

Go after her, you fool! Stop her! But he didn't move. All he could do was hope someone else would put a stop to her mad plan. Surely one of the Sisters was bound to see her, scurrying about in the early morning, looking all furtive and suspicious. *This can't be happening.*

The room seemed much emptier without Singay in it. And then Rose piped up, 'Could you tell me – what's a Jeffrey?'

So Pema told him about the marmole, how he'd been grabbed by the ice eagle and taken to the Abbey and how Singay had yelled at Pema for throwing stones …

It all seemed a long time ago now. *It's hard to believe it's still the same day. Though,* thought Pema with an enormous yawn, *I guess it isn't. It must be tomorrow by now.*

'You're tired. I don't think we can do much more until you've had some sleep. Let's make up some beds, shall we?' suggested Rose.

It sounded like a wonderful idea. There were plenty of

stripy blankets and cushions about the room. He didn't recognise the patterns woven into them, but he was too tired to ask Rose where they'd come from.

'What about you? Aren't you sleepy?'

Rose shook his head. 'Drivers are more nappers, really. Except for longsleep, of course, though that isn't something I could consider. Not having anyone to wake me, it would be much too . . .'

Pema didn't hear the last word. He was fast asleep.

Singay pulled out the rock without any difficulty, stepping carefully past the sleeping birds. No one saw her as she managed her errands in the Abbey. Back in the mews, she pushed her bundles through the hole in the mountainside. At the last moment she looked back. The birds stirred slightly, turning their hooded heads blindly in her direction, but she knew they'd forget her almost immediately. She crawled through the gap, and then shoved the rock carefully back into place, flush with the wall.

There was no question this time of leaving it loose.

'Bed! Thanks, Rose, that's just what I need,' she said as she came back into Rose's room. 'I'm shattered.'

Pema heaved himself up onto one elbow. 'Did you see Jeffrey?' he asked blearily.

Singay nodded. 'Yes, and he looked good. The wounds are clean and his nose was cold and wet.' She flopped onto the makeshift bed and started to shuck off her shoes. 'He's in good hands, Pema. The best. When you come back for him, he'll be as good as new.'

Pema watched her. She'd said 'when *you* come back' not 'when *we* come back.'

'What about the Sisters?'

A closed look came over Singay's face. 'That's taken care of. They won't worry.' She yawned hugely, making Pema yawn too.

'Time to sleep?' suggested Rose.

There was no argument.

The afternoon was drawing to a close when Singay and Pema woke up. At least, Rose *said* it was afternoon. It was hard to tell the time, surrounded as they were by the changeless silvery light. They felt groggy and stupid, until the Driver suggested one last thing that woke them up abruptly.

'It is sometimes my pleasure,' he said, 'to spend the end of the day on my observation platform, watching the sun set over the desert. I've always found it a very inspiring sight. I was wondering, as this is the last time, would you care to join me?'

He was surprised at their reaction.

CHAPTER TEN

The View of the Desert

High Land children always asked about the desert. It stands to reason that you couldn't grow up in the shadow of such an enormous thing as the Mountain without wondering what was on the other side.

'What's there? What's it like?' little Singay and little Pema would ask.

And the old storytellers would shake their heads and push out their lips. 'You don't want to know,' they'd say. 'You don't want to know about that terrible place.'

Though of course the children *did* want to know. And they'd wheedle and whine until they got every last detail the tellers could remember or devise.

'All right, I'll tell you, but don't blame me if you get nightmares! This is the way it was told to me, and many a sleepless night I've had for thinking on it.'

'Go on! Go on!'

'Well, then ... On the other side, beyond the Mountain, there's not a blade of grass, not a single tree. There's only the wasteland. A howling wilderness where nothing moves but the wind and the sand – and the monsters. Horrible misbirths of nature, crazed by the sun, mutated beyond a need for water in that waterless land, but not beyond a desire for it.'

'No water?' Pema would whisper.

'Not a river or a pool or a stream. No mist. No rain. No snow.'

'But ... why don't they come and get *ours?*' Singay would ask.

'Because ...' And here the teller would speak softer, no more than a murmur, so the children all had to lean in close to catch the words. *'Because they don't know it's here.* But someday, somehow, they're going to find out!'

When Singay and Pema had heard the stories, each in the safety of their own home, they'd giggled and shivered like the rest. They shivered now, too, but the inclination to giggle was missing.

'All right,' said Singay slowly. *I can't let them see I'm scared – especially not Pema!* 'We'll come to see your view.'

'Though you might rather be alone?' Pema suggested hopefully. *I have to go if she's going, but if I can find an out ...* 'As it's your last time, you might prefer some privacy?'

'That's right,' Singay agreed, a little too quickly. 'We'd be disturbing you.'

'Ah!' cried Rose. 'You're being tactful! Be reassured, my invitation is sincere.' He beamed at them. 'I know you'll love it.'

Pema and Singay exchanged sidelong glances and gave in.

Happily, the Driver led them out of the room. Not so happily, they followed. First along another corridor, and then up a long, curving staircase of shallow steps.

The low steps made sense, just the right rise for the Driver's little legs, but the corridor arched high above his head. Pema noticed the discrepancy but was too polite to comment on it. Singay had no such qualms.

'You're very short,' she said, 'but you made the ceilings

really high. Why would you do that? Seems like a lot of extra work for nothing.'

Rose shrugged. 'We built as the rocks suggested. Their memories are of enclosing shapes like this, beautifully vaulted bits of air. It feels good to them, the way the emptiness grounds them and yet they can lean into it.'

'The rocks? They feel good?'

Here we go again, thought Pema and butted in quickly. 'The light's really nice too. How do you do that?'

'It *is* pretty, isn't it?' said Rose. 'And easily achieved. As I said before, some part of all rock memory goes back to the time when it was space debris. All we had to do was introduce a little luminescence from our comet. Quite straightforward. Of course, we'd never ask them to do anything unnatural.'

'Of course not,' murmured Singay, and Pema grinned weakly at her.

They climbed on in silence for a time. Then Pema tugged on Singay's sleeve.

'Look at the light *now*,' he whispered.

The walls and ceiling and the long shallow steps were tinged with an amber glow, as if touched by distant fire.

Rose looked back at them with a big smile.

'Almost there!' he chirped.

As soon as he said that, they started to notice a grittiness in the air that made their eyes itch. Pema found swallowing difficult and Singay kept brushing at her face with her hands.

'Welcome to the other side of the Mountain,' said Rose with a flourish. 'Welcome to my desert view.'

65

He ushered them up the final steps onto a great platform of stone that thrust out from the side of the Mountain into mid-air. Before them, as far as the eye could see, there was nothing but sand, carved into billows and waves and towering dunes by the wayward winds.

'It's like skin,' murmured Singay, touching her face again. 'Warm skin. Like giants sleeping in the sun ...'

Pema saw this was true. The sand was the colour of copper, the colour of skin, though richer and deeper than the skin of anyone he'd met.

'Look.' He pointed towards the west.

The sun hung there, a huge luminous ball in the sky, just lipping the horizon. Distant dust particles in the air sparked and swirled in shimmering ribbons across its face. Gold blurred with bronze merged with deep, rich scarlet.

They stood together on the great prow of rock, looking out with wonder.

'Were the deserts like this before?' asked Singay softly. 'Before the meteor, I mean?'

Rose shook his head. 'No. They were just sand then. Very pretty, in their own way, of course. But *this* desert has meteor dust sifted into it. From the most fragrant galaxies you can imagine. Even the tiniest percentage, spread as thin as you like – one particle to a million million – is all it takes. It's magical, isn't it? Just *smell* it!'

They did as he said. They breathed in deeply, and realised something that part of their brains had been noticing all along.

'Nutmeg!' exclaimed Pema.

'That's right,' Rose agreed. 'Makes you want to sing, doesn't it?'

'If you're from space, how do you know what nutmeg smells like?' asked Singay.

Pema rolled his eyes and sighed, but Rose didn't seem to hear her question. He was rapt, as if trying to draw the view into his eyes to keep it forever. Singay chose not to ask again. For now.

It was getting too cold to linger long, anyway.

'Time to go,' said Rose. 'I'm glad I had the chance to show you that.'

'I'm glad too,' said Singay. 'Thank you.'

She really can be nice when she chooses, Pema was thinking to himself as he turned to follow them – when he caught sight of something out of the corner of his eye. He turned back, and stared out over the desert.

I guess it was nothing. And then, all at once, he saw it again.

There were *lights*, way out in the distance, flickering and shifting. They looked like low-lying stars, fidgeting on the northern horizon, or gigantic fireflies, or perhaps torches held high by a moving band of . . .

Monsters?

'Hurry up, slow-worm!' Singay called from the staircase. 'I'm freezing!'

Pema blinked, and the lights were gone. Shivering from more than the cold now, he hurried to catch up with the others but, for reasons he didn't understand, he said nothing to them about what he might – or might not – have seen.

CHAPTER ELEVEN

The Descent

'I can't tell what time it is, but my stomach says it's overdue for *some* sort of meal,' Singay announced after they had been walking for what felt like hours. 'Let's stop for something to eat.'

'There's a way down inside the Mountain, all the way to Jungle Head,' Rose had assured them. It was hard to believe any tunnel could be that long – it would take days – but the Driver must know his own Mountain.

Mustn't he?

Now that they were underway, and the great adventure had truly begun, Singay was so excited she wanted to hug herself, but Pema just felt sick.

Singay looked at him. 'It's really good of you to be doing this, you know.' She put her hand for a brief moment on his arm and then started to unpack the food. 'Thank you.' She didn't see Pema's face turn red. 'Breadcake, Rose?'

But Rose shook his head with a smile. Instead, he picked up a loose bit of rock, held it to his nose and made a deep snuffling sound. The rock seemed to go oddly out of focus for an instant, then he put it down and reached for another. He caught sight of the stunned expressions on his companions' faces and hesitated, the second rock halfway to his nose.

'Is something the matter?'

'What are you *doing*?' Singay choked.

'I was hungry. I'm eating.' And he snuffed at the stone. Again the rock wavered weirdly, but when it steadied it looked completely unchanged.

'You eat rocks?'

'Well, in a manner of speaking, yes. The minerals inside the rock. That's Driver food.'

'You eat rocks? *With your nose?*'

Rose thought for a moment, then nodded. 'Yes, I suppose I do. You know, that really is a very interesting way of putting it. I eat with my nose!' He looked quite proud of himself.

Singay spluttered breadcake crumbs all over herself and Pema laughed till he got the hiccups.

'If only the Great Gow could see us now!'

'Oh, how rude – talking with your nose full. I'm shocked and appalled!'

Rose waited politely till they finished laughing at their own jokes. 'This Great Gow,' he said, frowning. 'What *is* that, exactly?'

And Singay and Pema told him, interrupting each other in their eagerness to get across the full awfulness of the Abbess. Sitting in a silver corridor, with a silver man, they found the Great Gow's power to belittle and hurt already seemed far away and long ago.

One more strange thing, among so many.

Even the simple act of walking was different.

'Isn't this great?' said Singay with a grin. 'It's so *easy!*'

It's true, thought Pema. Moving down the endless gentle slope and shallow steps felt more like gliding than the kind of mostly vertical climbing he was used to. *You could do this forever and never get tired!*

But of course they did get tired, and when they did, they rested. When they were sleepy, they lay down and slept, and when they opened their eyes again, it was as if no time had gone by at all. There was no way of distinguishing day and night – the silvery light from the stone never changed.

For a while, a noisy river tumbled beside the path, making conversation impossible. Then it disappeared off into the rock again.

'Listen!'

If they put their ears to the wall they could hear its muffled voice as it followed its own route downwards.

'It's going to the Sea, too,' said Rose. His voice was bright with hope.

It'll get there quicker than we will, thought Singay. She looked across at Pema and wondered if he was thinking the same thing. *Quick, change the subject!*

'You're so lucky!' she blurted.

Pema looked surprised. 'I am? Why?'

'I'll tell you why: no sisters. My house is bursting at the seams with girls and there you are being an only one. You probably have your own bedroom and everything!'

As soon as the words were out of her mouth she realised she'd said the wrong thing. She should have remembered that Rose had been 'an only one' and terribly lonely for years and years. And Pema ... *He's thinking about his home. Snows, Singay, you're stupid. You want him to think about adventure! Change the subject AGAIN!*

'Rose, tell us more about Homeworld.'

That worked. The Driver's smile lit up and he began to

talk. And as he talked, the tightness in Pema's face eased. It was impossible not to be caught up in the wonder of it all. It was when Rose was telling them about the beautiful sunsets over the purple seas of Homeworld that Pema suddenly realised something.

'Rose, I only just noticed – you speak the same language we do!'

Rose laughed. 'We'd have trouble talking to each other if I didn't! But of course we didn't *arrive* speaking like you. We don't really use language at all when we're in space. Not being what you'd call an air-breathing people.'

It was a moment before he noticed that both Pema and Singay had stopped walking. They were staring at him, open-mouthed.

'Not a ... but, but how is that *possible?*' spluttered Singay.

'Oh it's easy, really,' he said cheerfully. 'I learned your language from the rocks. It's surprising, given what little use they have for such things, but a tiny portion of a rock's memory *is* given over to oral data. Bird song, animal sounds, the noises of different kinds of weather – and, in passing, human speech. Just one of nature's little oddities, but quite convenient, don't you think?' He beamed at her.

'No, I meant how is it possible not to *brea*—'

There was a bend in the corridor and suddenly they were reunited with the river, bounding and shouting its way down the Mountain.

'My goodness, we're coming to a noisy bit again. It's getting positively boisterous, that river, isn't it!'

He grinned at Pema and trotted ahead. *Is he joking?*

Pema wondered. But no matter how hard he watched in the days and nights that followed, he never saw the little man's chest move.

When Rose told them about the route through the Mountain, Pema had expected that the tunnel would look the same all the way down. He was wrong.

'Hey, Rose! This rock looks *different*. From the rock before, I mean. Look!'

Rose came up beside him. 'Of course it is. You're never going to be able to make an entire mountain out of one kind of rock. We used different rocks as they came to hand. With different experiences as well. Different memories to draw on.'

Pema frowned. *What does that mean?* he wondered. *Surely rock is rock?* But Singay had gone ahead of them and was calling back.

'Pema! Rose! You have to see this!'

They caught up to her at a point where the corridor opened out into a wide space. The river re-emerged here and flowed calmly across the flat stone, winding in and out of the strangest forest Pema had ever seen.

'What *are* they?'

When Rose explained about stalactites and stalagmites, the impossibly slow building up of raw rock, one drip at a time, one tiny grain of mineral after another, they could only stare.

'To think all this was here, for all that time, right under our feet while we were running up and down the Mountain,' whispered Singay to Pema.

He nodded. *Dawa would love this!* With a sudden stab, he saw his grandmother clearly in his mind, standing by their cottage, shading her eyes to see if she could see him coming back down the Mountain. Anger with Singay welled up inside him. *It's so easy for her! She WANTS to be gone from her old life.*

Then Singay turned to him, smiling, her eyes shining, and he found he couldn't be angry anymore.

As the days passed, the roof and walls and floor of their road kept changing, from speckled to banded, from red to grey, from marble-smooth to nubbly and rough. And as they walked, they talked.

He really loves his home, thought Singay as she listened to Pema tell about his gows and his grandparents and the cheekiness of his marmole. But deep underneath, she also thought, *I know he's changing his mind – he won't go back. He's going to come with us, I know it!*

Since Rose had left his singing rocks behind, he decided to teach Pema and Singay some of the simpler harmonies of Driver music. The songs were wordless and based on different kinds of humming.

'Though how a people who claim not to breathe can sing at *all* is beyond me,' Singay muttered.

'Really?' Rose smirked. 'Oh well, never mind.'

Pema hid a grin behind his hand.

By his rough reckoning, it was the fourth day of their descent. The rocks here were darker and the tunnel was lower and narrower.

'Brrr, this is a gloomy bit,' said Singay with a shiver. 'Let's sing.'

'Right,' said Rose. 'Let's do the humming song. After me, then.'

And they began.

They swung along at a good pace, humming away, concentrating hard on their parts – for even the easiest Driver songs were complex and convoluted, and there turned out to be many different ways to hum. They walked in single file: Rose first, then Singay, then Pema.

'Nnnn ...'

'Mm-mm-mm ...'

'Ahhh ...'

CRACK!

And the Mountain caved in.

CHAPTER TWELVE

The Language of Rocks

Singay screamed and threw herself forward onto the floor. The noise of rocks ripping out of the roof, the grinding of stone pressing down against stone – it was deafening, terrifying. And then ...

And then, nothing.

Dead silence, as if all the sound in the world had suddenly been cut off.

Panting with fear, Singay forced her eyes open. She saw a trickle of dust feather down from above. She saw a pile of rubble blocking the corridor. And she saw Rose.

He was standing there, statue-still, with a strange shine in his silver eyes. His hands were raised.

He's holding back the rocks. She didn't know how she knew that – she'd never seen anything like it in her life before – but it was as clear to her as her own name.

And then she realised what she *wasn't* seeing.

'*PEMA!*'

Horror rushed up her throat as Singay realised Pema was *underneath* the fall. *I've killed him! He didn't want to be here! I made him come!* 'Rose – is he – is he ... ?'

The alien light faded from the Driver's eyes. Without a word, he stumbled forward and began scrabbling at the boulders.

'Let me.' Singay pushed him aside and lifted stone after stone. She was afraid the whole heap would collapse, or slide forward like a rocky avalanche, but she was even more afraid of what she was going to find. *Crushed, mangled, broken.* The words kept yelling in her head. *Pema, please don't be dead!*

'There he is!' cried Rose suddenly. 'Pull him out – here, let me help!'

A space had opened and they could see him, stretched out on the ground. As they dragged him clear, Singay shuddered. He'd been lying in a narrow, Pema-shaped tomb, barely an inch of clearance above him. Jagged edges of rock reached for him on every side like teeth. His eyes were shut, and half his face was covered in blood.

'What happened?' Pema whispered, his voice hoarse with stone dust and shock.

She was so relieved to hear him speak, she wanted to cry. 'Stay still. Let me have a look at you.'

Carefully, she felt his arms and legs to see that if there were any bones broken. She wetted a cloth from their water bottle and sponged the blood from his face, parting his hair gingerly.

'Head wounds bleed a lot. They always look worse than they actually are. Aren't you glad I did a stint in the infirmary when I first came to the Abbey?' She knew she was sounding a bit mad, but she couldn't stop babbling.

Pema tried to grin at her, but only managed a shudder as some of the icy water dribbled down his back.

Neither of them noticed the Driver.

Rose had turned an ugly white, and the bones of his face stood out with a sudden starkness. He turned away from them and, with shaking hands, reached into his robes and pulled out a glittery bag on a silver cord. He managed to untie the knot, then tipped the bag and let a little of the powder flow out over the back of his hand. It sank instantly into his skin, like water sucked up by thirsty soil.

And the silver bag was hidden away again. The whole procedure couldn't have taken more than a few seconds, but even in that short time, the awful whiteness eased.

'Well, that's you,' Singay was saying to Pema, rocking back on her heels to survey her doctoring. 'Looking pretty good, too, I'd say.'

'Is he all right?' Rose whispered. 'Are you sure? Can he walk?'

'Yes,' said Pema in a tight voice. 'I can walk. Let's get out of here.'

They left the dark strata behind, moving faster now, in silence. Pema's head was pounding and he felt cold and sick, but he kept going as steadily as he could. Singay watched him anxiously.

'There's no danger now,' Rose kept assuring them. 'See – nothing but crystals here.'

It was true. The corridor was running now along a vein of quartz. Walls, ceiling and floor sparked light at them in every colour of the spectrum, but its beauty went unappreciated.

'Let's keep going,' insisted Singay.

'Please. It's safe, I promise. You have to rest. I . . . I'm so sorry . . . I have to rest.'

Singay and Pema stopped abruptly.

'Rose! What's wrong?'

'*You're* hurt!'

The Driver slumped to the floor and wailed, 'No, I'm ... It's all my fault! How could I have missed all that anger, and there was the blood, and ...' His words were swallowed up in tears.

'Was it seeing Pema's blood?' Singay hunkered down beside him. 'Don't worry, it just takes people that way sometimes. Sister Yi-mala, back at the Abbey, the sight of even just a little blood makes her come over all peculiar. She almost fainted one time when Sister Grale accidentally tipped strombomble juice down her front. I couldn't stop laughing! Just put your head between your knees for a bit. We can stay here for a few moments. Go on.'

Rose pushed her hands away, shaking his head. 'It was my fault – I wasn't paying attention. It was the singing. I was so enjoying our singing, I just didn't listen.'

'Listen to what?'

'To the *anger*. I mean, I could *hear* it, but I didn't listen. I didn't pay attention. Those rocks back there, they remembered people who dug into them and exploded and gouged and ripped them out of the earth, and they wanted to pay them back. Make them bleed. Time doesn't mean anything to them, so they don't understand that you couldn't possibly be the same people. They don't really think, you know.'

There was a horrified pause.

'So rocks don't think, but they can *hate*?' Pema's mouth went dry and he looked fearfully over his shoulder. 'They were trying to kill us?'

They were trying to kill us, and then Rose stopped them, thought Singay. But she didn't say anything. She suddenly couldn't think straight herself. It had been too long since they'd slept and too much had happened and Pema was probably suffering from shock and Rose didn't look much better.

'No more talking!' she announced abruptly, sounding uncomfortably like the Abbess. 'Rose says these crystals are safe. We're going to eat and then we're going to sleep, and I don't want any arguments.'

She didn't get any.

When they awoke, nobody wanted to talk about what had happened. There was an unspoken desire to just get moving. Pema was stiff and aching all over, but he wasn't going to let that slow him down. They walked briskly, until, once again, the rocks changed. The corridor opened out into a long chamber.

'Pema,' Singay whispered urgently. 'Look up!'

Pema flinched, fearing another rock fall, but the ceiling was still. Wiping the sweat from his hands, he squinted upwards. 'What *is* that?'

For a moment, he couldn't understand what he was seeing. He couldn't get the perspective right.

'So huge . . .' breathed Singay, and then it clicked.

He was looking at a gigantic skeleton in the ceiling, half-encased in the rock – a sea beast longer than a huge fallen tree, with a mighty rib cage and great fluted tail and fins.

And now that his eyes had adjusted he could see that the giant was not alone.

'They're *everywhere!*'

Walls, ceiling, floor . . . everywhere he looked he saw

shapes. One wall was encrusted with seashells, the other with things that curled round and round. As they stepped further into the cavern, they were walking over shoals of fish, with only the tracery of their bones to show where they'd once swarmed and swum.

Some pieces had fallen out onto the floor, but when Pema and Singay picked them up, they felt too heavy to be shell or bone.

'It's as if they're made of rock!' Pema exclaimed. 'But how can that be, Rose?'

'They're fossils,' Rose said.

They looked blankly at him. It wasn't a word they knew.

Rose scratched his head. 'Not an easy one to explain. In a way, it's another kind of memory.' He talked to them about bodies buried, subjected to enormous pressure and transformed over inconceivable stretches of time. Trying to imagine so much time made Pema's head spin. Singay walked ahead, busy looking and marvelling until, at the far end of the chamber, she paused.

'Rose? Can you hear that? Up ahead?'

Pema came up beside her. 'What? Wait ... Yes, I hear it!'

'Sounds like a waterfall,' said Rose. 'A big one. Come on!'

The noise was getting louder with every step, a deep, pulsing, roaring sound that they could feel through their feet. It pounded at them so that it was impossible to think. As they followed the passageway, it became much narrower, so that soon they were scraping through sideways. The silver light that had been with them ever since the first moment they'd crawled through the hole from the Abbey died away, until they were feeling their way in the dark.

And then, so suddenly it made them gasp, they pushed through a screen of hanging vines and were outside.

'Look!' yelled Singay over the noise of the water. 'We made it!'

They had come out beside a mighty waterfall. Ahead, they could see the river snaking away into the green haze of the Jungle. Directly below, laid out in a cluster of houses and gardens and sheds, was Jungle Head. And there, tied up at the pier, was a boat.

As if it's just waiting to take us away! thought Singay. She led them away from the waterfall to a point where they could hear each other without shouting. 'Time for your disguise, Rose!'

There wasn't much to it – a wide-brimmed hat, a shirt and trousers she'd brought from the Abbey. They were all too big for him, but the outfit hid most of his silvery skin. If you didn't pay close attention, he looked like a little boy who hadn't grown into his hand-me-down clothes yet.

'Perfect.' Singay gave the hat a final tweak. She turned to head down the slope. 'Come on, you lot, we need to get the tickets bought. That boat may be leaving any minute now. Let's get going!'

But when she looked back, Pema wasn't following. He was just standing there, slowly shaking his head.

'What is it? Hurry up! What's wrong?' she demanded. 'We need to go!'

'I'm sorry,' he said in a stricken voice. 'I told you – I'm not coming.'

CHAPTER THIRTEEN

Decision at Jungle Head

'I can't come with you,' said Pema. Each word hurt to say. 'I have to go home. Please understand. Wadipa and Dawa, my grandparents, they need me. The gows . . . Jeffrey . . .' He choked up. He hadn't wanted to think about this moment – for so many days it had simply been a case of putting one foot in front of another – but now, inescapably, he had to face what came next.

There was a horrible silence and then Rose was speaking, saying how of course they understood, how of course he needed to get back up the Mountain, back to his life and his work, how it had been good of him to have come as far as he had, how his family must be worrying.

And all the while Singay was standing there with a sullen expression on her face, while her thoughts battered around in her head. *You bake-brained idiot. You actually thought he'd change his mind. Just because YOU have nothing to go home to. You want him to be like YOU.*

Pema gulped hard. 'I'm so sorry. I . . .' His head was bursting with last minute advice. 'Remember the fare for the boat is fixed – from what I've heard the Borang don't haggle. Make sure you stock up first on food at Zeppa's shop, anything that will travel well. We don't know how long the journey to River Head will take. And Rose, pick up some rocks, all right? The boat might not tie up again very soon, or it might not be rocky where it does.'

The Driver nodded, his eyes huge and solemn.

He looks so little. So vulnerable. Pema felt sick.

'You see why I can't come down into the town with you,' he said, pleading with them both. 'If anyone in the settlement recognises me and word gets back to Zeppa, he'll be after me for answers – he's like a dugg with a bone, always has to know everything. I'd have to lie to his face about how I got here or else tell him everything about you, Rose. I know it's not what you want, so it's much better for me just to slip through town when it gets dark, get back home unnoticed and tell them everything I safely can – all about how I told the Abbess what I was supposed to, about the Mountain moving backwards, but she didn't think it was any of our business. They can't blame me for her saying that. But then I had to stay on because of Jeffrey. And then I came away without him, because I knew they'd be worried and then I'll go back up to the Abbey again and fetch him away. And once you get Rose back together with his friends, they can make it so the Mountain won't be walking anymore, and after a while everybody'll forget all about it ...' The words dried up, but there wasn't really anything left to say anyway.

Singay felt as if she'd been punched in the stomach. Rose just kept nodding bravely. Pema looked as if he were about to cry.

It was awful.

Singay and Rose sat in the barge and watched as the two Borang boatmen went about the business of preparing to cast off without exchanging a word or a glance.

'They don't talk much,' Singay said dully.

Rose looked at the boatmen with interest. It was almost as if he'd become the child they'd disguised him as, wide-eyed and awestruck at everything in this big new world.

Even with her mind ninety per cent numb, Singay had managed to buy the tickets and some supplies. As it turned out, the two of them were going to be the only passengers on this trip downriver, and that suited her. The Borang never asked questions, and this way there was nobody else to, either. *I won't have to pretend to be sociable.* It wasn't something she did well at the best of times, and this felt like anything *but* the best of times.

Rose watched the Borang, and the pier, and the sky ... anything, really, seemed to give him pleasure. Tears pricked Singay's eyes. She peered down over the side of the boat into the green water.

How am I going to manage? What was I thinking? She fished a forgotten piece of breadcake, gone stale and hard now, out of her pocket and dropped it overboard. It sank slowly into the dark greenness and then, just before it disappeared from sight, there was a sudden flurry of motion and something frighteningly large swallowed it and flashed away again.

Singay's heart contracted and she reared back and turned to Rose to tell him what she'd seen, when something even larger hurtled over the railing and knocked her onto the deck. She screamed and scrabbled away backwards and only then realised that the thing wasn't an enormous, razor-toothed monster come up out of the wet depths to rip her apart.

It was Pema.

She stopped screaming.

As the current caught the boat, swinging it out into the middle of the River, and the pier of Jungle Head was left behind, the three stared at each other.

'I . . .' said Pema.

'I didn't . . .' said Singay.

'I couldn't be happier,' said Rose, and he reached over and patted Pema on the knee.

'Me too.' Singay sounded choked.

'Thank you.' Pema found he was grinning so hard his face hurt. Then he suddenly turned serious. 'But I want you to know, I'm going to send a letter to Wadipa and Dawa on the next upriver boat. I'm going to tell them the truth. All of it. It's all I *can* do. I can't just say "Back soon!" – because we don't know how long this is going to take. And, well, I've never really lied to them before. Even if I tried to, what story could I possibly make up that would explain . . . *this?*' He waved a hand at the boat and the three of them and the darkening Jungle on either side. 'Rose, do you understand?'

The Driver looked at him long and hard. Then he nodded. 'I trust you. My life in your hands.' And then he gave Pema a wide, seraphic grin.

'Anyway, they might not believe you,' said Singay a bit huskily. 'You realise that?'

'Maybe not.' Pema shrugged. 'But then again, they might. They're not Abbess Great Gow, you know!' He gave a huge mock shudder, and added, 'I have to let them know. I can't leave them to worry.'

Just then one of the Borang came over and silently

handed out pallets and bedding. Suddenly the thought of being horizontal and unconscious seemed enormously attractive.

'Go ahead. I'm happy to look at the night,' said Rose. 'You sleep now. It's been quite a day!'

In no time at all, Pema and Singay were in their makeshift beds with nothing but the black sky above and the black river below, sweeping them inexorably along.

'Pema?' Singay said softly.

'Mmm?'

'What made you change your mind?'

There was a long silence and she thought perhaps he had already fallen asleep. But then he spoke out of the darkness.

'I watched you and Rose from up by the waterfall. I watched you going into the store and then coming out again, and then going down to the pier, and then disappearing onto the boat. And I found that every time I couldn't see you, my chest would hurt. Like a stitch, you know? When you climb too fast? And it struck me that if I let you go without me, I wouldn't be able to see you for most likely the rest of my life, and *choosing* to go through the rest of my life with a sore chest was probably one of the stupider things I could do. So I decided to come.'

'Oh,' said Singay, and Pema thought he could hear a smile in her voice. He smiled too, shifted a little on the hard pallet, and fell asleep.

CHAPTER FOURTEEN

The Jungle

The Borang were a strange, silent people with greenish skin and sad, soulful eyes.

'Though maybe to *other* Borang they're perfectly cheerful and chatty. Maybe they just don't talk to people like us,' suggested Pema.

'There *are* no people like us,' grunted Singay.

Two Borang manned the barge: one to steer, and one to manage the rhinophant that provided the return power. These hugely strong beasts rode the Borang boats downstream, and then dragged them back to Jungle Head again, plodding up the well-worn towpath along the eastern bank. The Borang obviously thought very highly of them. In fact they showed far more interest in their rhinophant than in their cargo or passengers.

At first the Jungle made Singay and Pema feel horribly hemmed in, in a way that being under an entire mountain hadn't. Perhaps it was the stillness, or the humidity, or perhaps it was the way the trees seemed to lean hungrily towards them as they passed.

It's like they're trying to suck the life out of us, thought Singay.

'It's hard to breathe,' she said.

'There's not enough air,' Pema sighed, fanning himself.

Singay had bought summer-weight clothes for herself and Rose at Zeppa's store. The Borang were willing to sell a spare set of trousers and shirt for Pema and she set to with needle and scissors to adjust them to his taller frame.

'What a relief!' he said, putting them on.

She wiped a hand across her face. 'What I wouldn't give for a breeze.'

Rose didn't care. He loved it all.

'He seems like such a child,' said Pema to Singay. 'I wonder how old he really is?'

'I wondered that too,' said Singay. 'But he said I wouldn't believe him if he told me.' She squinted at Rose with her head on one side. 'We've got used to him, I guess, and the Borang don't care, but we're going to have to be really careful nobody looks at him too closely once we get to River Head.'

Worry clenched in Pema's stomach. 'I think I'll go see the rhinophant.'

Time spent with the beast calmed him down. The massive, tough-skinned, ebony-coloured, viciously-horned, incredibly muscular rhinophant had its own enclosure at the stern of the boat, and its own schedule of feeding, resting, being cooled with buckets of river water, being mucked out and groomed. Pema stood at the railing of the enclosure for hours at a time. At first, the boatmen kept a close eye on him to be sure he wasn't bothering the animal in any way. After a while, though, they were satisfied and carried on with their work as if he weren't there.

'Need a hand?' Pema asked hopefully.

But they shook their heads at him, polite but firm. It was hard to argue with someone who didn't actually talk to you.

The rhinophant was like the Borang in that it was

almost completely silent, though it did have quite expressive, mobile ears. Pema thought he could tell quite a lot of what it (he wasn't entirely certain whether it was male or female) felt about things by watching the way it swivelled its ears.

'They really are magnificent animals,' Pema said to Singay and Rose. 'And complex and intelligent, you know? I feel like they're thinking truly deep thoughts.'

Singay looked over at the rhinophant and tried to see beyond the terrifying bulk and the piggy little eyes and the nasty horn. The animal chose that moment to lift its short tail and deposit a great big steaming plop of dung onto the deck.

'Deep,' repeated Singay. 'Oh yes, I can see it now.'

Pema just pulled a face and ignored her. It was too hot to quarrel.

In the course of the trip they passed two of the Borang's boats being dragged back upriver by their animals. Pema hung over the railing for as long as they were in sight, watching the steady, powerful plodding with admiration. But neither the Borang nor the rhinophants seemed to take note of the other boat's inhabitants, even to the extent of a nod, a trumpet or a wave. They stared a little, but that was it.

'I wonder if river duty is some kind of punishment for them,' said Singay. 'Maybe it's what they make Borang criminals do, with a vow of silence thrown in for good measure.'

'Hmm?' Rose was gazing at the trees.

'Eh?' Pema was gawping at the rhinophant.

'Nothing,' said Singay with a sigh.

In the days it took to travel down this stretch of the River, there were only a few real conversations in which everybody who took part was actually paying attention. The dark, slightly cooler night times seemed to encourage them.

'How much money do we have left?' Pema asked Singay one evening as they leaned together against the railing.

Singay pulled their money sack out of her pocket and handed it to him.

Pema looked serious when he felt how light it was, and even more so when he had counted it all out. 'I think we're going to have to stop soon and earn some money.'

'Stop and work?' Singay turned to him indignantly. 'That was my entire dowry – how can it not be enough?'

'I don't know how – it just isn't,' Pema snapped. Then he made a face. 'Sorry. But it may be a long way to the Sea, and we have to eat and pay for fares and places to sleep. So we need to think about work. What skills do we have?'

Singay bit her lip and scowled. *Do I have any skills?* She knew a bit about housekeeping and needlework from her mother, and a bit about first aid from Sister Menpa, and a very little bit about falconry from Sister Hodges. *But what good is any of that?*

'Is something wrong?' asked Rose, coming up beside them.

Pema looked at Singay and raised an eyebrow. *Best not to worry him.* She gave a slight nod of agreement.

'Nothing,' said Pema. 'Except that it's too hot.'

'We were wondering, though,' added Singay. 'What's it like, the Sea?'

As she'd hoped, Rose was distracted. He made a sound that in a breathing man would have been a great sigh of longing.

'The Sea is as beautiful a thing as the heart can imagine,' he said, closing his silvery eyes as if to see better the image in his head. 'It's . . .'

He opened his eyes and spread his hands in a gesture of apology.

'It's difficult to describe. I used to think that nothing could be more wonderful than the sweep of galaxies, with a solar wind in your face and a herd of meteors at your side and limitless space all around – but I was wrong. When you see it, you'll understand.'

And then, another evening, as the Jungle darkened around them, and they were all lying on the hard deck, ready to go to sleep, there was another conversation. At the time it hadn't seemed all that important, but Pema would remember it long afterwards.

'Rose?' Singay had said thoughtfully.

'Mmm?'

'You know all your stuff – your books, and the blankets and the rugs, and the little metal machines? Back in your room, I mean?'

'Yes?'

'Where did you get it all?'

'Oh, that's another story. I don't think . . .'

'Come on, Rose,' said Pema. 'We're past secrets, aren't we?' In the dark, he couldn't see the little man's suddenly uncomfortable expression. 'Did you make it all out of rocks somehow?'

'No, no. People just … brought me things,' said the Driver. 'From time to time. Things they thought I'd like.'

Singay sat up. 'You said nobody knew you were there!'

'Ah. Well, the people I mean weren't *your* people. No, no. It was the others.'

'What others?' exclaimed Singay, but Pema suddenly thought, *I know the answer to that.*

'The desert people,' he murmured. 'That's who it was, wasn't it?'

'That's right,' said Rose.

'You've met the monsters? The demons in the desert?' Singay's voice was shrill. 'But you *said*! You said everything died!'

'No, no. Not everything. Only the land-life that depended on green things was destroyed. The desert people never did, of course, depend just on green things and so they survived. Underground, mostly.'

'And did *they* call you Rose?'

The Driver gave an embarrassed little cough. 'Well, no. Mostly they called me God.'

There was a long, busy silence.

'Then the question is, I guess,' said Singay, in a strangled voice, 'why bother with us? Why the walking mountains and all the effort and all the time to make all this, when you already had them?'

'But we hadn't destroyed *them*!' Rose protested. 'What – didn't you *want* us to recreate you?' Surprise had turned to distress.

'No, no, it's not that. Of course not.' Pema tried to soothe him. 'We really *are* grateful. Aren't we, Singay?'

Singay lay down and turned away.

'Thanks be to Mother Mountain,' she muttered. 'Oh yes, we're grateful.'

The Mountain was moving. It shuddered under her, trying to throw her off, like a gigantic beast shivering flies from its flanks. Singay moaned. *Too small*, she cried without a voice, *I'm too small.* Something rumbled in the distance, growing louder and louder. When she turned to face the noise, she *saw* it, racing towards her. Tall trees toppled, rocks splintered, chasms opened and the green pastures disappeared into them. She couldn't run. She didn't even try – nothing could outrun *that*. The next second the earthquake reached her, knocking her to the ground and shaking her in its teeth like a furious dugg. Someone was calling her, demanding her help, but what could she do for anyone else when she couldn't even get to her feet?

'Singay! Singay! Wake up!'

'Get off! Leave me alone!' she protested, pushing out with her hands.

'No! Something's wrong with Rose. *Wake up!*'

Singay sat up abruptly. It was dawn, and the Jungle was loud with birdsong and the shrieking of unidentified animals. And there, lying far too still in the pale half-light, was Rose.

BOOK TWO

Look to the Sea

Go as secretly as you can, but remember – even in starlight, you will cast a shadow.

(Jathang saying)

CHAPTER FIFTEEN

Dangerous Ground

'I didn't know what to do!' Pema was almost sobbing. 'I woke up and he was shuddering, like he was having a fit or something, and then he just went like that – all rigid and not moving.'

Singay scrambled over to the little man. He looked awful. In a panic, she searched her mind for Sister Menpa's first-aid instructions and was just about to check Rose's airways when she remembered: *He doesn't breathe.* What next? Heartbeat. Should she check that? Would she know what she was checking for? *Do Drivers have hearts?*

She hesitated, afraid to do anything in case it made him worse. And then, to her enormous relief, Rose opened his eyes.

'Oh, thank goodness,' whispered Pema.

Rose gave them a ghost of a smile but seemed unable to speak. As if with enormous effort, he pawed awkwardly at his pocket.

'Is there something . . . ?' Singay moved the little man's hand aside and pulled out a silvery bag, tied with cord, containing something soft and light.

'Is this it? Is it some sort of medicine?'

Rose could barely nod. Singay untied the cord for him and then looked about for a cup or spoon to measure it into. But instead, Rose took the bag from her with trembling fingers and shook a tiny amount of something glittery and dust-like out onto the back of his hand. Instantly it disappeared, as if his skin had drunk it in. He repeated the process once more.

The effect was extraordinary. As they watched, his colour changed from dead white to a healthier silver, the tension in his limbs eased and, with Pema's help, he was able to sit up and lean against the railing of the boat.

'What just happened?' Singay's voice was shaky. 'Pema said you had some sort of fit.'

A single, silver tear rolled down Rose's face. 'I didn't mean you to be worried. It's all my fault. I . . . I got it wrong.'

'Got what wrong?' said Pema.

'The doses. I've been rationing myself, but I didn't realise just how much effect distance was going to have on my control – how much irradiant is drained just maintaining stability.' He stroked the sack unconsciously as he spoke, cradling it on his chest as if it were something infinitely precious and fragile.

'You are going to have to do better than that,' said Singay. Now that the panic was over, she felt impatient and cross. 'Is that the irri – irritant?'

'Irradiant.'

'In there?' She pointed at the bag. 'It's medicine you need? That you haven't told us about? And if you get it wrong you *pass out*!? Explain!'

'I'm sorry,' the little man said. 'It's difficult . . .'

Singay crossed her arms and scowled. 'Try.'

Rose looked at her nervously and bobbed his head. 'I'll do my best. Remember I told you how Drivers came to your world? Well, it wasn't as hard as you might think for us to adapt to living here. Right from the start we were able to access the minerals from your rocks, and although some of the flavours took a bit of getting used to, they were perfectly nutritious. But irradiant, well, that was another matter. It's your atmosphere, you see. It excludes most of the spectrum of irradiants, which is a good thing for *you*, of course, since they'd be poisonous. But without their ionizing effect Drivers gradually become . . .' He paused, gazing into their bemused faces. 'No, no, this isn't clear at all, is it?'

He slapped his forehead in frustration and tried again.

'You need to understand that space – up there – is awash with an invisible sort of . . . um, thing . . . that Drivers need to be healthy. We absorb it through our skin. Normally we never have to worry about getting enough of it, because it's everywhere. The way air is everywhere here. You can't see it, but you can't live without it, right?'

Pema and Singay nodded uncertainly.

'Good, right, well, irradiants are for us like the air is for you. However, there's a kind of invisible barrier around your world that stops the irradiants from getting through. They aren't good for you, in spite of being essential for us. Of course, we knew that would be the case, and we brought special powdered supplies with us – not as nice as fresh, obviously, but it does the trick.'

'All right,' said Singay. 'Irradiant. We don't have it. You need it. And is it the irradiant that makes you able to drive the Mountain?'

'Not exactly. The connection we have, our ability to hear stone memories or nudge the magnetic fields or make rocks do what we want them to – we can do those things because we're Drivers. But if the level of irradiants in our bodies starts to drop below a certain level, it's as if, for you, your air got too thin to breathe.'

'Like altitude sickness?' said Pema.

'That's right. When a human gets altitude sickness they become dizzy, am I right? And disoriented and confused. It's hard for them to concentrate. It's the same for me. I let my irradiant level drop too low and it gets hard for me to hold my concentration on the Mountain, keep it stable.'

'I dreamt there was an earthquake,' whispered Singay.

My grandparents! My home! Are they all right? Have they been hurt? Pema didn't dare say the words out loud.

Rose drooped. 'Like I told you, when I'm back with the others, the three of us will be able to ground the mountains properly, once and for all. Till then, all I can do is keep things under control, keep things steady.' He looked weary and sad. 'We had what seemed like a ridiculously large amount of powdered irradiant when we arrived,' he said. 'But we've stayed far longer than we'd expected and, now . . . I'm running out. It will get harder and harder for me to hold the Mountain in place.'

'And when it – this stuff – what happens when it's all gone?'

'Ah. Well. Then I die.'

'WHAT?!'

They couldn't believe their ears.

'So you're saying the Mountain wants to rip up the whole world, that there's no way you can permanently stop it without the help of the other Drivers, you're *dying* – and you weren't going to *tell* us?' shrilled Singay. Her voice set off a cacophony of Jungle birds, protesting raucously.

'I didn't want you to worry,' muttered Rose, hanging his head.

'I thought you trusted us.'

Somehow it was even worse when she spoke quietly.

'I don't see how we can do this if we keep secrets from each other,' said Pema.

'Stop looking at me like that!' cried Rose, scrambling to his feet. 'What about you? What about the fact that our money – Singay's money – is going to run out? You were keeping *that* a secret, weren't you?'

'Yes, all right, but that was different,' said Pema. 'We didn't tell you because we were thinking about *you*! It wasn't as if making you worry would make anything any better.'

'Exactly,' said Rose.

They stared at each other. They knew they were on dangerous ground. The truth was starker, more real to them, than it had ever been before.

They had to get Rose to the Sea.

'Oh, Rose,' said Singay, and then they were both crying. Pema would have joined them, but he was afraid if he started he wouldn't be able to stop.

'I'm sorry,' Rose sobbed. 'I shouldn't have kept secrets from you. I won't again. We're in this together, aren't we, and the sooner I can get to the other Drivers, the sooner we can fix the mountains in place.'

'And the sooner you can get all the irradiant you need. Save the Driver, save the world.' Singay gave a crooked grin.

'Right, that's settled, then,' managed Pema. 'No more—'

A rapidly approaching yodel interrupted him. He turned around just in time to catch an ample bosom in the face.

CHAPTER SIXTEEN

Lady Allum's Arrival

An extravagantly endowed lady swinging on a vine out of the Jungle, yodelling enthusiastically, had landed on Pema, who was now pinned flat on his back on the deck. He looked *so* stunned and *so* ridiculous that Singay and Rose burst into hysterical laughter.

The lady grinned cheerfully over at them.

'Nice save, lad,' she boomed at Pema as she clambered to her feet. 'I hope I didn't do you a mischief there? The Borang are so much better at the whole swinging on vines thing, but then they're a bit more sparely built.' She straightened her hat, grabbed Pema's unresisting arm and heaved him upright, as easily as if he were a feather's weight. 'Your parents aren't going to be any too happy with me if I've damaged you before we've even been introduced!'

'Nnn ... er ...' gasped Pema.

'We aren't with parents,' said Singay, wiping her eyes and trying to stop giggling. 'I'm Singay. This is Rose. And you've met Pema.'

The new arrival slapped Pema affectionately on the back, almost knocking him flat again. 'Oh yes, indeed – we're old friends, aren't we! And I am Lady Allum Broomback, of the House of Effulgence. Well, to be exact, I'm a fairly distant scion of a minor branch of the House of Effulgence. On my mother's side, you understand.'

'Oh?'

'Ah?'

Lady Allum gave a great guffaw. 'You have no idea what I'm talking about, do you? That's what I love about being out here in the back of beyond. Nobody knows your name, so you're free to just *get on*. No expectations, no restrictions. No "I can't talk to you because my House is allied to your enemy's House which makes you *my* enemy even if you're just a second cousin twice removed and quite a nice person *really*." Her broad, cheerful face suddenly turned solemn. 'Though not everyone who comes out of the City *is* nice. I picked up some pretty disturbing gossip when I was last getting supplies in River Head – cons and crack religions and all sorts. Best not judge all books by *my* cover, my new young friends.'

The City! thought Pema. 'You're from Elysia? That's by the Sea, right? That's a long way from here, isn't it?'

Singay gave him a warning look. In spite of Lady Allum's fabulously funny entrance, she *was* a stranger.

'A long way?' Lady Allum hooted. 'Leagues and leagues! Isn't it wonderful? My motto is keep your nose clean and the bleeders at arm's length. Hello, there!' She waved happily at the Borang and trotted over to speak with them. 'It's me again!'

Rose hissed anxiously. 'What did she mean about noses? Was she talking about the way I eat? How does she know about me? Oh, I knew it, I knew it, it's all going to go wrong!'

'Shh! Calm down!' Singay checked over her shoulder to be sure he hadn't been overheard. 'It's got nothing to do with you. It's just an expression. Careful – she's coming back.'

'Just dropped in for a lift, you see,' said Lady Allum as she approached them again. 'They're quite used to me hitching a ride to my next sector. *So* much quicker than hacking along on foot!' She plopped herself down on the deck with a contented sigh, pulled out a ferocious knife and began sharpening it with a file. 'Blunt your blade as soon as look at you, some of the stuff out there,' she added enthusiastically, tipping a nod at the lush green sliding past them.

'Get her to talk about something!' whispered Rose. 'Get her mind off noses.'

He gripped Pema's arm so tight it made him squawk. 'YOU – excuse me, you, um, live in the Jungle?'

'Lucky, eh?' She tried her thumb against the blade and went back to filing. 'I'm a zoo-otanist. Part botanist, part zoologist. Fertility's my field. You would not *believe* the rates of growth I've got notes for already – not to mention diversification patterns and environmental enigmas. Stop me when I get boring – I'm a bit of an enthusiast, don't you know. The Borang tolerate me, but there's no reason why you should!' Another hoot of laughter caused a flock of startled birds to fall out of the trees, screeching.

'Do they – the Borang – do they talk to you?' asked Singay, hunkering down on the deck. 'We haven't heard them talk at all! Tell us about them, will you? We're all really curious!'

But Lady Allum shook her head. 'No can do. They're a very private people, the Borang, and I agreed to respect that before they would let me even set foot in the Jungle, let alone wander about and study it. But I wouldn't mind finding out more about *you three* – you're a bit of a mystery yourselves!' She let out another of her raucous laughs. 'Oh, if you could see your faces! All right, I get it – *you're* a private people too. Never mind. If you were leafy or green or had paws I'd be prying away like mad, but *people* I can leave well enough alone.' And she put her finger to her lips, leaned back against the railing and peacefully closed her eyes.

'Oh,' said Singay, disappointed in spite of herself.

'Or,' said Lady Allum, opening one eye, 'I could tell you about zoo-otany?'

There was a unanimous chorus of 'Yes!'

Lady Allum sat up with a grin, took a breath so deep all her buttons threatened to explode, and began to talk.

She talked of compass point line surveys and biodiversity indicator species and how seismic tremors aided new growth by knocking down the canopy trees and letting in the light. She told them about Minkey Monkeys, whose fruit diet caused them to deposit poo – and the seeds in it – so regularly 'you can chart their paths through the tree tops by the saplings growing on the Jungle floor below. Always wear a hat around Minkey Monkeys, that's my advice.'

She spoke of the Lesser Spotted Trumpeting Butterfly, the only known species whose voice is audible to humans. It was such a specialist feeder that Lady Allum had only ever seen one specimen in all her travels, sucking the nectar from a rare Tarantella Orchid. 'Strange-looking flower, that – black and hairy and shaped like a large spider. No idea what sort of biological advantage that is. Not a lot, perhaps, which could explain them *being* so rare . . .'

She told them about the Salad Panda, an odd Jungle predator whose fur had evolved to resemble lush green salad leaves. 'It's a lazy beast, the Panda, just lies about in the shade, waiting for not-very-bright salad-eating rodents to come along and try to nibble it, and then WHAM – *it* eats *them*. The Jungle's ferly all right.'

They could have listened to her stories all day, and she could probably have gone on talking twice that long without running out of tales to tell, but all at once she looked round sharply at the trees and jumped to her feet.

'Whoops! I was so busy enjoying your company I almost missed my stop. Hello there!' Lady Allum shouted to the Borang, pointing towards the river bank. 'This is me!'

There was nothing they could see that differentiated that bit of the Jungle from any other, but the Borang nodded and edged the boat towards the place indicated. Lady Allum swung her knapsack onto her back and checked her big knife was secure in its sheath.

'Thanks!' she called to the Borang. They said nothing, though they may have blinked.

Lady Allum seemed satisfied. She swung herself over the railing and held on with one hand. 'You'll not say you met me, though, all right?' she frowned, suddenly anxious. 'When you hit civilisation? The Church Councils are all dead set against ferliness, and they've decided in their wisdom that my lovely great fecund mother here – the Jungle, don't you know – is officially not normal. They wouldn't think well of me and my zoo-otanising, if they knew about it. So if you don't find a need to mention me, I'll take it as a kindness.'

'Of course.'

'Not a word.'

She leaned forward at a dangerous angle and then reared back again to peer at them over her shoulder.

'Oh, cribbons – I just thought. You'd better mind out for the Protectors. They're always on the lookout for new labour. If they see youngsters on their own . . .'

There was no time for any more. The boat nudged the bank and Lady Allum Broomback, with a joyful yodel, flung herself forward and disappeared into the dense greenery of the Jungle.

'Good luck!' they heard her somewhat muffled cry. 'And remember – keep the bleeders at arm's length!'

Singay looked at Pema, bemused. 'What did she mean, Protectors?'

'I've heard stories about them from Zeppa,' he said slowly. 'Gangs of children chained together, men with whips. He said they steal them off the streets. I used to have nightmares about it, but I thought he was exaggerating.'

But Rose wasn't thinking about anything like that. He was gazing back at the place where Lady Allum had crashed into the undergrowth, and there was a goopy smile all over his face.

CHAPTER SEVENTEEN

Incident on the River Head Pier

'I hate this town,' said Singay, as yet another sweating citizen shoved her aside and she stepped into a garbage-clogged gutter.

Pema, Singay and Rose were lost. The town of River Head had grown up like a fungus, with smelly alleyways leading off dirty streets in an unkempt, foul maze, and it had taken no time at all for them to become completely turned around.

'I can't see where to go,' complained Pema. 'I don't even know which direction the River is anymore!' The buildings hemmed them in on all sides, and though the streets were crowded with people, there was no one he felt comfortable to ask for directions. Too many frowning faces. Too much hurry and haste.

'Everybody seems angry about something,' said Rose.

'Maybe it's because of those clothes they're wearing,' said Singay. 'They must be cooking!'

Pema shushed her anxiously. 'Careful! I think that's to do with the Church Councils. Wearing black is meant to show you're religious. Back home I heard stories about River Head. If half of them are true, well, let's just say they've got some strange ways we don't want to get on the wrong side of.' He wiped his face and pointed at a little girl playing in the dirt. 'Let's ask her where we can find a ticket agent – she doesn't look too holy. Er, hello?'

The little girl looked up – and shrieked. Heads turned to stare.

'What? I just—' Pema protested, but the girl wasn't screaming at him. The crowd parted hastily to make way for a tall man wearing black and carrying a wicked-looking whip. A word was whispered back and forth.

Protector . . . Protector . . .

'Where are your parents, little girl?' the man hissed. 'Don't know where, do you? You're coming with me – oh no, you don't!'

In a flurry of dust the girl scrambled to her feet and tried to run, but the Protector's whip licked out and wrapped round her ankle. The man pulled, dumping her onto her face in the street. He grinned and started to haul her in, hand over hand, like a gaffed fish. Pema waited for an outcry from the crowd, but no one moved to help her. They all just watched.

We have to do something – we can't just let this happen! Pema took a step forward . . .

And the ground shook. The heavy cobblestones in the street bucked and rocked and threw people off balance in all directions. The Protector was flung onto his back and his head hit the stones with an audible crack.

Pema heard Singay cry, 'Rose!' and he turned to see the Driver sagging in her arms.

'I've got him,' she called. 'Go untangle the girl!'

Pema raced to the girl on the ground and unwrapped the whip from her ankle. There was a deep cut and the blood was welling fast but the little girl was faster, burrowing away into the crowd the second she was free. Pema stared after her. To be honest, he'd been expecting some gratitude.

'Pema! Come *on!*'

All around them, people were getting cautiously to their feet. The Protector gave a moan, rolled over and was violently sick.

The little girl had the right idea.

Time to go!

Finally, they stopped running.

'Rose, you were *wonderful!*' Singay panted. 'But are you all right?'

'Yes ... no ...' Rose sprinkled a few grains of irradiant onto his hand and then firmly put the bag away. 'I'm fine. And look, there's a shop!'

It was part way along a noisy, smelly alley crowded with people, stray duggs and casually dumped rubbish, but from the outside it looked a little like Zeppa's store.

'What do you think?' Pema hesitated, but Singay gave him a shove.

'We have to try *somewhere* to find downriver tickets. Unless you fancy staying in this grunt-sty forever. Come on.'

As they stepped through the door, the first thing they saw was a table piled with High Land cheeses.

'See? It's a sign,' Singay whispered to Pema with a nervous grin.

The other goods weren't so familiar – strange fabrics, odd-looking foodstuffs, oil-powered gadgets.

The owner, a thin, dark-haired man, leaned on his counter and stared at them.

'Are you a ticket agent, sir?' asked Pema politely.

The man nodded and went on staring.

'I'd like three tickets to Elysia. Please.'

'You can't buy tickets for that far,' the man said, his face expressionless. 'Everybody knows that.'

'Oh ... ah ... I, um, but we're going ...'

'Of course we know that.' Singay shouldered him aside. 'How much is it to the next big town downriver?'

The man transferred his stare to her. 'That'd be The Smoke. River Head to The Smoke, that'd be ...' He considered for a moment, and then named a figure not far below the entire contents of their money sack. Pema gasped and Rose looked worried, but Singay just snorted.

'Oh yes,' she said, 'and that's likely, I *don't* think. We'll pay you a twentieth of that and you'll be lucky to get it!'

Then, as Pema and Rose stood by, open-mouthed, she proceeded to haggle as if she'd been doing nothing else her whole life. At the end of the process a price had been agreed that left both parties reasonably satisfied.

'Where'd you learn to haggle like that?' the man asked with a grudging respect.

Singay grinned at him. 'Lots of sisters at home.' Then, turning to Pema, she handed him the money bag. 'Pay up,' she said loftily. 'Little Brother and I will go and look out those supplies.'

'Everything's set price!' the man called after her as she dragged Rose off and Pema untied the money sack. He carefully counted out the right amount and then tucked the sack away into an inside pocket for safekeeping.

'Thank you,' he said politely, as the shopkeeper handed over their tickets. He turned to go but there was more . . .

'I shouldn't be saying this,' the man said, not looking directly at him and speaking very low. 'But the girl's got grit. So, a word to the wise. We see some pretty ferly things here, with the Jungle so close, and though I don't much like them, I believe in letting be. But there's others that don't think that way. They don't take well to oddities, and they make their feelings known, if you follow my meaning. I suggest you don't draw so much attention to yourselves.' And he nodded towards the door.

Pema turned to see Rose standing in a pool of sunlight. He was looking better, but he'd obviously forgotten he was supposed to be in disguise – he'd taken off his hat and was fanning himself with it while he turned over the shop's fascinating goods, his strange silveriness clearly visible.

Pema felt sudden sweat drip down his back that had nothing to do with the heat. Just then, Singay noticed what Rose had done and plonked his hat back on his head, but the damage was done.

'I . . . uh . . . we . . . uh . . .'

'Buy your "little brother" some make-up,' said the man.

'Thank you.' Pema swallowed hard. 'That's good advice. I—' But another customer had just waddled in, and the shopkeeper had already turned his attention away.

In amongst all the strangeness, the man had suddenly seemed like a friend. *Don't be so stupid*, Pema scolded himself and, clutching the tickets, he walked away.

'That boy's over young to be wandering about

unprotected,' commented the new customer, eyeing Pema suspiciously as he threaded his way through the displays. She was a fat woman with a tight, prissy mouth, wearing ostentatiously heavy black clothes. Her dress was so tight she looked like a sweaty sausage that'd been too long on the grill. 'Where's his parents?'

The shopkeeper shrugged. 'Shopping,' he grunted. He'd formed his own ideas about the unlikely trio.

Runaways. There were some bad stories about the customs *up there* – in the mountains. The short one they'd called their 'little brother' was clearly some kind of mutation, but the shopkeeper wouldn't get in their way. He'd have taken all their money if he could have – that was only fair! – but he wouldn't hand them in to the Church Council or the interferers either. Not even for the commission the Protectors gave.

'Humph,' said the woman sourly. 'Well, don't you try and cheat *me*! I know your kind.'

Unaware of the interest he'd left behind him, Pema rejoined Singay and Rose.

'Add make-up to the supply list. Rose is too noticeable.' When the others looked impressed by his cunning, he confessed, 'The shopkeeper suggested it. Come on, let's finish up and get out of here. The sooner we can get away from this town, the better.'

'What's that smell?' Singay screwed up her face in disgust.

They were walking along yet another alley between two rows of ramshackle storehouses, trying to find their way to the Downriver Pier.

Pema sniffed the air. 'That's grunts. And they're not very happy.'

'I wouldn't be happy if I smelled like that, either,' muttered Singay, trying not to breathe.

But Pema wasn't listening. The alley was coming to an end. As they stepped out from its shadows they saw, at last, the forecourt of a pier laid out before them, crowded and chaotic in the glaring sunlight, with the River and the barges beyond. And, in a corral almost directly in front of them, was a heaving herd of very unhappy grunts indeed.

'Who's packed them in like that?' Pema could feel the outrage climbing up his throat. 'Any idiot knows you can't crowd grunts.'

He started forward, and Singay suddenly realised that Rose wasn't with them. She turned to see the little man in his little boy disguise still standing at the alley mouth, gazing about with a fascinated and slightly gormless grin on his face. 'Hey! Come on!' she said, gesturing impatiently to him. Then she turned back to tell Pema to wait up . . .

. . . and saw that in that split second everything had changed.

A huge man was now squeezed in with the grunts, trying to shove one of them bodily through a gap in the corral nearest the barge. The grunt, being, as everyone knows, instinctively contrary, and already in a bad mood because of the overcrowded conditions, did not choose to go in the direction indicated. The stink of peeved grunts got worse, the man's curses became louder and more creative, and the usual dockside audience of layabouts and gawkers was gathering expectantly.

'HEY!' Pema shouted furiously at the man, striding towards him. 'STOP THAT!' he cried, just as the grunt broke free and plunged out of the enclosure and into the onlookers, scattering them to right and left. The big man fell over, bellowing, Pema disappeared into the chaos in pursuit of the grunt, and Rose and Singay could only stand by and try not to get trodden on.

'I've never seen him so angry!' Rose looked up at her, wide-eyed.

'Look at him now!' Singay replied, pointing.

There was a break in the crowd, and they saw Pema and the grunt, just standing there, staring at each other, oblivious to the fuss around them. Chirruping noises were exchanged, and then, gently, Pema put his hand on the animal's back.

Singay was just thinking it was all going to be all right, when suddenly a sharp-faced woman pushed her way forward, shrieking at Pema as she came. 'HOLD IT RIGHT THERE, YOU ROTTEN LITTLE THIEF! GET YOUR THIEVING HANDS OFF MY PROPERTY!'

'Are these your beasts?' Pema's anger flared up again and he put himself protectively between the animal and the screaming harridan. 'What do you think you're doing? Any fool knows better than to crowd grunts, so you must be worse than a fool, or else something even worse than that . . .' He stumbled to a halt as the sentence got away from him, and in the pause, her words penetrated to his brain. 'Th-thief?' he stuttered. 'What are you talking about?'

'I'M TALKING ABOUT YOU, YOU FLEA-BITTEN FILCHER! THAT'S A VALUABLE BEAST

YOU'VE GOT YOUR MITTS ON!' she shrilled, still at the top of her voice.

From where she was standing, Singay could clearly see how, while the woman was yelling at Pema, she also had one eye on the crowd, working them round to her side. But the red mist that came down on Pema whenever animals were mistreated had deserted him now, leaving him too tongue-tied and flustered to understand what was happening.

'But – but that's *ridiculous!*' he said. His voice had gone all high-pitched and desperate – even to himself he sounded guilty. 'Why would I want to steal your grunt?'

'Why would you want to? WHY WOULD YOU WANT TO? I've got eyes, haven't I? I saw how you BEWITCHED that valuable animal.' She grabbed him by the arm, her fingers digging in hard.

'Come on!' Singay whispered to Rose, desperately trying to find a way through the thickening crowd. But no one was letting them pass. An unexpected elbow in the face made her stagger backwards and clutch her nose.

Meanwhile, the man who'd been mishandling the grunt in the first place had no difficulty pushing his way over to the woman. Wiping the sweat and dirt from his face, he loomed at Pema. Pema was uncomfortably aware that the man's massive body had plenty of muscle under the fat.

'I saw what you did with that grunt, boy,' the man rumbled.

Snows. I'm for it now. Pema gulped painfully.

And then it got worse.

'Are those the ones?'

Before they could turn around, Singay and Rose felt

the heavy hands of authority taking firm hold of them by the neck. Another Protector stood over them. The path to Pema miraculously cleared and they were shoved forward.

'They with you?' muttered the big man in Pema's ear.

'No . . . yes . . .' Pema felt like a mouse between two cats.

'Shut up and follow my lead.' The big man beamed suddenly at the Protector, holding out his hands in welcome. 'Good day to you, Officer! I'm Klepsang Zale and this is my good wife, Ma Likpa. What seems to be the trouble?'

'Those are the ones! I'm sure of it!' It was the fat woman in the tight black dress, the one who had shown such interest in them in the shop. 'I saw them with my own eyes, bold as brass, loitering in a shop without clear and visible adult oversight. They need to be *protected*.' The woman's chins wobbled as she nodded vigorously.

Klepsang chuckled.

'Oh, but there's been a mistake,' he said amiably. 'They've got oversight. They're ours, Officer. Our children.'

'WHAT?' exclaimed Ma. She was clearly astonished, but she didn't let go of Pema. Even if she had, he would have just stood there anyway with his mouth hanging open.

'You must excuse my wife, Officer, she's a bit deaf.' The big man turned and bellowed, 'I WAS EXPLAINING TO THIS FINE PROTECTOR HERE THAT THESE ARE OUR CHILDREN.' Out of sight of the Protector he was winking madly at Ma Likpa. 'All three of them,' he added.

The Protector's eyes narrowed. He bent to peer at Rose more closely. 'They don't look like you,' he said, drawing his whip through his fingers in a speculating sort of way that made Pema's skin crawl.

'That's because they're adopted, Officer. We weren't blessed with kiddies of our own.' The big man gestured behind his hand at his wife and added in a loud stage whisper, *'Women's troubles.'* Ma's grip on Pema's arm tightened agonisingly, but she continued to smirk innocently at the world in general.

'No need to adopt children when we've got the Protectors,' muttered the fat woman in the black dress sullenly. She wasn't going to let her commission go without a fight.

The Protector ignored her.

'I heard your wife shouting at that one as I came near,' he said stolidly, pointing at Pema.

'A parent's prerogative.'

'She called him a flea-bitten filcher.'

'A family nickname. Against which there are no laws, am I right?' Klepsang pretend-cuffed Pema round the ear, gave Singay a quick hug and looked a bit doubtfully at Rose.

For a long, disconcerting moment the Protector just stared at them. Then, with a shrug, he put his whip away and stepped back.

'You may carry on,' he said.

The fat woman in black clucked her tongue loudly in annoyance and waddled away, sweating and disappointed. Klepsang grinned. He bowed to the Protector obsequiously before turning to Pema.

'Get them on board if you value your freedom,' he hissed in Pema's ear, detaching him from his wife and giving him a less than gentle shove in the direction of the penned grunts.

Pema looked helplessly at Singay and Rose, but the Protector was still standing there. *What else can I do?*

The escaped grunt trotting happily by his side, he went over to the corral and chirruped to the churning herd. A large female pushed her way through the others and stuck her nose through the fencing at him. He chirruped her round to the river side of the corral and opened the barrier. A polite invitation was issued and accepted, and together Pema and the lead animal – the matriarch – crossed to the gangway and walked sedately aboard. The rest of the herd came quietly, moving without fuss, though occasionally they expressed their opinion of piers and corrals and barges generally by lifting their tails and depositing large, wet, noisome grunt pats. Singay and Rose followed, placing their feet carefully and trying to look as if they were a useful part of the process.

Last to board were their unlikely saviours, the big man all smug and bland, his sharp-faced wife narrow-eyed and furious.

CHAPTER EIGHTEEN

Happy Families

'So, husband,' Ma snarled under her breath, 'perhaps you'd like to tell me now what this little charade is all about?' They were standing on the deck by the grunt pens while Pema and Singay filled the troughs with water and Rose got in the way. 'Or am I just to accept that you've suddenly got the brain-rot and we've got three extra mouths to feed?'

Klepsang gave his wife an unloving look. 'Use your wits, my dear. If you can find any. You only have to look at the tall boy to see he's one of the High Land freaks. And you saw what he did with that blasted grunt on the pier. Everyone knows High Landers can talk to animals. They can get any old beast to do any old thing. On to a boat. Off of a boat. Across the Overland ...'

He paused and let Ma's considerable cunning catch up. In spite of his rude comments, Klepsang had a healthy respect for his spouse's remarkable cold-blooded deviousness.

'Ah,' she said slowly, nodding her head. 'So, we protect them from the Protectors and the freak gets the meat to Cliffton for us, where we'll get twice the price we could get in a dump like The Smoke. Are you thinking we wouldn't have to pay him very much? Is that what you're thinking?'

'Not exactly. What I was thinking was that *they* would pay *us*.'

Ma sucked her teeth appreciatively. 'That would be a much better thing – for the children as well. For isn't it the truth that people don't value something properly unless they've paid for it?'

'It is, my dear, it is. They should thank us.'

'But gratitude's not a stable currency. Neither's fear if they figure out that the Protectors don't work beyond The Smoke. People might turn them against us. People always do.'

'Not if we make sure they *can't*. We're going to be such good friends to these strays that they won't be speaking to another soul.'

Ma looked up at her husband with a thoroughly unpleasant smile. 'Such good friends,' she agreed, and licked her thin lips.

Meanwhile, as they worked, 'the strays' were conferring together too.

'Do you have any idea what just happened?' Singay whispered urgently, as she emptied another bucket into the trough.

Pema shook his head.

'Pema – are you all right?'

'I'm fine.' But he was feeling completely wrung out. It always happened when he lost his temper. One minute he could take on the world and the next he went like an overcooked noodle. He scratched the nearest grunt behind the ears.

'Do you think they're just really kind people who have decided to help us out of the goodness of their hearts?' suggested Rose hopefully.

'No!' said Singay and Pema in chorus.

'No,' repeated Singay. 'They want something all right. What I can't figure is *what*.'

Pema looked up, and gave her a warning nudge. 'I think we're about to find out,' he muttered.

'This way, children. Mummy and Daddy want a word with you.' Klepsang loomed, and pointed to the prow of the barge.

Snows, he's so BIG! thought Pema. His mouth went dry every time he looked at the man's bull shoulders and huge fists.

All around, the other passengers were milling about, settling themselves here and there on the broad deck, and the captain was shouting orders in preparation for casting off. No one was at the prow, however, and they could talk there without being overheard.

Klepsang pointed a sudden sausage finger at them. 'We put ourselves on the line there for you, I hope you realise!' he hissed belligerently. 'Do you have any idea how much trouble we could get into, lying to keep you clear of the Protectors? Give me one good reason why we should go on doing that. Eh? EH?'

Singay, Rose and Pema huddled closer together like nervous mice.

'Now, now, dear, you'll frighten them,' Ma Likpa said in a voice like warm grease. 'But he's right, you know. You'll just have to tell us *everything*.'

They had their story ready and Singay told it well – their mother dead, their father remarried, an evil step-mother, the need to get as far away from her threats and beatings as they could, even as far as the Sea.

'Oh, Klepsang!' shrieked Ma Likpa, putting her hands up to her cheeks in horror. 'They're going to cross the

Overland! I can't bear it! These dear young people and that dear little boy, on that awful, awful road!'

'Um . . .' said Pema.

Ignoring him, Klepsang patted his wife consolingly on the shoulder. 'Now, now, my dear, you mustn't think of that. I'm sure they have made some arrangements. Of *course* they aren't thinking of travelling on their own.'

'Er . . .' said Singay.

Klepsang Zale sucked his teeth portentously. 'Oh no, no, no, that's *not* a good idea. You can't be aware of the dangers of the Overland if that's what you considering.'

'Do they even know what the Overland *is*, husband dear?'

'Uh . . .' said Pema.

So Klepsang told them.

It would seem that, at The Smoke, the River disappeared into a great canyon. There were terrible rapids for a long way, and no boat could navigate them.

'From there to the next big place, called Cliffton, we must travel along a high, barren plateau, on a horrible, dry, dangerous road. That's the Overland.'

'Dangerous?' said Pema.

'Yes. And not just the Protectors. There are wild animals that live on the Overland plateau – wulfs and scorpions and tarantellas – or you might wander off the road and die of hunger and thirst. Even *that's* not the worst. There's also . . .' Klepsang lowered his voice ominously, '. . . *the Jathang.*'

'What's the Jathang?' asked Rose, his eyes wide.

'Oh, don't tell them, Klepsang!' Ma squealed like a stuck grunt. 'Don't tell them – it's not fitting!'

'All right, all right, don't fret so. I won't. I won't tell

them about those vicious, ruthless, thieving, maiming, baby-eating savages, who lurk in a place no decent person could survive in. But you know, an idea *has* just come to me, and I'm sure you, my dear, who have such a kind nature, will agree to it with all your heart.' He smiled at Ma, who simpered back.

'What idea is that, dear?' she said.'Do tell us.'

So he did. He told them all about his idea of taking the three waifs along with him, providing them with his protection on the dangerous, deadly Overland, for a laughably small fee – his wife's kind heart wouldn't hear of charging more, he was sure, but he knew better than to embarrass them by asking any less.

'And if any of you felt you'd like to lend a hand, maybe, with the beasts, well, that might ease any feelings of being beholden you'll doubtless be harbouring.' His smile showed *all* his teeth.

Pema's heart sank. There was nothing about these people that he trusted. *But what else can we do?* He looked at the others. Rose nodded. Singay shrugged.

'All right,' Pema said hesitantly.

The big man grabbed his hand, swamping it in his own, and pumped it up and down.

'It's a deal,' said Klepsang Zale.

Looking disconcertingly smug, the couple began to walk away. Then, as if as an afterthought, they turned back.

'Just a word of advice, though, dears,' said Ma. 'I wouldn't do too much talking with the other passengers if I were you. Somebody might just get a bit too curious. If they don't talk to you there's no way they can find out that you're not who we say you are. That you're not our lovely little adopted family.'

'Why do they *really* not want us talking to the other passengers?' muttered Singay, wiping the sweat from her face. 'I can't believe it's because they think we'll suddenly start blabbing, "Hello, my name's Singay, and by the way, that big creep's not really my father."'

Pema shrugged, and dumped another scoop of grunt dung into the bucket.

'Does it matter? It's not as if we have any time to talk to anybody anyway.'

Ma and Klepsang were extracting every ounce of work they could out of Pema and Singay, while maintaining the illusion, for anyone who cared to look, that they were loving and attentive parents.

Rose, however, was a different kettle of fish.

'That is one *ugly* little boy!' said Ma to her husband. 'There's something really wrong about him.' She wrinkled her sharp nose with distaste.

'What do you expect? He's a freak.' Klepsang wasn't bothered. 'We won't get any useful work out of him, from the size of him, but what can you do? He's part of the package. And we can charge for him, dead weight or not.'

'Well, as long as he stays away from me.'

So Singay and Pema mucked out the grunts, and fed and watered the grunts, and pulled up buckets of river water to throw over the grunts to keep them happy and cool. And Rose spent his time in the bow, looking south, leaning forward as if by doing so he could get there one minute sooner.

On either side of the River there were rolling hills and rich fields of crops, many of which they didn't recognise. The barge, propelled by teams of men with poles, passed villages and towns and clusters of houses, stopping again and again to let passengers and goods on and off. Everywhere, there were people. Pema and Singay couldn't believe how *full* the Low Lands were.

As the leagues passed, they saw signs of tremors and damage – flattened barns, jetties tilted sideways into the River, chimneys that had fallen, knocking holes in roofs. They spotted oil-engine contraptions as well. It wasn't always clear what the machines were meant to do, and they were often lying useless when the farmers couldn't afford to fuel them. Klepsang and Ma scolded them for pausing to stare, but they made sure they noticed the gangs of children, chained together, working the fields or being marched by on the river bank.

The lines of mountains on either side pulled further and further apart until, one morning, Pema realised he couldn't see them anymore.

'So exciting!' crowed Singay when he pointed it out to her.

'Exciting,' he echoed, hoping he didn't sound as queasy as he felt.

They speculated amongst themselves about the next stage – the Overland.

'I don't know,' admitted Pema. 'I thought, after the Jungle, it was Low Lands all the way – that's how world-wise I am.'

It seemed to go on forever. But every day, they inched closer to the Sea.

CHAPTER NINETEEN

The Overland

'So *that's* why they call it The Smoke!' said Singay, impressed.

At last, a great cliff came into view, stretching away to east and west as far as the eye could see. It was monumental, massive – and yet even from where they were, raw rock showed where there had been landslides. The Smoke squatted at its foot, and towering over the town was a gigantic cloud of mist, rising up from where the River squeezed itself into a narrow canyon, wildly churning white water.

The colossal cliff, the raging water, the rising, shifting mist – it was a breath-taking sight.

'What are you gawping at?'

For a big man, Klepsang was quiet on his feet. None of them had heard him coming. But he wasn't looking for a chat with his counterfeit family.

Fists on hips, he was all business. 'We'll be coming into Pier 3. There's a road from there that by-passes The Smoke and heads up onto the plateau. I want us off the barge and up that cliff without any delays, so get yourselves organised *now*.' He turned on his heel, then seemed to notice that his tone hadn't exactly been that of a kindly father. He swung back with a benign smile, full of teeth, and patted Pema on the shoulder, causing him to stagger slightly. 'Well done, son!' he added, in case anyone was listening, and walked away.

Singay stuck her tongue out at his retreating back.

'Oh well,' said Pema, resigned. 'Maybe it's for the best. We'd just be tempted to spend money if we went into the town.' After paying even the first instalment of Klepsang's 'laughably small fee', their money sack was dangerously light.

When the barge docked, Pema and the matriarch led the way. Singay and Rose followed the beasts down the gangplank, dodging dropped dung. Klepsang and Ma were already off the boat and urging them on – from the comfort of a donkey cart.

'Where did *that* spring from?' muttered Singay crossly.

Pema pulled a sour face. 'Oh, don't worry, I'm sure we'll be invited to ride along.'

'Really?' said Rose. 'I've never ridden in a cart before!'

'And I've never seen grunts fly, but you'll see *that* before you get a lift from those two!'

There was nothing for it but to shrug and follow on. The grunts were certainly happy to be stretching their legs after being penned for so long, and there was a lot of cheerful barging and shoving in the ranks. With Pema keeping an eye on them, though, and the matriarch occasionally throwing an admonitory cough over her shoulder, their progress was well-mannered enough.

Then, as the road rounded the first corner of the town, they saw a cluster of sand-coloured tents, pitched on a grassy patch a little distance from the walls.

'Jathang,' muttered Ma, and spat over the side of the cart.

Jathang!

Their 'parents' had lost no opportunity on the journey

to tell them horror stories about the plateau people. Now their 'children' stared, curious to see what such unspeakably evil people would look like.

It was disappointing.

'But they're *tiny!*' exclaimed Singay.

They were indeed a small, tawny-coloured people – eyes, hair and skin all of the same light brown. Their clothes were tawny too, loosely-cut robes that stood out against the green grass, but would be perfect camouflage in the dry plateau above. As far as their thieving, maiming, baby-eating propensities went, they were giving nothing away.

'They're still taller than me,' said Rose wistfully.

'Nonsense – you're the perfect height,' said Singay.

'That's right,' said Pema. 'Just think what rubbish your cunning disguise would be if you were the size of, I don't know, Klepsang?'

The thought of Klepsang's big fat body bulging out of little Rose's clothes made them giggle. Ma Likpa didn't know what they were laughing about, but she scowled suspiciously on principle, which just made them giggle more.

The road skirted the town and then headed for the cliff, zigzagging up it in a series of switchbacks.

'Pace the climb!' Klepsang called from his seat in the cart. 'Don't tire out the beasts!'

He and Ma were quite a load for any animal to haul, and Pema watched narrowly as he geed up the donkey. However, it seemed to be pulling comfortably, so he returned his attention to the grunts. He chirped questioningly at the matriarch, but she just waggled her ears and started up the first leg of the zigzagging road without hesitation.

'Well, fair enough,' said Pema. 'Here goes!'

The grunts following her were not so calm, deafening everyone with their squeals and bellows.

'What are they yelling about?' Rose shouted. 'They were all chirrupy and quiet on the boat!'

'I don't think they've ever climbed anything before,' Pema yelled back. 'They get noisy when something's new.'

I hate grunts, thought Singay.

And it wasn't just the noise. All those pointy feet stirred the fine dust that lay on the road until it rose up in a beige cloud. Soon the grunts, along with Singay, Pema, and Rose, were completely coated – skin, hair, hooves and clothes. Pema saw Singay disgustedly trying to rub the dirt off her face with her sleeve. She only managed to make it worse, but at least Rose didn't need to keep topping up his make-up to look the same colour as everybody else.

It was a long climb. Singay and Pema had High Land legs, but the Driver was soon struggling. Pema took him up on his back.

'You don't weigh a thing!' he reassured the little man.

There was a bit of a melee when the herd reached the top – not all of the grunts wanted to stop this new activity so soon – but the matriarch exerted her authority with some well-placed shoves and squeals. The herd moved forward relatively calmly along the plateau road – the Overland. There was no sign of Ma and Klepsang, who were staying well ahead of the grunt dust cloud. Their 'family' peered around, anxious to see what this new stage of the journey was going to look like.

Then a hot wind came out of the south, dispersing the

obscuring, clogging cloud, and Pema, Rose and Singay were able to see the landscape that stretched before them.

It was a shock.

'I hope it isn't going to be too much for the animals,' said Pema anxiously.

Singay tried to make a rude noise, but her mouth was too dry.

The plateau was unlike any place she or Pema had ever seen – a stony, dusty, thirsty landscape whose ribs showed. Stretching away into the distance, all they could see was a flat scene of tumbled rocks and scree, scrub plants with leathery-looking stems and grey, spiny excuses for leaves, sharp-edged gullies like cracked skin and, heading straight across it, the road.

'No water,' murmured Singay, licking her dry lips.

'Like the desert,' said Pema, 'except . . .' He was going to say, *except the desert was beautiful*, but what was the point? Whatever this place was like, they had to cross it. Starting now. 'Let's go.'

With every step, every sense relayed the same message: *You don't belong here*. The broken surfaces of the road bruised hooves and feet; bitter-tasting grit got down everyone's throats; the blaring glare of the sun hurt their eyes. In the emptiness, there were no familiar sounds – even the distant scream of a bird of prey, no more than a speck high up in the brassy sky, echoed weirdly. And if dryness could *have* a smell, the dust that rose up with every step reeked of it.

The herd and their keepers followed the Overland, hour after hour, in a kind of dreary dream. Then, as the sun finally began to set, the road dipped down into a broken valley, and the first Way Station – one of the hostels spaced out along the route, each a day's march apart – came into view.

'At last!' croaked Rose wearily.

Holding pens with welcoming feed and water troughs immediately caught the attention of the herd, but the lead grunt and Pema managed to keep things orderly as they settled in.

As soon as the work was done, and not a moment before, Klepsang Zale and Ma Likpa appeared, carrying food and blankets.

'Well, I expect you'll be ready for a good night's sleep, am I right?' Klepsang beamed at them. They stared back, dusty and dishevelled.

'We've brought you your suppers,' said Ma. 'Here you are.'

'Wait! Aren't we staying in there?' exclaimed Pema, pointing at the Way Station.

'No,' said Ma, sounding surprised and affronted.

'Rooms are very expensive, and we're already doing you all quite a favour,' said Klepsang.

'Quite a favour,' agreed Ma.

Pema, Singay and Rose looked at each other. What could they say?

They did their best to clear away stones and hard lumps from the ground by the pens, laid out their bedrolls and lit a fire.

'I wonder if they have bath tubs at the Way Station?' said Singay, looking longingly through the fading day at the building. Welcoming yellow lamplight was beginning to spill out of the windows. 'Warm water ... some soap ... lavender oil ...'

Pema caught his breath. His grandmother Dawa used to put lavender oil into his bath water at home whenever he was sad, or sore, or she just felt like mollycoddling him a little. For just a moment he thought he could remember the warm, purple scent, and how it made him feel ... but then the dry smell of the dust and the sharp tang of the pens and the smoke from the campfire swept over him and the memory was gone.

Homesickness squeezed his heart so tight he nearly cried out. He got up. 'I'm going for a walk.'

As he padded off into the darkness, Rose murmured to Singay, '*More* walking? Is he all right, do you think?'

Singay poked the fire. The temperature was dropping as the light faded. 'I expect so,' she said. 'Sometimes you just have to be by yourself for a bit, you know?'

Night had fallen. At first, away from the fire, everything seemed uniformly dark. Then, as his eyes adjusted, Pema began to pick out the details in his surroundings. The darker humps became the shapes of spiny shrubs and outcroppings of rocks, and he could see the black slits of gullies eroded by streams and flash floods long dry. A part-moon came out from behind the clouds, and its light reflected off the paleness of dry soil and stone.

He found himself a rock to sit on and stared out across the plateau. Stealthily, the spell of desert lands washed over him. He became aware, as he had not been during the harsh glare of the day, that this place had its own surreal beauty. He let his mind empty until there was nothing of him that was separate. He became part of the night breeze, the moonlit shapes, the great empty distances of tumbled scree and broken rock, deep-shadowed rifts in the ground and sudden blank inclines and . . .

'What *is* that?' Pema muttered crossly.

So high-pitched it was practically not even a sound, there was an irritating, insistent vibration coming at him out of the wilderness. It was unlike any cry or call or communication he'd ever sensed before, and yet it was inescapably clear what message was being sent.

Someone, or something, was in serious trouble.

CHAPTER TWENTY

Dasu and Ker

For a moment, Pema hesitated. *I can't just go off – it's dangerous out there. I should go back to the others.* Then the call intensified in a way he could feel in his bones.

He didn't hesitate anymore. Slipping and stumbling, he blundered forward. Spiny bushes tried to catch hold of him, loose pebbles rolled out from under his feet, dry ditches and ankle-wrenching cracks appeared without warning in his path.

Where are you? Hold on – I'm coming!

Glancing up, he saw that clouds were lipping round the moon. He gritted his teeth and hurried on. *If the light goes, I'm lost.*

There was a new despairing note in the cry, then the clouds covered the moon and he put on a final burst of speed – and, without warning, the earth disappeared from under his feet.

'SNOWS!'

An avalanche of sand and stones and sharp grit swept him down the side of a deep gully and half-covered him when he hit the bottom. He was scratched and bruised with the breath knocked out of him, and he wasn't sure how he was going to get out again, but he had at last found the source of the cry.

There was just enough light to see a tail and two back paws sticking out from under the treacherous scree. Pema scrambled over and tried to clear the dirt away but more fell down around his hands. He realised to his horror that the distress call had gone silent. There was no time to be delicate. He grabbed hold of the motionless paws and heaved.

The entire side of the ravine began to collapse on top of him. Encumbered by the animal, he could only stagger backwards, and slammed into the opposite wall. Between the rising dust and the falling dirt it was hard to find breathable air, but at last the landslide trickled to a stop.

The treacherous moonlight reappeared. Pema spat dirt out of his mouth and looked to see what it was he had in his hands.

It was a small dugg, with a longish body and short legs and wiry, dirt-caked hair. It wasn't moving.

Pema laid his ear to its side. He thought he could just hear the flutter of a heartbeat, but he couldn't be sure. *I need better light – I need to make a fire.* But what with? He looked anxiously to the left, but that way seemed blocked. *If I can just get out of this gully,* he thought, turning to the right.

It was then that he realised he was no longer alone. Long, low shapes moved in the shadows. There was a rasping growl, an answering snarl.

He wasn't the only one who had heard the cry for help.

Cold sweat trickled down his back. Moving with painstaking slowness, he shifted the dugg to one arm and stooped. His fingers closed around a sharp-edged stone. He stayed crouched, staring into the darkness, desperately trying to find a target.

There! A flicker of movement.

With a wordless yell, Pema straightened, and threw

with all his strength. There was a yelp of pain, claws scrabbling, then silence. For moment, he stood frozen, every sense straining. Had it worked? Had he driven them – whatever they were – away?

No. The shapes flowed back, and in the moonlight Pema caught a glint of teeth. He groped for another stone . . .

. . . and a flaming angel leapt down the gully wall from behind him, right over his head like a shooting star. It flailed its wings, shrieking at the predators, thrashing a trail of fire back and forth, and Pema had a horrifyingly clear glimpse of the creatures that had been stalking him.

Their bodies were huge and lean and covered in rough hair, their feet were clawed, their hackles raised high over narrow shoulders, lips pulled back in snarls to show, impossibly, *fangs* – and then, suddenly, they were gone. It was as if they'd never been there.

The angel turned, and became a girl in a robe holding a torch.

'What did you think you were *doing*!' she said sharply, thrusting the light at him, and then gasped, 'Dasu? *Dasu!*'

Suddenly, as if by magic, the limp little body in Pema's arms squirmed into life and flung itself at the stranger.

'Dasu, Dasu, you daft dugg, where did you go? I've been looking for you everywhere! Are you hurt? Are you all right?' The girl hunkered down, doing her best to examine the wriggling animal, who was doing *its* best to lick any bit of her it could reach. 'Don't you know those wulfs would have you in shreds as soon as look at you?'

'Those were *wulfs?!*' Pema gasped. 'But they were huge! And their *teeth!*'

'Plateau wulfs. They're venomous. Fire's the only thing they're afraid of. No one but a fool would walk in the wild at night without a torch prepared.' She looked up at him, her eyes glittering strangely.

'Here, hold Dasu while I make a fire,' she said. 'I need to check properly he's all right.'

The girl moved about purposefully in the dimness, collecting and laying dry shrub branches and carefully applying the torch.

Who is she? Pema thought. *What's she doing out in the wild?* He was uncomfortably aware of how alone he was. *Nobody has any idea I'm here.* He hugged the warm dugg closer for comfort and was rewarded by the rasp of a wet tongue across his chin.

'Let me see him.'

In the light from the fire, she felt along the dugg's legs and back, murmuring to him, checking there was no tenderness in belly or chest, nothing to make him flinch. Then she nodded and set him down.

'He'll be stiff in the morning, but no real harm done. He's still just a pup, and a dim-witted one at that. He ran off after a rabbid, which is bad enough, but the wulfs would have had him in three bites if you hadn't come by, so I guess we're in your debt. My name is Kerkerbabu, but mostly I'm called Ker.'

She smiled. Her teeth were disconcertingly sharp-looking.

'Um, I'm Pema.' Then a bit of dry bush fuel caught and flared up and he saw the girl clearly for the first time. Saw the small build, the angular face. The tawny skin, and hair, and eyes.

'You're *Jathang*!' he spluttered, scrambling awkwardly to his feet.

'Pema. Strange name.' Ker was ignoring his outburst. 'So, tell me, Pema, how did you find my beast? How did you know he'd got himself into trouble?'

'I heard him.' Pema rubbed his face with one hand, smudging even more dirt over it. *What's she going to do to me?*

'You heard him,' she said, lengthening out the words speculatively.

'Yes. Well, I didn't know it was *him*, specifically, but I heard something in trouble – not a grunt, they sound different. Actually, I've never heard *any* animal that sounded like yours before, but it was pretty obvious he was in some sort of distress. So I came to see what was wrong ...' He trailed off, unsure what the look on the girl's face might mean.

'That's surprising,' she said, 'since Jathang duggs are mute.'

Pema stared at her. 'But that can't be right – I *heard* him.'

Ker shook her head. 'No. Hearing him isn't possible. We breed our duggs to be voiceless.'

'Why?'

'Why do you think? As you so astutely pointed out, we're Jathang. We're travellers, hiders, the people of the moonlit flit. We're hunters of wary prey in a land short on cover. Just how useful do you think a dugg with a big yap is going to be to us? I thought even you people could figure out *that* much.'

'Who people?' said Pema, more offended than

grammatical. 'Those aren't *my* people.' He shrugged a shoulder in the general direction of the Way Station. 'That is, I'm *with* them because I'm travelling with them – we met them on the barge, and I'm looking after the beasts. But *I* come from the Mountain. I—' He stopped abruptly. *Pema, you fool – shut your mouth!* He was opening himself up to a whole host of questions it would be hard to answer.

But the question she *did* ask was, 'How much are they paying you?'

'What?'

'For driving the beasts,' Ker said impatiently. 'That's what you said you were doing. And I want to know, how much are they paying you for doing it?'

'Er, nothing.' *What is she talking about?* 'But they knocked off half the fee for the trip.'

The girl raised her tawny eyebrows. 'You're joking, right?'

'No ...'

'Boy, have *you* been conned!' she snorted. 'Whoever you're travelling with should be paying *you* to herd their beasts for them. There's an official hiring market in The Smoke, with set fees and contract-signing and everything.' She paused and leaned back. 'But you didn't *go* into the town, did you?'

'But they said ... they said they were saving us ... that we'd be picked up by the Protectors ...'

She was shaking her head at him. 'Protectors don't come onto the Overland.'

'Of course they do – why wouldn't they?' Pema knew he sounded sullen. He *felt* sullen.

Her grin was not very nice. 'Jathang don't *like* Protectors.'

'Well, but, hang on, how would *you* know about rates of pay and stuff? Your people are banned by the towns – you're not even allowed in!'

'Says who? We don't go into towns because we can't stand the smell, not because anybody's tried to tell us not to! And I know what they should be paying you because my cousin did that route not two seasons ago, with just a small herd of beasts, and *he* made enough to get married on! Yes, they've conned you, boy, coming and going.'

'All right, I get it.' Pema stood up abruptly. 'You don't need to keep telling me.'

Immediately, Dasu the dugg started up his inaudible wailing again and, without thinking, Pema bent down to comfort him.

Ker bit her lip.

'I apologise,' she said, not sounding at all comfortable about it. She reminded him suddenly of Singay. 'This is not how I should be thanking you for rescuing my Dasu, is it?' She thought for a moment, and then nodded to herself, as if she'd come to a decision.

'Are you stopping at Cliffton or going on?'

'We're going on.'

'Right.' And she began to search about on the ground. 'There. That'll do,' she said, as if to herself, holding up a small, smooth, flat pebble and squinting at it in the firelight. Then she pulled a lethal-looking knife from her belt and began to scratch a pattern on the stone with it.

When it was done to her satisfaction, she held it out to him.

'When you get to the pier below Cliffton, look for a

boat with *that* marked on its bow. It won't be obvious – it's only meant to be seen by us – so you'll need to look carefully. That'll be a safe boat to take passage on, and if you show the captain this stone, she'll give you berths.'

'Why should she?'

'Hm? Oh, she's my auntie. And now,' she said, leaning over to throw sand on the fire, 'I'll take you back.' She stood up and tucked the dugg under one arm. 'The moon's set and we don't want either of you getting into any more trouble!'

Pema wanted to say he didn't *need* her help, but really he was just too tired to argue about anything anymore.

Sooner than he would have thought possible, they were back at his own camp. The fire had died down to the embers, and there was nothing of Rose and Singay to be seen except two blanketed humps on the ground.

He turned and said, 'Thank . . .' but the Jathang girl was already gone.

'You all right?' came Singay's sleepy voice from one of the heaps.

'I'm a dupe and an idiot,' replied Pema.

'Fine,' she muttered. 'As long as you're all right.'

In the darkness, Pema grunted ruefully, curled up in his blankets and fell asleep.

'Pema? Pema! Come on, it's time to get up!'

Sometimes when people wake, they find that the resolutions of the night before have simply and utterly dissolved. But *sometimes* when people wake, they find that what had been no more than a good idea the night before has become immutable, urgent and written in stone.

'Time to get to work,' was all Singay said, but that was all it took.

Kicking his blankets aside, Pema stood up. He looked strangely taller. 'Not yet,' he said, in a voice they'd never heard before. 'Singay. Rose. Come with me.'

Klepsang and Ma were sitting in the Way Station dining hall, just finishing an excellent breakfast, when they realised they had unexpected company.

Fists clenched, Pema stood over them. It was his turn to loom. In a level, icy voice he said, 'You will stop cheating us. Now. I will tell you what a fair rate is for the work we are doing for you, and then you will pay us – half now and the rest when we get to Cliffton.' He paused for the briefest second and then added, 'And there will be no more of this nonsense about our not staying in the Way Stations or threatening us with Protectors. The Protectors don't come onto the Overland. You knew that. And now, so do we.'

All around the room, travellers stared, food halfway to their mouths. Ma was rapidly turning scarlet and Klepsang made astonished gargling noises before turning furiously on his wife.

'You've let someone talk to them, haven't you?' he snarled. 'You stupid gow. I give you one simple job – keep them away from people, don't let people talk to them – one simple little job and you can't even do *that* right! What did I ever do to deserve you?'

Ma Likpa squared up to him, thin-lipped with rage. 'No – body – talked – to – them,' she spat each word out, separately, like poison pellets. 'Not – one – soul.'

'I see,' said Pema, steel in his voice. 'You no longer wish us to help you with the animals. Goodbye then.'

He turned on his heel to go, but before he could take even one step, the pair were out of their chairs and holding on to his sleeves.

'Sit down, dear boy,' smarmed Klepsang.

'Have some breakfast,' oozed Ma.

'Money first,' said Pema. 'Half now and the rest when we get to Cliffton.'

Klepsang and Ma automatically tried to haggle, but this new version of their dupe was having none of it. It took no more than a few moments before everything was settled. But even such a short time was enough for Pema to feel his anger-fuelled fearlessness starting to drain away ...

'Get me out of here,' he hissed desperately to Singay.

Snows! thought Singay. She could see he was turning white and starting to sweat. Grabbing Rose with one hand and Pema with the other, she hustled them out of the Way Station and out of sight round a corner of the building.

Pema slumped onto the ground and buried his face in his hands. Rose and Singay sat down on either side and stared at him with wide eyes.

'That was a surprise,' said Rose.

'I'll say! You were *amazing*!' said Singay. 'Are there really no Protectors on the Overland. How did you find out they were cheating us?'

'Somebody told me,' Pema muttered. Then he groaned and clutched his head. 'I can't believe I just ... Did I really just walk into a crowded room and threaten Klepsang and Ma?'

'You really did!' said Singay.

Pema groaned again. 'I feel awful.'

'But why?' asked Singay. 'You were magnificent!'

'I put Rose's life in danger. So stupid . . . so stupid . . .'

'You aren't – you *didn't*!' exclaimed Rose. 'You've been looking after me all this way!'

'If I'm stupid about money we might not have enough to get you safely to the Sea. That's not looking after you.'

'But Pema, they tricked *all* of us!' Singay put her arm around his shoulders. 'If it weren't for you I'd probably be as old as Ma before we found out what was going on, and you'd have a long white beard! And we'd *still* be hiding from the Protectors!'

Pema gave a ragged laugh. 'That doesn't make any sense,' he said shakily, 'but thanks.' He took a deep breath and stood up. 'Snows, I feel like I've done a day's work already!'

'And here comes another,' said Rose. 'Come on. Let's get started. The grunts are waiting. And tonight, thanks to our hero, it's beds and a roof.'

'And lavender oil in a bath!' cried Singay.

'If it's there to be had, you'll have it,' said Pema, sounding suddenly fierce again. 'Or I'll want to know the reason why!'

CHAPTER TWENTY-ONE

Cliffton

A few weeks later, just as the sun was setting, they dropped down from the high plateau and spent the night on the outskirts of Cliffton. First thing the next morning, Pema settled the grunts into one of the selling pens, made sure they had clean water and fresh food, and scratched the matriarch behind her big ears.

He was sad as he made his way back to the others.

'What, Klepsang and Ma aren't coming to say a loving goodbye?' said Singay, looking about.

Pema snorted. 'Still snoring.'

'Good thing they paid us last night for getting the grunts here. That was the job, beginning to end.'

Pema didn't answer. He just started walking, and Singay and Rose trotted after him.

'Yes, we did it, just like we said. Job done,' Singay continued in an irritatingly chirpy voice. 'You know, I wanted to ask you, Pema – do grunts have much of a homing instinct?'

'Yes, they do. Very strong.' *Why is she asking all these questions? Why can't she just leave me alone? And what's that squealing I'm hearing?*

'So *that's* a good thing too – because I loosened the fence at the back of the pen,' she said. 'No, keep walking! Don't even turn around!'

'What – you – what?' spluttered Pema.

She gave him a companionable shoulder shove and started to laugh.

'The look on your face!' she giggled.

'Were you in on this?' he asked Rose, who only smiled sweetly.

Pema shook his head in amazement. 'And all this time I thought you didn't like grunts very much!' he said.

'I don't. But I like Klepsang and Ma a whole lot less!'

'Well, maybe our visit to the great and good town of Cliffton should be a short one . . .'

Klepsang and Ma stood looking at the empty pen.

'What do we do now?' wailed Ma. 'Go after the grunts?'

'No,' said Klepsang through gritted teeth. 'Those grunts are long gone. No, we go after those brats. We get even.'

As if on cue, a squad of leather-clad Enforcers with their heavy sticks strolled into view.

'Thank goodness you're here!' squealed Ma.

'You're . . . glad to see us?' asked one of the men. He was the youngest member of the group and his leather was so new it still squeaked. He was thrilled to be on duty, but he'd been expecting a bit more terror and awe from the general public.

Instead, this ghastly woman lunged forward and grabbed him by the arm. 'We've been *longing* for you,' she said breathily, ignoring the young man's desperate attempts to back away. 'Ever since those terrible fiends got hold of us, all the way back before the Overland.'

'Fiends?' barked the Chief Enforcer. 'Explain yourself, madam!'

'Yes, wife,' said Klepsang. 'Explain yourself. And put the boy down.'

Ma reluctantly released the young man and explained all about the three strangers who, disguised as innocent children, had wormed their way into the much-too-trusting couple's confidences. How they had preyed upon their pity – 'Such poor little souls they seemed, lost and all alone in the great wide world ... how could we not try to help them?' They had taken advantage of the gullibility of two upright citizens. 'Especially my husband. He's got such a big heart – it's really no difficulty at all to trick him.'

By now, a curious crowd had gathered and, as one, they turned and looked at Klepsang, who plastered a simper onto his face and did his utmost to look as green as grass. It was a singularly unpleasant sight.

'So, my good woman,' the Chief Enforcer said, turning back to her with a slight shudder. 'What did these deceiving children actually *do* to you?'

'Children, Your Honour? Oh no. They aren't children, sir. They're ...' Ma let her voice drop so that the Enforcers and the enthralled crowd had to lean in close to hear as she whispered the word. 'They're *demons*. Who caused an entire herd of grunts to *vanish*!'

Cliffton was impressive. It had tall, white, uniform buildings and wide streets. There was nothing haphazard about its grid layout, perfect pavements and straight thoroughfares – it was the most organised place they'd yet seen.

'It even smells good!' exclaimed Singay. 'Remember the stink at River Head?'

'It's not hard to smell better than River Head,' Pema replied. 'Right.' And he checked that Ker's pebble was still in his pocket. 'The Pier is in this direction.'

The Enforcers were looking anxious.

'And where are they heading?'

'Heading south, Captain, Your Honour,' Ma said. 'Looking for a boat to take them on to the City, that sink of sin, Your Honour, sir.'

The Chief Enforcer had explained to the couple that they didn't need to call him that, but they were only simple folk, after all, and it would be churlish to insist.

'You'd best hurry, Captain,' urged Klepsang. 'The way to the Pier will take them right through the heart of the town.'

'Like an evil arrow, sir,' added Ma.

'Uh, yes, like an arrow, and who knows who might be, um, pierced, evilly, by them on their way?' Klepsang gave his wife a look.

'And Father Impeccable is holding a rally in the Square today to add to the Tower of Faith – starting any time now!' squawked the youngest Enforcer.

There was a chorus of horrified gasps. Thanks to Ma and Klepsang's vivid rhetorical fireworks, most of their audience now had a picture of Rose, Singay and Pema as three slavering demons with blood-stained tusks and mesmeric eyes, though still, confusingly, at the same time, apparently just three children. The thought of these devils rampaging through their fair town and into the very midst of a rally of unsuspecting religious townsfolk – well, it didn't bear thinking about.

'If you hurry, you might catch them!' urged Klepsang and Ma yet again, but this time it turned out they were talking to themselves. The Enforcers, and the crowd, were already on the hunt . . .

'Come on, Rose! We've got to stay together!' Singay urged, but still the Driver tried to hold back.

'I want to go another way!' he wailed. 'There's something wrong up ahead. I don't want to go this way!'

The happy mood of earlier had completely evaporated. They'd been caught up in a crowd of Cliffton citizens heading into the centre of the town. Mostly people were on foot but there were oil-engine chairs and sedan chairs as well, carried by burly serving men. Their passengers were arrogant-looking ladies and gentlemen, but what were they doing in the midst of the common crush?

Pema managed to drag the others to the edge of the procession, aiming to shelter in a doorway of one of the fine buildings that lined the street. But Singay was swept back into the flow and, rather than be separated from her, Rose and Pema had to follow her in.

'They must all be going *somewhere*, and as soon as they get there, we can break free,' Pema tried to reassure the distressed Rose, but in truth they were all more than a little scared by the mass of people and their relentless press forward. They'd never seen such a crowd before. It was all too breathless and intent, and with a kind of panic just under the surface. *Like a herd, just before it stampedes*, thought Pema, feeling sick. It wasn't an angry crowd – if anything, it was a purposeful and happy one – but with a brittle kind of happiness that could so easily flip into its opposite.

An old woman beside them stumbled and would have fallen if Singay hadn't steadied her. 'Thank you, dear,' the woman said. 'Everyone gets so excited, they don't always notice someone who isn't so spry anymore. We're almost there, though, aren't we? There's more room in the Square.'

'Is that where they're all going – the Square?' Singay asked. She kept a hand on the woman's arm, as there was another surge forward.

'Of course! Didn't you know?' The old woman's expression started to sharpen suspiciously, but Pema broke in.

'We're new in town,' he said. 'Just in off the Overland.'

'Oh, well, that explains it. You're in for a treat then, and no mistake! Father Impeccable is holding another auction at the Tower. I *always* go to the auctions. I've never won a bid, of course – well, it's not likely, is it? – but I always take part. Even someone as poor as I am can have faith, Father Impeccable says. Look! Look! There it is! The Tower of Faith! Isn't that the most amazing thing you've ever seen?'

Pema and Singay could only stare, but the Driver clutched at his head in sudden agony.

'Oh no,' he whimpered wildly. 'No, no, no . . .'

CHAPTER TWENTY-TWO

The Tower of Faith

The Tower of Faith rose into the air like a staircase from a nightmare. The fine, white buildings that made the sides of the Square were tall, three and four storeys high, but the Tower was taller still. It was shaped in an impossible spiral that swerved and bulged its way precariously upwards.

'What's holding that thing *up?*' exclaimed Singay, as the crowd swept them further into the Square.

'Faith, of course,' said the old woman. 'The dear Father is in charge of the building. He allows us to be part of it, by bidding on each new block of stone. That's why we're here! With his blessing, we help the Tower to grow higher and higher.'

Rose moaned again, louder this time.

'Is the little boy ill?' the old woman asked solicitously. 'I know these big crowds can be upsetting for some. Here, let him sit down.' She metaphorically unsheathed her elbows and shoved her way over to a bench. The spectators currently using it to see over other peoples' heads were summarily dislodged, and Rose, shivering and whimpering, collapsed onto the seat.

'He's starting to attract attention,' Singay whispered to Pema.

'We've got to get him away,' he whispered back, but before they could spot an escape route, the crowd around them suddenly went still.

'*He's here!*' the old woman breathed.

As if from nowhere, a figure had appeared on the platform.

A short, overstuffed woman with a cauliflower hairstyle climbed up beside him, introducing herself as Madame Phophor, Chairwoman of the Tower of Faith Steering Committee, wittering on about the fair town of Cliffton and what a decent, righteous place it was to live, and all the while the man held every eye. Pema and Singay could see him clearly, could see that he was medium height, dark haired, with dark eyes, modestly dressed, but the rest of their perception was flooded by his charisma. There was something about the way he held himself, the way he moved his head, the look in those dark eyes . . .

And then he smiled and somehow each person in the Square was sure the smile was meant for them alone.

'And now,' Madame Phophor shrilled, '*dear* friends, it is time for the first token of your faith.'

Throughout the Square there was the sound of hundreds of people reaching for their cash.

'What's happening?' Singay whispered to the old woman. 'Who *is* that?'

'Shush, it's the auction!' she hissed, her eyes fixed on the man as her fingers fumbled with her purse. 'It's Father Impeccable. Who else?'

The old woman called out one of the very first bids, for a tiny number of coins, but the look Father Impeccable sent in her direction couldn't have been more loving if she'd offered him a fortune.

'Bless you,' he said, and turned his attention to the next

bidder. The old woman sighed joyfully and seemed utterly, deeply content.

Baskets miraculously appeared and began passing from hand to hand, criss-crossing over the heads of the crowd until they reached the next bidder, who threw in their coins.

The bidding worked its way quickly through the poorest. Now it was the turn of the newly better-off, whose careful accents occasionally let their owners down in the excitement of it all, as they called out higher and higher figures. Then, the positively rich took over. Servants now called out the bids, and letters of promise with seals and crests landed in the baskets with hardly a sound. Until a voice announced a huge – a handsome! – offer.

The Square went still.

Father Impeccable looked enquiringly at a veiled lady in an oil-engine chair. All the other bidders were silent. The lady inclined her head infinitesimally, confirming the bid.

'Done!' said Father Impeccable. His smile was beatific, and his voice throbbed with emotion. 'Thank you, my dear, dear friends.' And everyone felt blessed.

'Now what?' whispered Pema.

'Now the block gets taken up to the very top of the Tower and placed there for everyone to see how strong our faith is,' answered the old woman.

'What – that fancy lady's going to climb up there carrying that great big stone?' said Singay.

'Of course not. Don't be silly. One of her servants will do it.'

A young man in a servant's uniform now came forward and, with difficulty, picked up the stone. Father Impeccable placed his hand on the block in a final gesture of blessing and stood aside.

The young man put his foot onto the first step of the Tower, and began to climb. They could see his arms shaking from the strain of the weight, and his Adam's apple bobbed up and down convulsively. Higher and higher he climbed. Pema and Singay couldn't take their eyes off him. As he neared the top, the whole crazy structure started to shiver in time with his footsteps, or perhaps in time with the pounding of the blood through his veins. At the final turn of the spiral he suddenly lost his nerve, and what should have been a delicate, precise placing of the block of stone at the very top was more of a terrified fumble.

They stopped breathing.

Did the Tower sway? Did the entire structure quiver, right down to its base?

Would faith be enough?

There was a long, long moment . . .

. . . and the Tower didn't fall.

The crowd let out a sigh, and the servant scuttled back down to the safety of the ground. The veiled lady modestly accepted the applause of her well-dressed neighbours for her piety. Father Impeccable reappeared on the platform to begin the auction for the next stone.

'Not happy, the stones aren't happy,' wailed Rose. 'The tower is wrong – it's going to fall! The whole thing is going to fall—'

'Rose! Don't!' said Singay, her voice sharp with fear.

'Shh,' whispered Pema anxiously, but it was too late. In his distress, Rose's voice had been too loud, too clear.

Heads turned.

'What was that?'

'Did you hear that boy? Did you hear what he *said?*'

'Blasphemy!'

The crowd drew back in horror, leaving a circle of clear space around the bench where Pema, Singay and Rose crouched. Whispers rippled out, like the hissing of threatened snakes.

'Blasphemy . . . blasphemy . . .'

At the same moment, at the edge of the crowd, a squad of Enforcers had appeared, pushing forward towards the Tower. Using their sticks, they prodded and shoved past people too distracted and too tightly crammed together to easily make way. The press of bodies bulged outwards around them.

It was unclear whether it was this, or the smaller displacement of people from around Rose, but the packed crowd moved closer to the foot of the precarious Tower. And closer still. Until someone jostled someone else, and the person behind them was shoved sharply backwards and bumped into the base of the structure.

There was a heart-stopping moment, and then Singay screamed, 'LOOK OUT! IT'S GOING TO FALL!'

Stone blocks shifted and groaned, grating against each other, and the whole mad structure began to tremble and tilt, further and further over the sea of trapped bodies below. The people stood, frozen, but even if they had found the will to move, it would have been impossible to run.

They were going to be crushed – there was no escape. Any second now the stones would be crashing towards the ground. It had already begun—

And Rose stood up.

He was small and odd-looking and scruffy, a childlike figure standing on a bench, and yet he possessed an undeniable power to rival Father Impeccable's hypnotic charisma. Paying no attention to the sea of faces around him, the little Driver raised his hands.

The stones of the Tower, already committed to the embrace of gravity, slowed. They still fell, but now their descent was in slow motion. They swirled gently around each other, and settled their crushing weight onto the ground as delicately as autumn leaves. The crowd was frozen. Mesmerised. It was bizarre, beautiful, unbelievable . . .

When it was over, the stones of the Tower of Faith lay on the ground. No one had been killed. No one had been injured. And Rose, his eyes closed and his skin the ghastly colour of something dead, had collapsed.

'It's them!' shrieked the youngest Enforcer. 'The demons! They destroyed the Tower of Faith! They destroyed it!'

Father Impeccable stood on the platform, alone and unmoving. His dark eyes were focused on the Driver, and there was a look of suppressed excitement on his suddenly calculating face.

The crowd parted abruptly to let the Enforcers through.

'Demons! Get the demons!'

The final rush seemed to take the three fiends completely by surprise. Heavy black bags were thrown over their heads (everyone knows you shouldn't look a demon in the eye), their hands were tied and, as the crowd bayed and cheered, they were dragged away to Cliffton Prison.

CHAPTER TWENTY-THREE

Locked Up

'Got some company for you, Noksam. A bevy of demons, but don't worry. They're not full-grown, and this one's sick.'

It had been a nightmare. They'd been pushed along with the bags over their heads, not able to see where they were going, shoved and jostled and yelled at.

'You're for the rope, you are!'

'We know what to do with demons in *our* town.'

'Hang 'em now, I say. Why wait?'

'No, no, we'll do it by the book. Make 'em suffer.'

And all the while neither Pema nor Singay knew what state Rose was in. Somebody must have carried him from the Square – he couldn't have made it otherwise.

Inside the prison there was more shoving, then the sound of a metal door clanging shut behind them and then someone was pulling the horrible bags off them and fumbling with the ropes tying their hands.

'Demons indeed!' the stranger was tutting crossly. 'Really, this town ... There you are. Are you all right? I'm Noksam.'

They were in a cell. Everywhere they looked was cold stone, from the floor to the walls and the stone bench down one side. There was a tiny barred window high up, and hardly room to move. The cell was not designed to house four.

'Oh dear, the little one really doesn't look well, does he.

Here, put him on the bench. Did they hurt him, the great bullies?'

'No,' said Pema. 'Not exactly. He's sick. Could you, er, excuse us a moment? We, um, we have to give him some medicine.'

'Of course, of course.' And their cellmate politely turned his back to give them what privacy he could.

Rose looked tiny, laid out on the thin prison blanket, but his eyes were open and he managed the ghost of a smile as they bent over him.

'The bag,' he whispered. 'It's in my pocket.'

But when Pema found the irradiant sack and drew it out, he thought he must have made a mistake. 'This *can't* be it – it's so light!' He looked over at Singay in horror.

The little Driver didn't say anything. He was shaking as he took the bag from Pema and thrust his hand inside. They watched intently – they could see it doing him good, starting to bring his colour back – but then, far too soon, Rose brought his hand out again and hid the bag away.

'Wait – you need more,' Singay protested, but he shook his head.

'That's all I can spare,' he murmured. 'I'll rest now, I think. I can't . . .' His words died away as his eyes closed.

Singay tucked the blanket round him and then just stood there, feeling helpless.

Questions pounded in Pema's mind. *What's going to happen to him? How can he possibly be controlling the Mountain in the state he's in? What's happening back at home?* And, louder than all the rest, *Are they really going to hang us? Are they? ARE THEY?*

'Please, sit! I'm sure it's been a difficult day.' Noksam squeezed over to make room for them at the other end of the bench. It was strange having their cellmate acting like a solicitous host, but it was comforting too.

'We're sorry to be crowding you like this,' said Pema.

'Not at all, not at all!' said the man. Now that they looked at him properly they saw he was meagre and middle-aged, with a constantly flickering, anxious smile. 'The prison's always full to bursting these days. Besides, I won't be here all that much longer.'

'Oh, are you being released?' asked Singay, thinking that perhaps this was the cell for people due to be let out.

'Released? Well, yes, in a manner of speaking. I'm pencilled in to be hanged early next week.'

'Pencilled in . . . *what?*'

'Well, they don't want to say a definite date in case it doesn't come off. It's this summer flu that's going around. Quite nasty. You want to stay clear of it if you can. Anyway, the hangman's been taken bad with it, and hasn't been able to leave his bed, but he sent word he hoped to be up and about by the middle of next week at the latest. Personally, I think you can't be too careful with these things. Try to get up too soon and you find yourself flat on your back for twice as long again afterwards. I think he should stay home for a while longer, I really do. But, of course, I would say that.' He smiled apologetically. 'But enough about me. Please, do tell me, what did you do? To end up here, I mean?'

'Nothing,' said Pema.

'They think we're demons,' said Singay. 'But we're *not*.'

She'd meant to sound outraged, but the words came out as more of a wail.

'Of course you aren't,' Noksam tutted sympathetically. 'Utter nonsense!'

'And you,' said Pema, since this was apparently jail etiquette, 'what did you do?'

The man looked modest.

'Oh, I'm nothing so exciting as a demon! I'm just a thief. Well, at least, that's what I'm going to be hanged as. In actual fact, I'm an accountant. *Was* an accountant. I looked after my employer's money. Adding up and subtracting numbers all day, every day – that was me!'

'What did you steal?' asked Singay. He seemed such an unlikely criminal.

'Oh, money,' said Noksam. 'Stick with what you know, I always say. Twenty-three years of blameless bookkeeping, and then snap! One Monday morning, not long before lunch, I just started cooking the books, as they say in thieving circles. Not that I know any other thieves, not to speak to. I got caught before I could meet any.' He shrugged apologetically.

'Why do you think it happened?' asked Pema. 'The "snap", I mean?'

'I've had time to give that quite some thought,' said Noksam, 'and in the end, I've decided the oil's to blame.'

'The oil?'

'Yes. You see, in the beginning my employer earned roughly 2.67 times as much as he paid me, and I never considered for a moment that there was any unfairness in the arrangement. He manufactured household goods, and I did the books. But when he moved into oil-engine gizmos, suddenly he was earning ten, then fifteen times as much as me. He was a good man – he gave me a raise – but it didn't touch the percentages. And so, as I say, snap! It was definitely the oil that did it for me. That, and religion.'

'You started to feel guilty?' asked Singay.

'No,' the man said, sounding faintly surprised. 'Not that I've noticed. No, it was my employer's wife. She gave a lot of money away to that Father Impeccable – you know, the one who's auctioning off chunks of that Tower to the rich folks? Well, maybe she wanted to prove her faith or maybe she just wanted to swank a little, but it was a big enough sum that my employer had to come looking for a place to take it from and, well, it wasn't exactly there anymore.'

'I can't believe they're going to hang you just for taking money!'

'Oh, they hang you for most things in this town.'

Singay looked at Pema, her eyes wide.

'They wouldn't do that to *us*,' he said quickly. 'I'm sure they're just trying to scare us.'

'I wouldn't bank on it,' said Noksam cheerfully.

There was a pause, then the accountant-thief said, 'I'll tell you something for nothing, though. Speaking as a thief, you understand. That Father Impeccable has himself a nice little earner there, with that Tower of his.'

'How do you mean?'

'Elegant and ingenious, like all the best scams. High risk, of course, but you have to expect that. That's a lot of money they're giving him. And extremely simple accounting required!'

'It's a *con?*' gasped Pema and Singay.

'Oh yes,' said Noksam. 'But it's got a definite time limit. Mark my words, one of these days that thing is going to fall down, and somebody is going to get hurt!'

Pema and Singay looked at Rose. He hadn't moved.

The cell fell silent. Prison time passed – slow and inexorable.

Singay heaved a weary sigh and, to Pema's great surprise, leaned her head on his shoulder. He peered at her, going slightly cross-eyed.

'Singay? What's wrong?' It was a stupid question. *We're in jail, accused of being demons, and we're going to be hanged. What could possibly NOT be wrong?*

But it was Rose she was thinking about.

'Look at him,' she murmured. 'Look at what we've done to him. He's dying.'

Pema tried to comfort her. 'We were trying to help him. He'd no chance of getting home if he'd just stayed inside the Mountain.'

'I guess. But at least he would have been *safe*. Safe, and comfortable and happy, with his singing stones and his projects and the desert people thinking he was a god. We dragged him away from it all. Was it just because I thought I deserved an adventure?' She sighed sadly. 'Do you think he wishes he never met us?'

'Not once.' It was Rose's voice, no more than the thread of a whisper.

Pema felt Singay stiffen beside him and then relax. Greatly daring, he took her hand. She didn't pull away.

Out in the town, the man they called Father Impeccable was busy tying up loose ends. He'd sold the blocks of stone from the ruined Tower back to the builder who'd supplied them in the first place. For a profit.

'I know you'll be marketing them as relics before the week is out,' he said when the builder tried to haggle.

His own financial affairs were always in readiness for a speedy exit. One of his first investments, when the Tower money had started to come in, was to buy a ticket south on one of those oil-fired speedboats. He carried that ticket in his pocket, always. But the next departure wasn't until morning, which meant he had time for one more thing . . .

He found Madam Phophor still in the Square amongst a crowd of twittering ladies. He separated her out from them with the skill of a champion shup dugg. As they stood together, every eye was fixed on them, hungry with curiosity and envy. Madam Phophor patted her meticulous, cauliflower-like hair and tried not to smirk.

Father Impeccable's voice was deep, intimate, low.

'My dear, there's something I want you to do for me.' His eyes held hers, telling her what she wanted to hear – that she was special, she was special to him, so much more than those others.

'Anything, Father, you know that,' she breathed. 'You just have to ask.'

Of course, his eyes said. *I know.*

'Wait till it gets dark, and then, this is what I want – I *need* – you to do for me.'

He whispered into her ear for a while, and then handed

her a bag that clinked agreeably along with a small object. One last look from his mesmerising eyes, and he was gone.

Madame Phophor's heart beat fast. The demons weren't demons . . . but she was to pretend they *were?* These were strange things to have asked of her – very, well, *odd*. But for Father Impeccable, she would do *anything*.

CHAPTER TWENTY-FOUR

What Demons Do

'Evening, all!'

The prisoners blinked, rubbing their eyes in the sudden glare from the jailer's lantern. His voice was too loud in the cramped space. Pema's brain felt cold and sluggish and Singay had a whimper stuck in her throat.

'Evening, Jopi,' said Noksam politely. 'Thanks for bringing the gruel. And how has your day been?'

'I'm glad you asked,' said Jopi the jailer, setting the food down on the floor and leaning comfortably against the cell door. 'The ferliest thing happened. I've just had a visitor – an extremely *generous* visitor – who, for reasons not mentioned to me, wished to remain anonymous. Now, to be honest, having a visitor of *any* sort is a pretty unusual event for me. It's a lonely job, being a jailer. If it weren't for the prisoners, like your good selves, I don't think I'd have the chance to pass the time of day with a living soul from shift start to shift end, and that's a fact.' He shook his head sadly.

'But you had a visitor today,' Noksam reminded him.

'That's right. She – oops, well, now you know it was a lady, but I'd be grateful if you'd all forget it as soon as possible. This visitor – who said she was representing someone else, who *also* wished to remain anonymous – made the following suggestion to me, backed up with a satisfyingly persuasive sack of coins, but that's just between you and me, which was …' They could see him working his way back through the sentence to find out where he was meant to be going, and then, with a happy smile, starting up again with, 'That said person did not think that justice was being served, killing young people and children *generally*, and you three young people and children *specifically*. Even if you *are* demons. Which she didn't seem to have entirely made up her mind about. Nevertheless, she thought that the best thing would be for you to *vanish*, the way demons do. Disappear. Walk through walls, pass through locked doors. That sort of thing.'

'Don't be ridiculous,' exclaimed Singay. 'We can't do anything like that. We're not demons at all.'

'Ah, now that's the clever bit. Apparently, as long as people *think* you're demons, which it would seem that people do, then they'll believe you can. The lady suggested I let you out and then just lock the door of the cell behind you, go and sit in my guardroom and deny all knowledge. As neat a jailbreak as you could ask for, and none of this having to knock your jailer over the head or tie him up in any uncomfortable sort of fashion whatsoever, which is more usual in such a scenario.'

'A jailbreak?' exclaimed Pema.

'A jailbreak,' said Jopi. He beamed round at them, but the smile faded as he turned to the accountant-thief. 'But not you, Noksam, I'm afraid. There's nobody thinks *you're* a demon.'

Noksam gave a resigned smile. 'And no more I am, Jopi. No more I am.'

'No – wait – we can't just *leave* you here!' cried Singay.

Turning to the jailer, she said, 'Don't you realise he's pencilled in to be hanged this week?'

'Or next,' added Noksam helpfully. 'Summer flu permitting.'

Jopi shrugged regretfully.

Singay drew an indignant breath, but before she could speak, someone else did.

It was Rose. He still looked like death warmed over, but he was sitting up.

'Demons eat people, don't they?' he said. 'Body and soul?'

'That's what I've heard,' said the jailer. 'But what would your point be in mentioning it, eh?'

'Well, poor Noksam here has been trapped in a cell with three demons for quite some hours now. Who knows what might have happened to him in that time? Demons get hungry, I expect, just like anybody else.'

The little Driver and the jailer looked thoughtfully at each other for a long moment.

'Body and soul,' said Jopi slowly. 'But not, if I understand these things, *clothing*.'

Rose nodded. 'That would be most convincing, I feel. No blame could possibly be placed on the custodian in such a situation.'

'Can't be expected to control hungry demons. Wouldn't be reasonable,' Jopi agreed, nodding sagely. Then he took a step towards Noksam.

'What in the name of Snow are you *talking* about?' demanded Singay, but Pema was beginning to get the inkling of an idea. He grabbed Singay's arm and swung her to face the door. 'Don't turn around,' he said.

'Yes, please don't,' said Noksam. He sounded a bit muf-fled, as if someone were vigorously pulling his shirt over his head.

Jopi chuckled. 'Don't worry, a blanket or so missing is not going to be noticed. Here, use my belt.'

'Can I look yet?' asked Singay, exasperated by not knowing what was happening.

'Soon . . . not yet . . . almost ready . . . Now!'

Pema and Singay turned, and there was Noksam, look-ing like a pleased – if embarrassed – scarecrow, wrapped up in a prison blanket. He pointed down at the stone floor and grinned.

'That's demonically clever, wouldn't you say?' said Jopi. 'No offence!'

The jailer had taken the accountant-thief's clothes and laid them out on the stone floor in the shape of a man, flat-tened and contorted as if the body had been sucked out by extreme force.

'That's the most ridiculous thing I've ever heard of,' exclaimed Singay. 'And it just might work!' She could feel hope ballooning inside her. *We're going to get out – we're going to get out!*

Jopi chuckled smugly.

Pema turned to Noksam. 'But what will *you* do now? Where will you go?'

Noksam put his head to one side, thinking. 'Well, I find I prefer accountancy to thievery, and from what you say, upriver there's not so much oil to get in the way of the numbers. So that's the what and the where for me, I'm thinking. Though I also think it would be no bad idea to drop off at my rooms first and put on some clothes!'

He hitched his blanket up a little more securely, smiled shyly and trotted out of the cell.

They were about to follow when Jopi suddenly turned, blocking the door.

They stared in horror.

He lied to us! thought Pema.

It was all a horrible game, thought Singay. *He never meant to let us go!*

But the jailer had just paused to rummage in his pocket. 'Goodness, there was me almost forgetting. I was supposed to give the smallest demon this.' And he bent over and presented Rose with a small metal disc.

'What is it?' asked the Driver, bewildered.

'No idea,' replied Jopi, stepping into the corridor. 'Come along!'

He led them through the jail, to the front door.

'Look at that! There's even a bit of fog, for easier disappearing into. Nothing but the best from Cliffton Prison!' Then, as they hesitated on the threshold, he added, 'Off you go!' before moseying cheerfully back to the guardroom to count his cash.

CHAPTER TWENTY-FIVE

Through the Fog

Madame Phophor made her way back to the Square with a light step and a quickly beating heart. She had taken time after her errand at the prison to go home, change into her best dress and freshen up her make-up and hair. *Just a way of showing respect,* she said to herself in the mirror. *It's good to show respect.*

Father Impeccable had told her to meet him by the platform where the Tower of Faith had so recently stood. It was fully dark now, and as she arrived a fog was beginning to blur the light from the oil lamps around the Square.

She hurried forward, a bit breathless.

'Well, I did what you asked, Father. Father?'

There was no one there.

She peered about, searching for that well-loved figure. She began calling his name, tentatively at first, and then more and more wildly, while questions and fears raced desperately about in her brain. *Where is he? He said he'd meet me. What can have happened?*

When the answer came to her, she staggered and almost fell with the horror of it. *They couldn't have!* But what other explanation could there be? Father Impeccable certainly wouldn't have just walked away without waiting for her. It *must* have been those awful, evil, dastardly … Her mind found its way to vocabulary she didn't know she knew, but even that wasn't adequate to express what she was feeling.

Those people had taken the gift of freedom that the Father had given them – *through me!* – and used it against him. While she had been foolishly, thoughtlessly wasting time on her appearance, they had circled round here and vanished Father Impeccable!

She realised there were tears running down her face. *Stop that immediately*, she scolded herself with a big sniff. *This isn't the time for crying – this is the time for finding those demons, forcing them to un-vanish the dear, endangered Father and then to punish them to the fullest extent imaginable.* And her imagination was more than up to the job.

What Madam Phophor needed just then was a mob, preferably one with flaming torches in their hands and unleashed fury in their hearts. What she *had* was the Tower of Faith Steering Committee, which was just as good.

If not better.

The three demons had almost made it to the Pier when they heard the sound of an angry crowd coming up behind them.

'Run!' cried Singay, her heart leaping into her mouth.

Pema was carrying Rose on his back. 'Hold tight!' And he plunged forward.

The Pier was a maze of wooden wharves, sporadically lit by pools of lamplight that were weirdly fuzzy-looking in the fog. They could feel the jetty swaying under their feet as they ran and knew they were over water now. All Singay could think of was getting them onto a boat – any boat! – and out of sight before the hunt could catch up with them. But Pema, as he pounded along, was scanning frantically from side to side, peering closely as one boat after another loomed up out of the murkiness, and then running on again.

She tried to stop him. 'Wait! Pema! What's wrong with this boat? Or that one? We need to get on board somewhere and hide! What are you looking for?'

But Pema just gritted his teeth and ran faster. He was going so fast he almost ran right past it. As Ker had said, the sign was not obvious – he just caught a glimpse of it out of the corner of his eye.

Someone had painted the Jathang rune as part of a decorative border round the boat's name.

Pema stopped so suddenly that Singay shot by him and had to turn back.

'What are you doing?' she gasped, holding her side. 'Have we lost them?' She tried to still her breath to listen.

Pema set Rose down and pointed up at where the name of the boat showed in the lantern light. 'This one! We want *this* one.'

The others read the name in silence. Singay turned to Pema.

'The *Aubergine*? We just ran past all those other boats so we can hide on the one named after a vegetable?'

'What? It's called what?' Pema looked up. He hadn't noticed anything but the rune. 'No, never mind that now. There's no time to argue. Come on!' He tried to herd them towards the gangplank that angled up onto the *Aubergine*'s deck.

'But why *this* boat?' Singay stuck out her chin, set to argue every step of the way, but then Rose commented quietly, 'The jetty is still wobbling, even though we are no longer running on it. I think the people who are looking for us might be about to arrive.'

There was a moment of frozen horror. Then Singay babbled, 'Vegetables — you gotta love 'em!' and, grabbing Rose between them, she and Pema pelted to the gangplank and raced up it at full speed.

CHAPTER TWENTY-SIX

The Aubergine

The moment their feet touched the deck, a man the size of a barn loomed up at them. His face was all squashed and bent, as if someone had been using it for a punching bag.

'Sorry, no passengers this trip,' he rumbled.

'Oh, but listen, we're being chased!' Singay wailed, but Pema interrupted her.

'I need to speak to the captain. Right away.'

'Eh?' said Singay and the big man in unison, while Rose murmured, 'Oh dear, you don't want to sound rude. What makes you think *he's* not the captain?'

'Oh, he's right, sir,' the big man said earnestly to Rose. 'I'm not the captain.'

Singay shoved Rose behind her protectively. 'And *you're* mistaken – he's not a sir, he's just a little boy, aren't you, Ro— Roger?' It was a shock having Rose addressed as an adult, when so many people had accepted his child disguise. *What can this giant see?* she wondered, when sudden shouting from the pier made her crouch in fear, dragging Rose with her. Pema took one look over the railing and dropped down beside them. The big man looked down at the three, bemused.

'What's wrong?' he asked in a too-loud whisper. 'Are you hiding? Why are you hiding?'

'Shh!' hissed Singay. 'Please!'

Pema clutched at the man's trouser leg. 'Look, right, we're

in trouble, but it wasn't our fault. You've got to let me speak to your captain. I *know* she'll want to see me! Please, if you'd just give her this.' And he thrust the marked stone Ker had given him on the plateau into the big man's hand. '*Please!*'

'Hey! You there!'

'Don't tell them we're here,' Singay whispered frantically.

'You up there! We're searching the boats on this jetty and we have reason to believe you may have dangerous demons aboard,' came a voice of self-appointed authority from the pier below. Others in the mob were muttering to each other.

'Wouldn't it be safer just to burn it now?'

'What are we waiting for?'

'But we don't even know if they're on this boat—'

'Burn it anyway!'

'Down to the waterline!'

The big man leaned over the railing and called down to the heaving mass of torchbearers, 'Hello, my name's Bob. Can I help you gentlemen and ladies?'

There was a growl from the crowd. They were not here for polite conversation.

'We're chasing three demons in disguise who have vanished, or possibly even *killed*, a priest,' said a rather dumpy middle-aged woman. It was Madame Phophor, though the excitement of the chase had left her cauliflower coiffure in an unrecognisable state. 'We're going to search this boat of yours from deck to doorknob until we find them. And then we're going to deal with them the way they deserve. And you too – don't think we won't! – for taking on criminals as passengers.'

Bob shook his head. 'It's not my boat, ma'am. I'm not the captain,' he said calmly. 'And I'm sorry, but we have no passengers on this trip.'

'You're sure about that?'

'Oh yes. I may not be the captain, but I *do* know whether or not we've accepted any passengers – and we haven't.'

At this point Bob stepped up onto the gangplank and the sheer size of him was made clear to the group below. Some of the torch-holders backed away so quickly they were in danger of falling off the other side of the pier, and the comments that drifted up to the deck of the *Aubergine* definitely shifted in tone.

'Well, of *course* he's sure.'

'What do you think – the man doesn't know who's on his own boat?'

'Goodness me, if that's just a crewman, imagine what the *captain* must be like!'

'We'll be on our way, then. Now that I think of it, I expect it was one of those other boats they boarded.'

'Yes. We're going. Leaving you in peace. Um, goodnight!'

Madame Phophor was not easily cowed. She was a short woman, and when *everyone* you meet looms over you, you become less impressed by it, as a rule. Her voice could clearly be heard as they bundled her away, arguing with her Committee about how they should stop behaving like this *immediately* and search that boat *properly*. But this time she was being briskly overruled.

Bob stared after them, a troubled look on his big, crumpled face. He lifted his hand to scratch his nose, only to discover he was still holding Pema's stone. 'Ah. Right. You and your rock and my wife. Well, I can't imagine she's still asleep after all the hubbub. You'd better come with me.'

He led the way towards the stern of the boat and ushered them inside the steering-house.

'Captain Gata?'

'Well, Bob? What was all the fuss about?'

'Them, Captain. Oh, and this.' He handed over the stone.

The captain was a tiny woman. She had obviously just got up from the bed in the corner and was busy running a comb through her tawny hair. She had light brown skin as well, and tawny eyes and . . .

'You're a Jathang!' exclaimed Rose. 'How exciting!' For a moment enthusiasm overcame his weariness and, before Pema or Singay could stop him, he babbled, 'We've been hearing all about you being throat-slitting barbarians who would rather steal than work, and you have to keep travelling because no decent town will let you inside its walls and, and, what was the other thing? Oh, I remember – you eat baby, though I never found out baby *what*. I'm so glad to have a chance to meet you!' The little man beamed, oblivious to the pool of horrified silence he'd created around himself.

Gata's face was unreadable. She leaned forward and stared into Rose's innocent, silvery eyes for a long moment. 'You travel with a straight-speaker, it would seem,' she said at last to the other two.

'We travel with a suicidal fool,' muttered Singay, not quite quietly enough.

The woman nodded. 'They are often one and the same.

You should know that the Jathang are a people of many rules and complex customs. At the same time we have always found room for the one or two who live outside the safety of rules and beyond the constraints of custom. The suicidal fools, the innocents, the ones who speak without calculating the price. They have a place.'

'That's very enlightened,' said Pema tentatively.

'And in your case, it's also very lucky. Imagine what I might have done to you if we didn't appreciate certain forms of candour?' She smiled at them, slow and wide, revealing sharp, white teeth. 'And you can stop gawping at me like a numpty, Bob, any time now!'

He certainly was looking astonished. Then a radiant smile crossed his face and he clasped both his hands over his heart. 'Oh, Gata, you are *fabulous* when you do that!'

The little woman gave him a regal sort of wave and giggled.

'You mean, you're *not* Jathang?' spluttered Singay.

'Oh, I'm Jathang all right,' said Gata. 'I'm just not all that traditional about it. It's good fun messing with people's pre-conceptions – you should have seen your faces! Though I did mean it about the little one there. He does seem to be somewhat out of the ordinary. And now, perhaps you'd like to tell us how you came by this safe-passage stone?'

'Yes, we'd be interested to hear that too,' muttered Singay, staring at Pema meaningfully. He blushed, but before he could explain, Gata turned her attention suddenly away from them. 'What's wrong, Bob?'

The big man shuffled his feet and looked uncomfortable.

'Ah, Captain, I think I can hear that overexcited group

of townspeople getting closer again. I think they're coming back.'

'My husband has excellent hearing,' the captain told them. 'That being the case, Bob, and all things considered, I think casting off round about immediately might be no bad plan. I'll wake the Philosopher, and we'll be on our way.'

'Righty-tighty, captain wifey,' said Bob cheerfully. But then he stopped and his face fell.

'What is it, Bob?'

'Er, Captain, I'm not sure, but I think I may have said, pretty categorically, that we didn't have any passengers for this trip.'

'Bob is uncomfortable with lying,' Gata told the three in a stage whisper. 'We always try to accommodate that.' Then she raised her voice again. 'And who said anything about them being passengers? I've just taken these good people on as crew.'

Bob beamed, and it lit up his big ugly face like a lamp.

'Casting off, Captain, dear,' he bellowed cheerfully, and took himself off.

'Crew?' said Pema.

'Casting off?' said Singay.

'The Philosopher?' said Rose.

The captain of the *Aubergine* smiled her sharp-toothed smile.

'Later,' she said. 'Later.'

CHAPTER TWENTY-SEVEN

Gata, Bob and The Philosopher

'Later' turned out to be some way downriver from Cliffton, moored on the eastern bank, just as the moon was setting. The new crew hadn't had much to do with getting them there, though they managed to get in the way quite a lot. The real crew were tolerant, however. Not counting Ferdinand, the ship's pet ferreck, there were only the three of them: Captain Gata, Bob and the Philosopher – a tall, thin man with no name.

Singay found this disconcerting. As they waited for him to bring breakfast for them all (it was his turn) she turned to the captain and asked, 'But what do we *call* him? We can't just go around calling him "Philosopher"!'

'Yes, you can,' said Gata.

'And you don't find it a bit . . . odd?'

Gata returned her gaze steadily. 'Do you have a problem with things that are odd? That must be inconvenient.'

Singay could feel her face turning red. 'Oh no, not at all. I just—'

'Is something the matter?' The Philosopher stood in the doorway with a laden tray in his hands.

Singay jumped up to help him. 'Nothing at all, Philosopher. Except I'm starving!'

'There's just one thing, though,' said Rose suddenly. 'I don't eat food. I eat rocks. With my nose.' And he pulled a stone out of his pocket.

Singay froze with a plate halfway to the table.

Pema buried his face in his hands. *What's come over him? First he says all that stuff about eating babies and now he's telling them everything – they're going throw us off the boat or take us back to Cliffton or who knows WHAT they'll do to us!*

Singay felt tears pricking – it was nice on this boat and she was so tired.

But the Auberginers hardly blinked.

'Fair enough,' said Captain Gata. 'And after breakfast, would you like to look around the boat?'

And that was that.

The *Aubergine* was a surprising vessel. She was a cargo boat, but that was almost a sideline. A good half of her, both above and below deck, was given over to experimenting with various ways of producing power, each more ingenious than the next.

'The *Aubergine*'s a hybrid,' said Bob proudly.

'Come along – we'll show you everything!' said the Philosopher.

And they did. They showed them the Reverse Windmill Apparatus and the Bifurcated Paddlewheels. They explained the workings of the prototype Streamjets and the experimental Lurch Mechanism. When Singay tried to act intelligent by asking about oil engines, both men were quite scornful, and explained in *enormous* detail how utterly lacking in interest and challenge the new devices were, until the captain arrived.

'Need rescuing yet?' she said, peering up at them with a grin.

'Oh, er, not at all.'

But she took them back on deck anyway.

As the *Aubergine* trundled downriver and the days passed, Pema and Singay were sad to see that Rose didn't pick up. The experience at Cliffton had drained him and, though he didn't say as much, they feared that keeping control of the Mountain, all those leagues behind them, was becoming more and more difficult.

'I just need to rest,' he said, and so they left him in peace.

In spite of their worries, it was a peaceful time. After its tumultuous passage through the canyon, the River seemed to relax too. It spread out and flowed more gently now through level countryside.

'This is the Plains,' the Philosopher told them.

They'd never heard of it. Farms and clusters of houses and big estates covered every inch of the land, and boats of all kinds travelled up and down, including the noisy, smelly speedboats Bob and the Philosopher so despised. But the *Aubergine* felt serenely separate from it all.

There was plenty of work for Pema and Singay to do. With so many different machines on board, there was always something that needed tinkering with. They got very good at finding things like the twelve-bore spanning winch from the toolbox, and knowing how hard to bang on the pipes of the Reversible Windmill Apparatus when it jammed up. The project that was really holding everybody's attention at the moment was the Philosopher's newest idea – Solar Storage Lamps. Working on this seemed to require everyone involved becoming smeared to the eyeballs with

grease. And Bob was busy adapting the Bottom Scrabbler
– a sort of miniature dredging machine in the prow – for
collecting nice, cool river rocks for Rose to inhale.

In a company of eccentrics, they fitted right in.

'Have you noticed how they've asked hardly any
questions?' said Pema. 'I mean, they ask questions all the
time, but it's mostly ones like "Should it be making that
sound?" or "Do you think I could get this to go faster if I did
that?" But they haven't asked us anything about what we're
doing on their boat.'

'I know,' said Singay. She smiled at him. 'It's wonderful.
And I haven't had a single dream!'

I haven't seen her so relaxed since . . . ever! thought Pema.

Rose was resting on the deck one afternoon, with Ferdinand
the ship's ferreck curled up on his lap, when the others came
to join him.

'It's so strange,' said Pema, flopping down beside the
Driver on the warm wood. 'I can remember every second of
when things were going wrong, but the time we've been on
the *Aubergine* just seems to blur.'

'Just because you can remember something, doesn't
make it important,' said Singay, leaning back against the
railing. When she noticed Pema staring up at her in surprise, she poked at him with her foot. 'What – only Rose
gets to be gnomic?'

The little man opened his eyes. 'You think I'm gnomic?'
he murmured. 'How wonderful.'

It was a golden time.

And, as everyone knows, golden times don't last.

CHAPTER TWENTY-EIGHT

Welcome to the Flats

'Goodbyes don't get any easier,' said Pema. He was carrying Rose on his back as they climbed away from the River. The Driver was very quiet. In the moonlight he looked deathly, but then so did they all.

'Oh, I don't know,' said Singay. 'It wasn't hard saying goodbye to Ma or Klepsang. Or that mob at Cliffton. Or—'

'All right, all right. You know what I mean.'

Singay sighed. 'Yes. I do.'

But Gata and Bob and the Philosopher hadn't actually *said* goodbye. They'd made sure everybody was kept extremely busy right up until the last moment, and then had simply said, 'Here's your pay. No time to argue. When you reach the crest of the hill, take a moment, look back. And travel well!'

At which point they'd more or less booted Pema, Rose and Singay off the *Aubergine*. The fact that it was long past midnight wasn't significant – at this point in the River the tides came into play, and the *Aubergine* would start her return journey when the incoming tide was there to help push her on her way.

'I didn't cry,' said Singay. 'I'm glad about that, anyway.'

'Me too,' said Pema, though it wasn't clear whether he meant he was glad he hadn't cried or glad *she* hadn't.

As they neared the top of the rise, panting a little, they

paused. Pema set Rose down gently. Then, without a word, they all three turned and looked back.

They could see her – the *Aubergine* – lying in mid-river, a dark smudge on the light grey, moonlit surface of the water. It had been their whole world for a while, but now . . .

'It looks so small,' murmured Singay. 'It looks—'

Pema grabbed her arm. The smudge had suddenly exploded into a dozen points of light. 'Look! Look! They did it!'

'The Solar Storage Lamps!' cried Singay.

'Look to the stars!' murmured Rose.

The lamps were indeed like a sliver of night sky hovering on the surface of the water. Then the *Aubergine* up-anchored and the incoming tide began to sweep it back towards the heart of the land. The lights grew smaller, and smaller, until they winked out of sight in the distance.

For a long moment the three stood there, looking north. Then, squaring his small shoulders in the dawn light, the Driver turned towards the Sea.

'Almost journey's end, my friends. Almost journey's end.'

Singay helped him back up onto Pema's back and they took the last few steps to the top.

The expectation with any hill is that once you reach the summit, you'll start going down again, but not this time. This hill was broad on top, with a dip in the middle. As they crossed it, the sun rose, and with every step the same thought danced in their heads: *The Sea! At last we're going to see the Sea!*

Aren't we? Singay felt suddenly queasy. 'You know, Rose, things may have changed some. In all this time. You need to expect that, or you'll be disappointed.'

'Oh, of course,' Rose agreed. He was sounding stronger. 'Shorelines shift, things like beaches and bays come and go. But I think you'll understand when you see it why I'm not too worried about the *Sea* changing!' He laughed, but Singay still looked worried.

Pema was watching her. 'Have you had another dream? Is there something you want to tell us?'

Singay shook her head and tried to smile. 'I just can't believe we're so close, and any second now, Rose will hear them, the others, and get his irradiant and save the world and . . .' And now she *was* crying.

'Hush!' said Rose. 'Put me down.'

Pema set the little Driver on his feet. Side by side, they took the last few steps to the final crest of the hill.

'There it . . .' The triumphant words died away as the full vista opened out before them.

The Sea was gone.

Rose moaned.

Spread out before them in the full light of day was a vast expanse of black muck, divided up by hundreds of channels and pools. The rays of the morning sun glinted off multi-coloured slicks. Growing like a many-fingered mould over the surface was a network of ramshackle houseboats, joined haphazardly by walkways and bridges. The whole scene was crawling with movement: bodies and boats; laundry hung out to dry, flapping like the flags of a hundred battles; sounds of hammering and bickering and babies crying. In the distance, a great wall sliced across the nightmare. It was too far away to get an accurate sense of height, but it looked enormous.

And beyond that ...

'What *is* it?'

Higher than the wall of stone was a wall of fog that obscured the view in a great cloaking curve from east to west.

'Where's the City? Where's the Sea?' stuttered Pema, but Singay was staring at Rose.

'You still can't hear them, can you.' It was a statement, not a question.

Silver tears spilled onto his thin face and he spread his hands helplessly. 'I don't understand. It's all wrong. I can't ... there's no ...'

'Hey! Budge over!'

They spun round just as an enormous wicker basket full to overflowing with leafy vegetables loomed up behind them. Singay pulled Pema and Rose aside as it trundled past without slowing. Underneath the greenery was a man, bent double so that only his muscled legs showed. And he was not the only one. As they looked about, they saw that there were trails zigzagging all over the hillside, all aiming at the point where the River spread out into the mud flats. And the trails were dotted with travellers, heavily laden and hurrying downhill.

'Wait! What's going on down there?' Singay called after the man. 'We're strangers here.'

The man didn't stop. 'Embarkation Pier,' he called over his shoulder. 'Buy your disc at the Disc Shed. Better hurry!'

Then he took his own advice and powered off down the hill.

'Thank you so much,' muttered Singay bitterly.

Rose just stood there looking small and frail, saying nothing as he stared out over the vast horrible mess.

Pema put a hand on his shoulder. 'Well, we didn't come all this way to stop now. I'm not surprised you can't hear the other Drivers with all *that* in the way.'

Singay rallied. 'That's right. We just need to get past all the muck and the smog and out to the clean Sea.'

'But *how?*' Rose's voice was tremulous.

'We'll just have to go and find out,' said Pema. 'Come on!'

The focus of all the hurrying was a pier, but firmly on the solid shore, running alongside a channel in the mud. There were dozens of people clustered about, yelling and waving their arms at dozens of small boats in the channel. The people in the boats were standing up, shouting back, gesticulating, even sometimes reaching up and grabbing hold of prospective customers by their trouser legs. The closer the three got, the louder the noise – and the stronger the smell from the churned-up water – became.

It was like a market day where there was only one product for sale – transportation – and no one was allowed to speak below a bellow. Some of the boats had oil-powered engines, and these attracted the more prosperous-looking fares. They saw the man who'd passed them on the hill clambering into a much less impressive boat powered by nothing more advanced than human muscle and an oar.

In the scrum, no one paid any attention to the little

ragged group at the back of the crowd. Pema, Singay and Rose watched, bewildered, as the ferry-ers and the fares sorted themselves out. There seemed to be a system involving the exchange of small metal discs.

'Look at those!' Pema shouted into Singay's ear, while at the same time trying not to breathe in. 'They're like the one Rose has!'

The metal circles did look remarkably like the one Rose had been sent in prison, back in Cliffton, all those leagues ago. The Driver fished it out of his pocket and handed it to Pema.

Already the crowd had mostly dispersed, and the little boats were scurrying away down the muddy channels as fast as their owners could take them, all heading for the strange barrier on the horizon.

'The man said we should go to the Disc Shed,' said Pema.

'There,' said Singay, pointing. It was the only building on the pier, so it seemed a good guess.

They ventured nervously inside. The shed was dimly lit, and empty except for an official-looking man sitting at a counter, tidying things away. Without looking up, he held out a free hand and rumbled, 'What kind?'

'I'm sorry?'

'What kind of disc do you want to buy?'

'I . . . we're not sure. We have this?' Pema held the metal circle out.

'What are you doing here then?' the man snapped. 'You've already bought your disc – why aren't you on your way?'

'I . . . we . . .'

The man got up impatiently, grabbed Pema by the arm and marched him out of the shed.

'House Priority discs embark over *there*,' he said, pointing along the Pier. 'But you're too late now. All the boats are gone. Come back next tide.'

'But . . .'

'When is that, sir?' said Singay, pitching her voice to sound sweet and young.

The man did not seem impressed. He threw a casual glance at the mud beyond the pier.

'Ten hours,' he said. 'Give or take. To the Wall. But you're talking tomorrow morning to get into the City, House Priority or not.' And he walked away.

'What?' said Perma

Rose sank down on the pier, too weary to stand up anymore.

'What's he *talking* about – that's not a ten-hour trip! We can *see* the wall!' exclaimed Singay, gesturing.

'He didn't say it took ten hours to get to the Wall,' said a new voice from behind them. 'He said it was ten hours till the next low tide.'

For a second they couldn't see who had spoken. It was only when they let their eyes drop low enough that they saw two tiny children squatting in a boat, a boy and a girl, staring up at them out of two sets of identical black, beady eyes.

CHAPTER TWENTY-NINE

Twins

And it wasn't just their eyes. Pretty much everything about the pair seemed identical, from the expressions on their faces and the way they held their heads tilted to one side, down to the mud-coloured clothes, the mud-coloured skin and the mud-coloured hair.

'Er, hello,' said Pema. 'Who are you?'

'I'm Zamin. He's Za,' said the girl. 'Got any money?'

'What do you think?' said Singay. 'And we've got one of these.' She nudged Pema, who showed them the disc. They appeared quite impressed, exchanging glances and nodding at each other. 'Right, then,' Singay continued. 'How much to get us to the City?'

'She really enjoys it, doesn't she,' murmured Pema to Rose as they watched yet another epic battle of wills played out over the value of half a coin.

Rose gave him a wan smile but didn't answer. Pema patted him carefully on the shoulder. *That's good. He's saving his strength for the next bit of the journey.* He wished he believed himself.

As soon as the price was agreed and the money changed hands, the twins ushered Pema, Singay and Rose solicitously on board. There was just room for them to sit amongst the wicker storage baskets and general boat gear. Though it looked thoroughly mucky, the craft didn't seem to be about to fall apart or sink. Not immediately, anyway.

Zamin took up the sculling oar, Za cast off the mooring rope, and they headed into the noisome maze of mud, canals, rickety walkways on stilts and grubby houseboats moored amidst a haphazard forest of slimy poles.

'First,' said Zamin, 'you'll need a place to stay for the night. We eat at Granny Geyma's table, so we'll take you there.'

'That's ridiculous!' protested Singay. 'Look – we've paid you to take us to the City, to Elysia. We don't want to stay the night, we want to go to the City.'

'Which is on the other side of the wall, right?' added Pema.

The twins nodded.

'So it can't be more than an hour away. We saw from the hill.'

'That's right,' said Zamin. 'The Wall is about an hour away. But you can't get to the City till the morning.'

'You wasted the tide,' said Za. 'It's too late to get through the water-gate today. Sure, there's another low tide this evening, but nobody's going to let you into Elysia at that time of night. So, obviously, you'll need a place to stay.'

'I have no idea what you're talking about.' *But what are you going to do in the middle of a swamp, Singay – walk away?* 'We want to go to Elysia, and we want you to take us. Now. That was the deal.'

'Look, let me explain,' said Zamin, sounding unbearably superior. 'You don't seem to understand – there's City Time, right, and there's Flats Time, and they're not the same thing. In Flats Time, high tide is when you sleep. Low tide is when you work.'

'The way the birds used to,' murmured Rose.

The girl paused and gave him a strange look. 'Fancy you saying that. Granny sometimes tells stories about long ago, that she heard from *her* Granny, about when there was no Wall and no City and the Flats had nobody living on them but birds. Thousands and thousands of birds. That was the story, anyway.' She shook her head and then repeated, 'Fancy you saying that. Well, anyway, that's Flats Time. *City* Time, now, that's what the rich people go by. They sleep in the night, and do business in the day, and pay no attention to what the tides are at. Flats Time is nothing to them!'

'Are you saying we really can't get to the City today?' asked Pema slowly.

'We've told you that about six times!' As she spoke, Zamin swerved their boat suddenly to avoid an over-laden punt coming in from a side channel. She stood up, gesticulating wildly and spouting language that made the passengers blink. 'Besides,' she continued, sitting down again as if nothing had happened, 'what's your hurry?'

Pema and Singay looked at each other helplessly. What could they say? They couldn't tell these tiny, wild strangers what their hurry – their *desperate* hurry – actually was, and even if they could, it didn't seem as if it would make any difference.

'You've got a disc,' said Za. 'A good one too – House Priority. The rich people all belong to different Houses. And you've got money.'

'Yes.'

'Then we'll take you. Tomorrow. The gate'll be open from about first light.'

'And you know your way in the City?' asked Pema doubtfully.

Zamin waved a casual scull. 'The City's easy. It's the Flats you can get lost in.'

Suddenly Za lunged half over the side of the boat with a cry and plunged his arms up to the shoulders in the muck. Zamin dropped the oar and grabbed him by the belt.

'Pull! *Pull!*'

There was a horrible slurping, sucking sound as Za wrestled with something unseen in the mud.

'Open that basket!' Zamin yelled over her shoulder at Pema as the struggle grew wilder and filthy water splashed everywhere and everyone.

Pema managed to get the lid off one of the wicker baskets just as the twins dragged something ghastly on board. There was a glimpse of a thick snake-like body covered in grey slime, with a collection of sharp, snaggled teeth at one end. Singay screamed as it thrashed blindly in her direction – and then somehow Za had it bundled away in the basket and the lid tied down. Panting and covered in muck to his eyebrows, he grinned triumphantly at them all.

'What *was* that?' squeaked Pema, mud dripping down his face.

'Vomerine eel,' said Zamin proudly. 'Specially good eating in a vomerine.' She licked her lips and gave her brother an appreciative shove.

'You eat things that live in *there?*' Singay swallowed hard, looking around at the slurping landscape with a sick expression on her face.

Za nodded enthusiastically. 'You'd be amazed what

good munching there is, if you know where to look. And not just eels. There's slugs and mudworms, too, though a lot of them are poisonous.'

'Poisonous?' Singay and Pema exchanged anxious glances.

'Hey! Za! Zamin! What'd you catch?' A shout came from a group of children wading in the deep sticky mud.

'Oh, nothing much. Just a vomerine.'

'Vomerine? You lucky pickers!'

'Oh, I *love* vomerine!'

'Yeah, well, so what – *I* found a glass eye and a practically new razor and loads of other stuff I'm not telling *you* about!'

Za made a rude gesture at the boaster, and Zamin picked up the oar and began to scull forward again. 'Elysia dumps its rubbish over the Wall. Wonderful things a clever picker can find. Whole set of false teeth one time – remember that, Za?'

Her brother grinned.

Singay shuddered.

Zamin noticed, and shrugged. 'It is dangerous, at that. A lot of things in the mud don't like being found, so they grow poison spines.'

'And teeth,' added Za. 'And stings and snaggy scales. And some of the garbage from the City has sharp edges. Broken glass and stuff like that.'

'Still, good pickings.'

'If you're clever!'

'What do you do with all these things you find?' Pema asked, trying not to look as revolted as he felt.

'We take them to Granny. Granny Geyma. We work for her. She gives us a cut on everything we find—'

'Ninety/ten, straight up.'

'And then she either sells it or she puts it on her table.'

'Who is Granny?' With a pang of homesickness, Pema saw a picture of his own grandmother in his mind.

Singay, too, was thinking of Dawa and the loving way Pema spoke of her. 'Do you work for her—'

But before Singay could finish her question, Zamin pointed with the scull.

'Look,' she said. 'There she is!'

And all thoughts of benign elderly relatives disappeared.

CHAPTER THIRTY

Granny Geyma's Table

Granny's establishment looked just like any of the hundred other ramshackle, wonky structures they'd passed. This one, however, had Granny Geyma sitting on its porch.

She was more of a heap than a woman. In spite of the heavy, humid heat, she was bundled in dozens of mud-coloured shawls and skirts. Her face was a muddy grey, and she had practically no hair at all, and yet there was no mistaking the power in her gimlet eyes.

'Look what we brought, Granny!' called Zamin.

A gnarly hand came out from under the pile of shawls. Zamin scrambled onto the porch and tipped coins into it. The old woman hefted the handful, as if weighing it, and while she did so, she considered Pema, Singay and Rose as if she were weighing them as well. It was unnerving.

'Look, we don't want to put you out . . .' Pema began.

But Granny Geyma had made up her mind. 'Pay now.' She named a price. Singay didn't even consider haggling over it. They climbed out of the boat and stood in a row on the rickety porch. Singay tried not to stare at the way the old woman's scalp showed through her wisps of hair.

Granny Geyma selected a coin, grunted 'Catch!' and pinged it high into the air. The twins scrambled to grab it, but a last-minute hip shove from Zamin won her the prize.

'That's not fair!' Za whined.

His sister flaunted the tiny coin before pocketing it

firmly. Then, with a bobbed sort of bow, they headed indoors.

Pema, Rose and Singay hesitated a moment, and then started to follow the twins. But as they passed Granny, a bony old arm suddenly shot out and clutched Pema by the sleeve.

'Him.' She jerked her chin at Rose. 'Is it catching?'

'Catching?' squeaked Pema, and then tried again in a lower register. 'Uh, catching?'

'He's sick. Is it something that can spread?'

'Oh. No, ma'am, it isn't. It's just . . . him.'

For another moment, she continued to stare into him. Then, with a nod, Granny Geyma withdrew her hand.

'Follow the noise,' she said.

They followed the sound of voices, as the old woman had told them, down a dingy corridor and pushed through a sacking curtain.

The noise cut off as if sliced by a knife as dozens of sharp eyes turned towards them. The diners at Granny's table were all children. It was impossible not to notice how many of them were missing fingers and toes, some whole hands and feet. Scavenging in muck that harboured so many poisonous, angry things demanded a high price.

The twins beckoned them over, and the babble of voices started up again.

'Where have they all come from?' Singay whispered to Zamin.

Zamin shrugged as if she'd never thought about it before. 'Just anywhere, I guess.'

'It's true,' said a boy from the other side of the table. 'All sorts end up on the Flats. We get washed downriver with the other muck and fetch up at the foot of the Wall.'

'Fetch up at the foot of Granny Geyma, you mean!' laughed somebody further along.

There was a general sniggering, but a little girl sitting next to Singay leaned close and whispered, 'Don't worry. She never kicks the ones who can pay.'

Singay smiled weakly.

Mismatched bowls were being passed round. Grey tentacles, globby bits floating in mud-coloured gruel, and something that looked horribly like an eye floating on the top.

Pema and Singay exchanged appalled glances.

Fortunately, it was a short meal. Pema and Singay could only pick at the unidentifiable food, and Rose sat silently. But the others tucked in with enthusiasm, and the table was soon cleared of every scrap.

'High tide,' announced Zamin. 'Sleeping room's along here.'

She and Za showed them another bare room. Children were already curling up on the floor.

'I think I could sleep now,' said Rose, and lay down.

But for Singay and Pema, it was all the wrong time.

'Is there somewhere else?'

'All right, come out on the back porch. You can sometimes catch a breeze, this time of day,' said Zamin.

If there *was* a breeze, it was too faint to feel.

Singay wiped the sweat off her forehead and turned to the twins. 'Before we head out tomorrow, I think we need to tell you some things.'

'What kind of things?' Two identical looks of suspicion appeared on their faces.

'Well, it isn't actually Elysia we want to go to – it's beyond, out the other side, to the Sea. Can you . . . ?'

But the twins were already shaking their heads.

'We're Flatters,' said Za bluntly. 'That's House stuff, that is.'

'We'll get you into the City and to the House on your disc and that's it.' Zamin rubbed her eyes and yawned. 'We're going to sleep now.' And the twins turned towards the sleeping room.

'Zamin? Za?' Pema called quietly after them. 'Thanks for helping us.'

Za looked odd, as if he weren't used to thanks, but Zamin shrugged. 'We get a cut,' she said, and then they were gone.

Pema and Singay stood in silence. All around them, the Flats had settled into a vast, hot, stinking lethargy, as the Flatters took their rest and the sun beat down.

Pema wiped his face. 'I can't remember what it feels like to be cold,' he said. He'd lost track of the seasons. Could it really be almost time for the first snows at home?

After a bit, Singay leaned sideways on the railing and looked at him. She heaved a sigh. 'What are we going to do, Pema? We're so close, and Rose still can't hear the other Drivers. What if, after all this, what if they're really . . . not there?'

Pema shook his head wearily. 'Too soon to be talking like that. I don't think we can tell anything for sure yet. Somehow, somewhere, we need to find a boat that's big enough to take us right away from all this. We need to get out onto the open Sea. If we can get far enough away from this, from *everything*, then he'll be able to hear them. Even just catch a whisper.'

'If only we could have got the *Aubergine* past this mess. I bet *she* could have gone out to Sea, no bother,' said Singay.

Pema nodded but didn't speak. The silence drew out between them. Singay glanced across at him. He looked so sad. She felt her heart go out to him.

'You know, maybe it'll be like the way your Jathang girl's stone led us to the *Aubergine*. Haven't you noticed? At first everybody seemed to be against us, but then there was some mystery lady who got us out of jail, and Gata and Bob and the Philosopher, and now Zamin and Za. It's like our luck has maybe turned. I know we're not there yet, but there are people to help now. Unlikely people, but still . . .'

Pema looked at her. 'So according to you, we'll go to this House place and whoever lives there will just decide for no reason at all to help us get out to the open ocean. That's what you're predicting?'

'Pretty much. What do you think?'

'I think you're trying to cheer me up.'

'How am I doing?'

Pema grunted, and then gave her a half smile. He wasn't convinced, but something inside him had loosened a bit.

'We should probably try to sleep now,' he said.

They went back into the airless shack, and found themselves a place to lie down in the sleeping room. All around them, Granny Geyma's children were breathing in the fetid dimness. There was the occasional sigh or whimper. Rose was asleep too, but restless.

'There should be birds ... thousands and thousands ... the mud remembers birds ...' they heard him whisper. Then he was still again.

CHAPTER THIRTY-ONE

Beyond the Wall

'Is it any cooler? I don't think so.' Singay fanned herself and then gave up with a sigh.

Pema shook his head. He sniffed experimentally. 'I may just be getting used to it, but I don't think it *smells* quite so bad.'

'Not sure I'd go that far.'

Rose said nothing.

In the east the sky had begun to pale, and they were back in the twins' boat, heading for the Wall. All around them, there were sounds of activity – voices calling out, clattering pots, the thin wailing of babies and the thunk of punt oars being settled into oarlocks.

This is it, thought Pema. *We've come all this way to get to this place. To get Rose to this day.* He glanced over at the little hunched shape in the stern of the boat, and then looked quickly away again.

Nothing can go wrong today, thought Singay, chewing her lip. *Not one solitary thing. If one thing goes wrong, EVERYTHING will go wrong.*

As Zamin sculled them through the morning murk, the silent tension grew and grew, until Singay thought she was going to scream, and then, rising up in the dawn light, beyond a final huddle of houseboats, there it was. The Wall. Wordlessly, she nudged the others.

'Snows!' said Pema.

It loomed above them out of the muck as if it had grown there, like a work of nature, its skirts all muddied up to the high-tide mark and the weed-draped water-gate like a tattered rip.

'Got your disc?' Zamin was all business now. 'Give it to Za. They won't be expecting a Priority to come in on a boat like ours.'

There was already quite a scrum in the open water before the gate, and more boats were arriving every minute. Some of them must have come straight from the Embarkation Pier, right across the Flats, in the dark. The oil-engine boats jockeyed for position simply by revving their motors and shoving the smaller craft aside. But the smaller boats had the advantage of manoeuvrability, and nipped in and out of the crush.

'We're going to be sunk!'

Then, with a great slurping and sloshing of water, the gate groaned open.

'Priority discs first! Priority discs only!' Pairs of guards emerged, shrugging off slime-smeared greatcoats and setting up checking stations on either side of the gate. The oil-engine boats all tried to surge forward at the same moment, but Zamin slipped between two of them and reached the guard post first.

The man looked down at them impatiently.

'You deaf?' he barked. 'I called for Priority discs. Scum comes after . . .' His words trailed off as he saw the disc Za was holding out with a cocky air.

The guard narrowed his eyes. 'How did you get hold . . .' he began, but the impatient revving of motors reminded him of his position. Muttering crossly, he waved the little boat on with poor grace and turned his attention to the more obvious Priorities.

The tunnel smelled dank, and drips from the slime-smeared ceiling splashed onto them, making them shudder. The sound of Zamin's oar echoed strangely, and every moment Pema and Singay expected the guard to change his mind – call them back, tell they weren't allowed to go any further, it had all been a mistake – and then, suddenly, they were out the other side.

Singay gasped.

'Rose! Look!' whispered Pema.

In the time it took to travel through the thickness of the Wall, a breeze had sprung up, the smog had dispersed and, in the light of the rising sun, the City lay before them, gilded with gold.

Elysia. This was what all the towns they'd passed on their journey down the River had been aspiring to. Cliffton, The Smoke, and dozens of no-nothing places in-between, all dreaming, all thinking, *I know I'm small now, but someday I'm going to grow up to be just like the City.*

Everything was writ large – the canals spread wide, the buildings towered, the open spaces had awe-inspiring proportions, windows and doors and colonnades were all built on a larger-than-human scale. Everywhere they looked they saw vivid colours – on the mosaic walls, the shop awnings, the clothes of the citizens, each costume more elaborately, satiny and eye-catchingly jewel-like than the last.

And we look like something the rat dragged in. Singay thought suddenly of Lady Allum in her rough Jungle clothes, and wondered how she could have turned her back on all this.

Faces, shop displays, glimpses into courtyards and hallways – images leapt out at them in brilliant focus, burned into their eyes and then were gone. It was the essence of Elysia, all this colour, light, motion, never still, always a new pattern. The Philosopher had said you could never step in the same river twice. It was like that here. If you blinked in the City, when you looked again, the City had changed.

Hold still! thought Singay. *I want to see it all!*

Zamin sculled deftly though the busy traffic on the main canals, dodging boats of all sizes and modes of propulsion. There were little gondolas piled with flowers, flat-bottomed barges piled with garbage heading for the Wall and the Flats beyond, and ornate, powerful launches. Zamin explained these belonged to the different Houses, with intricately painted emblems to announce their owners. They all had up-tilted prows that made them look as if they scorned even the water they passed through. And because this was the City, that actually made some kind of crazy sense.

It wasn't just oil-engine launches they were seeing – there were machines and gizmos powered by oil on every side. Motorised sedan chairs teetered along, threatening to dump their wealthy occupants into the canals, while motorised winches raised heavy loads to upper storey windows.

Then, as the sky clouded over and it began to rain, Pema suddenly grabbed Singay's arm.

'Did you see that?' he hissed in her ear. 'That man – the fat one – see his umbrella? I swear it just opened by motor!'

Singay could only shake her head in amazement.

The rain fell hard, making pockmarks on the pretty, coloured oil slick of the water, and making visibility poor, but fortunately the twins seemed to know where they were heading. In spite of all the noise and chaos, there must have been some sort of right of way in effect, since they saw no collisions, though several times their little boat was almost swamped by the wakes from oil-engine craft twice their size. It was only when they'd moved away from the central district, through a maze of back canals and into the residential area, that the traffic calmed down a little.

Here the colours were more muted – rich umbers and ambers and faded reds – and the noise and frenetic movement of the shopping district were replaced by the barely audible purr of enormously tasteful, supremely confident wealth. As the rain continued to pour down, it only served to make the buildings seem more sleek, and the viewers, rapidly becoming soggy in their out-of-place little boat, feel less worthy. Singay and Pema exchanged nervous grins.

They passed palace after palace, turning from time to time.

But getting closer to the Sea? thought Pema. *Surely we're getting closer to the Sea.*

'Can you hear them?' he whispered to Rose. 'Can you hear the other Drivers yet?'

Rose just shook his head and huddled in on himself.

Pema looked across anxiously at Singay, but before she could say anything, the boat bumped up against a pier.

'This is it.' Za sounded odd. Zamin hurriedly tied their mooring rope to a rusty ring and jumped out.

'Come on, get out,' she said. 'We're here.'

'Are you sure?' Pema looked around doubtfully.

The residence they had come to was as large and imposing as any they'd seen that day, but it was also long deserted. The walls were cracked. The colourful paint was flaking away. Dirt from some higher-than-usual tide smeared the marble paving. At various times, repair jobs had been started on the mosaics or the window frames or the decorative metalwork, but nothing was finished, and now it would take a lot more than piecemeal patching to turn back the decay.

Singay frowned. 'This doesn't look like a place where they'd have any help to spare for *us*.'

'Yes, well, looks can be deceptive,' chirped Za. Zamin clipped him across the head.

'I'm going to knock on the door,' she said. And she trotted off, Za in tow.

The others stood up to follow them, but then Singay put a restraining hand on Pema's arm. 'This feels . . . I don't know, does this feel all right to you?'

Something snapped inside him. 'Feel all right? Of course it doesn't feel all right! It feels all *wrong*! So what do you suggest we do – go home?' Then he sighed and rubbed his face with his hand. 'Sorry, sorry. I just . . . sorry.'

'So close,' murmured Rose. 'We mustn't quarrel now.'

'Of course not,' said Singay, trying to smile reassuringly at the wan little man. 'Let's go.'

So it was as a soggy party of five that they stood before the great door. Its wood was dried and splitting, and the metalwork was so rusted it was starting to come away.

Zamin thumped on the door with her fist, hard, three times. For a long moment, nothing happened. Then . . .

'Did you hear that?'

'Hear what?'

'Somebody called. Somebody said, "Come in."'

And, with a grunt of effort, Zamin shoved the door open a crack.

'What are you doing?' exclaimed Pema, but the little girl was sliding inside.

'Wait! I didn't hear anything!' Singay could feel panic rising in her chest, but the others were already following Zamin's lead, sidling into the dimness beyond the door as if they had no will of their own.

She gave in. *At least we'll be out of the rain.* She made herself shove in after them.

It was true, there was no rain inside, but there was about all she could say for it. What had once been an impressive grand hall was now an echoing, derelict space, edged by shadows. All the beautiful furnishings it must have held were gone, and the smells of damp and despair were all that remained.

Surely no one lives here . . .

'Excellent,' said a voice. 'You've come.'

CHAPTER THIRTY-TWO

The Mighty Fallen

I know that voice, thought Pema.

'It can't be,' murmured Singay.

But it was.

The charismatic holy man they'd last seen all those leagues back in the Square in Cliffton, spiriting the money of the crowd into his pockets, was standing before them, here and now.

'Father *Impeccable?*'

'Father?' he said. 'Oh no, no, I'm done with all that. Purely secular now, I assure you. You may call me *The* Impeccable. And do you know *why* you may call me *The* Impeccable?' While he was speaking he was also edging round them, so that they had to turn to keep him in sight. When he was between them and the door, he paused and his teeth glinted like pearls in the dimness.

'Can't you guess?' He waited. 'Give up?' No one seemed able to speak or move or escape from his horrible game. 'Well then, I'll tell you! You can call me *The* Impeccable because that's who I am! The one and only, last remaining son of the House of Impeccable, late unlamented of this City.'

There was a blank pause. He tutted. 'At this point in the conversation your eyes are supposed to go wide and I should be seeing lots of round little O's where your mouths are. Instead, you act as if you'd never even heard of me. Most disappointing.'

Then, unexpectedly, he turned to the twins.

'Though obviously you two dear little rascals have heard of me.' He grinned at them. 'By the way, you must remind me what I owe you. I'm sure you wouldn't like me to forget *my* end of our bargain!'

Slowly, Pema and Singay turned to look at the two Flatters. Rose sank down in a heap on the dank floor and covered his face with his hands.

'What does he mean?' Singay asked the twins, her voice dangerously quiet.

Zamin shrugged. 'He paid us. To keep our eyes open for three that looked like you, carrying a Priority disc with his crest on it. We were to tell him as soon as we saw you and he'd pay us more. Bring you to him direct, more again.' She paused. 'It was business.'

'We were good at it, too,' put in Za. 'Nobody suspects a couple of kids hanging about.'

'*We* certainly didn't,' said Pema, and a fleeting twinge of discomfort crossed the twins' faces.

Impeccable laughed.

'Why are we here?' asked Rose quietly, lifting his head.

'I'll be happy to tell you, but first let us go up to my private chambers. It's a little vulgar to talk business in the hall, don't you think? After you.'

Why don't we run away? thought Singay. *He couldn't stop us all. Why don't we just run away?* But there was something about Impeccable, some horrible mesmeric power . . . They let him herd them up the grand staircase, and on, deeper into the heart of the ruin.

'I'd mind that step – the rot's got into it. And along this corridor it's best to stay to the left.'

Mildewed walls, rotted tapestries, glimpses of the weeping sky where the roof had collapsed . . . it was a wonder the building still managed to stand up at all. But Impeccable moved through the devastation as if he were completely at home.

'Welcome to my suite,' he said and, with a grand gesture, he ushered them through a set of doors and into a large, shuttered room.

Like the entrance hall, it must once have been beautiful, an elegantly proportioned, light, lovely space. But not anymore. Damp stains showed everywhere. The parquet floor had warped and splintered. In the dim light they could see it was bizarrely furnished with broken bits and mismatched pieces, the rejects of a wrecker's yard.

It was the saddest room they'd ever seen.

'Sit down. Sit down,' said their host, as if oblivious to their dismay. 'You'll forgive me if I secure the door.' Unlike everything else in the room, the locking system was in excellent condition. No one would get into Impeccable's inner sanctum without an invitation. No one would get out, either.

They sat on a collection of mismatched chairs and stools. When Impeccable was satisfied with the door, he joined them, placing himself so that he was the focus of their attention – and suddenly it was the Square at Cliffton all over again. His voice took on the warm, chocolatey tones of the orator once more.

'I can see you are wondering what place this is, but I'll tell what it *was*. It was the House of Impeccable.'

His words echoed and died and rose again.

'Let me tell you about us. The Impeccables were among the first of the Houses to strike it rich, out in the oilfields, among the first to discover what lay beneath the waves. All that buried treasure. Being among the first, our prestige was without limit. Unfortunately, our oil claims *weren't*. Oh, they supported several generations of Impeccables, but then we began to hit the bottom of the barrel. When the fields started to yield less each year, my father could have taken heed. He could have funnelled our wealth into buying new sites, building new rigs. Instead he funnelled it into pretending nothing was wrong. When there was no longer enough for that, he borrowed. By the time my father finally did the decent thing and died, we were inescapably in debt to the House of Grandiloquent. They *owned* us, down to the last tapestry and teaspoon. The first moment they could, they dismantled our rigs and did all the things my father should have done.

'Of course, they couldn't touch *me*. If I'd suddenly died it would have been extremely embarrassing for them. So they just took away everything of value that could be sold, let the servants go and left me with the shell of a building I couldn't afford to keep up.

'I remember the day their steward came – they didn't even bother to send a member of the family! I remember my nanny crying – oh yes, I was just a child! – I remember her crying, "Let *me* stay, at least. What will become of him?" And he said, "What will become of him? Why, he's free to become anything he likes!" And he was right. I was completely free. Free to starve. Free to hide in corners, all alone, when the noises of the night in this empty house shook me with terror the way a dugg shakes a rat. Free to plot and plan my revenge. Free to miss . . .'

They watched as his words trailed off into memories. When Impeccable spoke again, his voice had changed. It had a mad quaver to it.

'She was nothing to him – just one more extraneous crone! But I loved my nanny. She was always there, always on my side. Presumably he sent her back to the Flats, but he might as well have sent her to the moon. Of course, he may not have known I cared specially about her. It may have been no more than a simple economy on the part of the family. They'll pay for it, nevertheless. Oh yes. Not long now.'

He gave himself a shake, and became brisk again. 'Which is, of course, where *you* come in. Allow me to introduce the setting of my grand plan.' He walked over to the shuttered windows and flung them open.

'There they are,' said Impeccable, a curious note of longing and pride in his voice. 'The oilfields.'

As far as the eye could reach, a greasy sea slurped and swayed around the legs of hundreds of enormous grey structures, metal skeletons that had somehow taken root in the salty water and twisted up towards the sky. Huge metal heads nodded hypnotically. Gouts of flame shot out of the tips of the towers, and died, and shot out again, adding yellowy-black smoke to the low-lying smudge of cloud. The air on the incoming breeze tasted tinny and wrong.

'Oh no,' murmured Rose.

They could hardly look away. All this horror had been hidden from sight behind Elysia's proud palaces and fine municipal buildings. It was like a festering disease behind the City's fair face.

'Beautiful, isn't it,' murmured Impeccable.

'All that metal – that must be why Rose hasn't been able to hear the others,' Pema whispered urgently to Singay.

Singay nodded. 'We've got to get away from here,' she whispered back. 'We've *got* to!'

Impeccable was pointing. 'You can't actually see the Grandiloquent oilfields from here – I do hope that won't be a problem?' And he turned his mad eyes suddenly on Rose.

The little man shook his head slowly. 'I don't understand.'

'Then I'll explain. I was asking whether having a clear line of sight was necessary. For the little job I want you to do for me.'

'Me? A job?'

'Oh, *do* keep up. Why else would I have arranged your dramatic jailbreak back in dear old Cliffton? Why else would I have given you the Priority disc and paid our little friends here to be on the lookout?'

'*You* got us out of jail?' exclaimed Pema, but Impeccable didn't answer him. He was focused intently on the Driver. There might have been no one else in the room.

'What job?' Rose's voice was low, each word like a stone dropping into water.

'I saw what you did at Cliffton. You can control rocks. You know what they're about to do, and you can make them do what you want them to do. Which means . . .' His eyes glinted with greedy excitement. 'Which means you can make them do what *I* want them to do.'

216

'And what is that?'

'I'll tell you. What I want is for the rock over my enemy's oilfields to crack and let the Sea flood in. You see the beauty of it, I'm sure. *They'll* be ruined, utterly, and with a threat or two, or ten, of doing the same to the other Houses, I'm pretty certain I can be as wealthy a man as even *I* could wish to be. The House of Impeccable will rise again!'

There was a long silence in the desolate room.

'That is the stupidest thing I have ever heard in the whole of my very long life,' said Rose quietly.

'Says you!' retorted Impeccable, suddenly sounding like a rude little boy.

Rose stared at him. 'You must understand – the oil is contained in rocky chambers, honeycombing the seabed across this whole area.'

'Well, yes. We'd figured out that much by ourselves,' said Impeccable, examining his nails.

'Then you should also be able to understand that now that you've emptied the chambers, they are weaker and more likely to collapse. And the collapse of one chamber could lead to a cascade of similar collapses throughout the oilfields.' Rose pointed out of the window. 'The whole thing could cave in on itself. Then the seabed across this entire section of coast would drop and the water would rush in. An earthquake or even a series of earthquakes would be more than likely, along with a giant, destructive wave crashing into the shore.'

'Could. Maybe. Might.' Impeccable wagged a finger at the Driver. 'I can tell you're bluffing. Embroidering. You're powerful, oh yes, but not as powerful as *that*. Not so powerful you can make earthquakes and the end of the world.' Then he snapped his fingers. 'Or maybe you *are* that powerful. In which case, you can use that power to make sure *none* of that happens! There! Got you coming *and* going!'

'You're mad,' said Rose.

'And you're lying,' replied Impeccable. 'I saw the way you controlled the stones of my oh-so-lucrative Tower – you let them down as easy as a feather. You're just trying to raise the price. Don't think I don't appreciate that, though. I do! And believe me when I say, you will be *well* paid.'

'You don't understand!' cried Pema and Singay in chorus.

'*What* don't I understand?' snarled Impeccable, swinging his mad focus abruptly to them. They stepped back involuntarily.

'Rose can't do what you're asking him to do because it'll kill him,' said Pema, trying to keep the tremor out of his voice.

'Controlling rocks *uses him up*,' said Singay urgently. 'Can't you see how much worse he looks now than when you saw him before in Cliffton?'

'You think he looks worse?' said Impeccable in a carefree tone. 'Really? He looks fine to me.'

'He's *not* fine. It was saving all those people back in Cliffton – including *you*! – that made him as ill as he is. And now you want him to kill himself for you? Why should he?'

'That's right. Why should I?'

Everybody turned and stared.

There was an expression on Rose's face that Pema and Singay had never seen before. His cheeks were drawn and there were hard lines marking his forehead and mouth.

But most unsettling of all was the look in his eyes: it was alien and angry, a look utterly at odds with the person they thought they knew.

Singay took a tentative step towards him. 'Rose?' she said, but it was as if he couldn't hear her anymore.

'Why should I?' he snarled again, not at anyone in the room, but over their shoulders, at something or someone they couldn't see. 'Why shouldn't I do what he's asking and then let it all go wrong at its own sweet pace? I'm dying – why should I care who else dies too? All because of a mistake, so long ago. That's all it was. It was just a mistake. When do I get to stop *paying*, that's what I want to know. I've paid and paid for all these years, and for what? So that things like *him*' – suddenly his eyes focused on Impeccable with a cold clarity – 'can flourish? Horrible, tiny-minded, evil-spirited creatures like him, like Klepsang and Ma and the Protectors and the people at Cliffton and all the others like them – so *they* can grow fat and prosper? And produce hells like the one we just left, like the one we've just seen?' His body was shuddering violently now. 'Is this the world I've lost all those years for? Is this the world I'm supposed to die for?'

'Works for me,' said Impeccable cheerfully. 'Now do what I'm telling you.'

'No,' said Rose.

Impeccable shrugged. Then, quick as a snake, he grabbed Singay by her hair and twisted so hard she screamed. A vicious-looking knife blossomed in his hand and he held it against her throat.

'Wrong answer,' he said.

CHAPTER THIRTY-THREE

Into the Fields

It was as if Impeccable had thrust his knife into the Driver. With a wail, Rose collapsed onto the floor. 'I'll do it I'll do it I'll do it,' he babbled tearfully. 'But not from here. I can't from here – it's too far. I'll need to be closer. Directly over the chamber.'

Impeccable's smile was like a wulf's. 'Of course. Every workman knows his trade. I bow to your superior knowledge in these matters.'

I won't cry, Singay told herself. *I won't give him the satisfaction.* But the tears were brimming already. Impeccable was strong, and he was hurting her, and she was deathly afraid. She blinked hard, and a few hot tears spilled over onto the hand that held the knife.

'Oh, now, don't take it personally,' said Impeccable. 'You must see you really were the obvious choice. It was either you or the other little girl – girls are traditionally the best hostages, of course – and, well, as we know, a Flatter's not all that valuable. Not to mention the fact she and the other brat just betrayed you. Nobody might want to bother keeping *her* safe.' He glanced over at Pema. 'You, mountain boy, look in the top drawer of that chest – there should be some rope in there . . . Good. Toss it to me.'

Pema's mind was racing. What could he do? This couldn't be happening! *It's up to me. I haven't a clue. I think I'm going to be sick. What should I be doing?!*

'I'm perfectly happy to slit her throat, you know,' Impeccable said mildly as he finished tying Singay's hands behind her back. 'That old definition of a hero being somebody who gets other people killed is right on the mark here, if you were planning anything noble. I've no problem with using this knife. Though you can believe me or not. It's nothing to me, either way.'

'He means it, Pema,' said Rose, his voice infinitely weary. 'I'm going to do what he asks.'

Singay tried to turn towards him. 'No! Rose, you can't! It'll kill you!' Then she gasped in pain as Impeccable pulled back on her hair again.

'Leave her alone!' wailed Pema. 'Rose, it's not possible. What about the cascade? The cave-ins?'

'I will do everything I can to dissuade the surrounding strata, at least until some sort of evacuation plan can be implemented.' He looked without hope to Impeccable, who snorted and shook his head.

'Rose,' said Singay, 'did you mean all those things you said?'

Rose smiled sadly at her.

'In other words, just bluffing,' smirked Impeccable. He adjusted his grip on Singay. 'We'll be on our way now. There are the keys, boy, for the door, and I'll have the whole lot of you in front of me if you don't mind. You too, Flatters.'

They did as he said.

'Fortunately, maintaining a launch *is* something I've been able to do,' he continued, ushering them all forward. 'There are some standards you just don't slip below. Turn left, down those stairs.'

The boathouse must have been spectacular once, with beautiful mosaic walls, a vaulted ceiling, and moorings for half a dozen launches. Only one boat remained, tied up at the far end of a decaying pier.

Impeccable looked at it smugly. 'I've kept her paintwork fresh and oil in her engine. Now, stay close and behave, girl. I don't think you'll be able to swim far with your hands tied.'

Singay shivered. *I can't swim at all!*

The twins cast off at Impeccable's instructions and soon they were on their way, slipping through the back canals and the rain, heading out to the oilfields.

Heading out to the Sea.

There were guarded checkpoints along the way, but all it took to get past these was a launch with a crest and a driver with a supercilious manner. A dozen scenarios raced through Pema's mind: of wrestling Impeccable to the deck, seizing the launch, speeding away from the horrible oilfields and out to the clean Sea and Rose's friends. But Impeccable kept his knife – and Singay – close at all times.

On and on, they threaded their way, under the bellies of the huge storage tanks and between the metal legs of the rigs. There was a heavy smell in the air, and spilled oil smeared the surface of the water, leaving metallic colours swirling in their wake. Machinery thunked ponderously, never resting, as the pumps dragged oil up from the depths and the drills whined through the rock below the water, blindly searching for more.

Pema leaned closer to Rose. 'Are they there?' he whispered. 'Can you hear the others?'

'No talking!' barked Impeccable. 'Be quiet and enjoy the ride.' *He* certainly seemed to be. He snuffed up the stink of oil as if it were a fine perfume, and stared greedily around at the rigs and tanks.

'Right,' he said finally. 'This is it. Tie up there.'

The crest of the Grandiloquents was plastered everywhere. The tank they were moored to, and the rigs and other structures surrounding it, all proudly proclaimed the House that owned them.

'This is as close as it gets,' said Impeccable, licking his lips. 'Do it *now*.'

'I just wanted to get home,' moaned Rose.

'And so you shall, my dear fellow, so you shall. With the money I'm going to pay you, you'll have enough to go anywhere you like. A more than generous payment for this one *little* thing.'

But Rose wasn't paying attention to him anymore. Singay and Pema recognised the strange, remote look on his face. He was reaching out to the rock beneath them, listening, preparing to manipulate and control.

'Oh, is he doing it?' clamoured Impeccable. 'Has he started doing it? Has he?'

'Shut up,' said Singay.

Impeccable put both his hands over his mouth like a child and his eyes sparkled with malicious excitement.

They could hear the plashing of the waves against the side of the boat, and the thudding of the drilling rigs, and the screaming of gulls in the sky above, but it was as if a pool of silence had formed around the Driver.

What is he hearing? It was hard to imagine – the babble

of all those rocky voices, then closing in on the voice of the chamber walls, feeling for the weaknesses, the line of stone most likely to be persuaded to shift, ever so slightly, just a little more, to let in the whole mighty volume of the Sea.

They could see him struggling, when he was only encouraging the stone to do something it was willing to do already, but then the truly hard part came. The boat shuddered and rocked as the chamber flooded and collapsed, and then Rose was faced with the entire coast's irresistible desire to do the same. It was like dropping a boulder into a lake and then trying to persuade the ripples not to spread.

For one long, impossible moment, the little man did it. They could see how the effort was using him up, devouring him from within – yet still he held. And held . . .

Then, as if lightning had suddenly struck him out of the clear, blue sky, his whole body jerked. His head snapped back, his spine arched, and he flung his arms up and out. His mouth was wide open in a silent scream, more horrifying and intense because the sound of it was beyond their hearing.

Then, just as suddenly, he folded in on himself and collapsed into the bottom of the boat.

'ROSE!' yelled Pema.

'You've killed him!' Singay struggled to go to him, but Impeccable held tight to her rope.

'Nonsense – he's just tired. He's—'

Before he could finish his words, the world began to shake.

CHAPTER THIRTY-FOUR

Higher!

There was a muffled roar from below, a sound so deep they felt it more than heard it, and all around the surface of the water began to judder and jump. Rippling out from where they were, rigs suddenly flared and then stopped, metal screamed and groaned, shaken from the foundations. In the distance, in slow motion, one of the structures toppled and fell.

There was a sudden, pressing silence.

'No,' whispered Impeccable.

And the level of the Sea began to drop. Within a breath, the launch was tilting backwards.

'Loose the mooring rope!' screamed Zamin.

Impeccable didn't move, frozen in disbelief.

'Get out of the way!' Pema shoved him aside and struggled with the knot, desperate to get it undone before the weight of the boat dragged it impossibly tight. It was raw luck that his fingers found the right bit to pull. With a wet screech, the rope shot through the ring. The launch lurched level, then dropped as the Sea disappeared under it, down, down, and all the while, there was a horrible sucking sound as the water was drawn into the chambers below.

And then, it stopped.

The launch floated in a shallow gulley of water, surrounded by dripping, slime-streaked rocks. Panting, they peered up, following the barnacle-encrusted metal leg until, high above them, they saw the body of the tank, like a strange, bloated spider.

'Hey! *Hey!*'

It was an oilman, his face all creased up and urgent. He leaned over the railing of a walkway and scanned the little group anxiously. He bellowed down to the twins, ignoring everyone else.

'You're Granny's, aren't you?'

'Why? Who wants to know?' yelled Za.

The oilman made an impatient gesture. 'Ditch that – I've no time for muck. I've eaten at Granny's table myself, so I'm telling you this for nothing – get some height! *Now!*'

'What are you talking about?' demanded Impeccable, but the man had already disappeared.

For a moment, no one moved.

Then Impeccable knocked Singay viciously aside and lunged for the leg of the tank. Slipping and swearing, he scrambled up the criss-cross metalwork, sending gobbets of green seaweed down onto their heads.

The wet sliminess seemed to galvanize them.

'Untie my hands!' demanded Singay hoarsely. The twins rushed to her while Pema bent over the fallen Driver and gently raised his head.

'Rose?' he whispered.

Rose's eyes flickered open for a moment, and shut again.

'Singay, tie him onto my back – I need my hands to climb.' As she busied herself with the ropes, he barked at the twins, 'Za, Zamin, get out of here.'

The pair hesitated for only a second, then fled after Impeccable.

The moment Rose was tied onto his back, Pema gave Singay a shove.

'Go!' he said roughly. 'Climb – hurry!' She didn't argue.

He checked the ropes round Rose once more, and followed.

Up and up he went, each handhold festooned with slippery seaweed, the placing of each foot precarious. The stink from the exposed mud rose up after them, overpowering in the close, still air. Pema didn't look down. He focused every nerve, every muscle, every panting breath on dragging himself and the friend on his back to whatever safety lay above. A sudden hot wind burned sour at the back of his throat, and his skin prickled, the hairs standing up. He could hear a distant rumbling, and his own rasping breath, and the pounding of his heart, and finally, a voice.

'Pema! Come on! You're almost there!'

It was Singay, calling down to him from above.

He risked a glance up and there she was, peering intently over the edge of the walkway, her head framed by a brilliant, cloudless blue sky. *That sky's all wrong*, he thought. *Why's it so blue?*

'Hurry!' cried Singay.

With a final surge he reached the platform, his breath rasping in his throat, his hands cut and bleeding from the raw metal of the tank's leg. But he knew there was no time to rest. *We need to get higher.* The staircase that curved round the outside of the tank was only a few paces away. It had proper steps and a handrail, and was perfectly, wonderfully free of seaweed and slime. Pema felt a stiff little smile begin to form on his face as he stumbled towards it. *We're going to make it*, he thought. *We're going to . . .*

Then he saw the others – Singay, Za and Zamin. They were huddled together at the bottom of the steps, staring. He turned to see what they were looking at.

CHAPTER THIRTY-FIVE

Out of the Depths

The ocean had disappeared. As far as the horizon, Pema could see nothing but lines of buckled rock, twisted and tilted in ranks like shattered teeth. Great boulders and blocks were draped with swathes of rubbery seaweed, brown and fleshy, and interspersed with oily pools and films of slime. Fish flapped frantically. Things with legs scuttled, trying to get out of sight. There was an obscene smell.

Pema had a sudden flash of memory, of Rose speaking lovingly about the Sea as a thing of such glory, such beauty. *Not like this.* What they were being shown was not meant to be seen.

And there was the silence.

'Too quiet,' someone moaned. 'Too quiet!' All the relentless thudding of machinery had ceased. The wind had died away. There was a pressure on his ears, like deafness, that only stopped just this side of actual pain.

Then he saw it.

The wave.

The sight came before the sound, like thunder trailing lightning. It already filled the skyline and was racing towards them before the roar of it caught up.

'We need to get higher!' Singay tried to shout the words, but her voice sounded small and weary, and her feet refused to move.

Then her eyes met Pema's and, straightening her shoulders, she led the way at a run.

Four pairs of feet pounded up and around the sheer side of the tank. At first the clanging metal of the steps drowned out all other sounds. But soon the howl of the approaching wave, hundreds of thousands of tons of water relentlessly on the move, beat at them with a wall of noise.

'Climb! *Climb!*' shouted a voice from above.

The top came so suddenly they almost fell onto it. It was wide and flat, and crowded with oilmen, staring in rigid terror at the horror that seemed to be reaching up to engulf the sky. Singay caught sight of the twins, clinging to the man who'd told them to climb.

And then time ran out.

Flinging themselves down, they wrapped their arms round the railings and braced.

'Hold on!' yelled Pema, though no one could hear over the roar, so loud it was like an enormous fist of sound, pounding bodily against them, harder and harder.

The tank shuddered and rang like a gigantic, dissonant bell as the wave smashed into it, exploding round the curve of its walls. Lethal shards of metal slammed past, propelled by the volume of bottle-green water on either side. Blinded, battered, crushed by unbearable weight, the whole world was submerged – even the sun had drowned. Time stopped beneath the wave.

Then they became aware of a light approaching, something they could sense even through tightly shut eyelids.

This is what dying feels like.

And then, impossibly, the light surrounded them. The wave had passed.

We're still alive.

They clung to the railing, bruised and sodden, throats raw with salt water, eyes burning, but gulping down air once more. For a long time, that was enough. But then, they looked around them.

On the top of the tank, drenched, bewildered men stirred. Some started to move towards injured comrades. Some hugged their knees, shaking. Some turned, and turned again, staring about, as if uncertain where the great wave could have gone.

Singay and Pema dragged themselves upright.

'This must be a dream,' whispered Singay. 'It can't be real.'

Acrid smoke and steam wreathed around the tanker. There was a hot, erratic wind that shredded and shifted the cloud, revealing nightmare shapes in the greasy swells of the Sea. Twisted metal shards cut the surface and disappeared, appeared and sank, over and over, all that remained of the oilfields' platforms and gantries and cranes. There were things drifting between the rigid, broken structures. Pema squinted, trying to focus on what they could be.

Bodies. So many bodies, face down in the Sea. The way they moved was horrible, as if they were turning gently in their beds.

Later! Think about it later! shrieked Pema's brain. *Think about Rose!* Even with soaking clothes, the body on his own back weighed next to nothing.

'Is Rose all right?' he croaked. 'Help me get him off my back!'

Singay, too, had been standing as if poleaxed, but Pema's voice brought her back with a jolt. 'Rose? Rose!' she cried.

She scrabbled with the wet knots and managed at last to free the Driver from Pema's back and lay him gently down.

His silvery skin was almost translucent now, and the bones of his face stuck out sharply, as if the flesh that covered them had melted away. At that moment he looked more alien than they had ever seen before, more unearthly, more . . . far away.

'Rose! Here, take this! You must!' Singay dragged the irradiant sack from his pocket and thrust it into the little man's lifeless hands. 'Rose!' He didn't respond. She took the bag back, fumbling with the knot, trying to untie it, but she was crying so hard she could barely see. Even soaked with seawater, the bag weighed almost nothing now. Maybe if she turned it inside out – maybe there was still just enough left. Maybe . . .

A hand reached over her shoulder and took the bag. She was pushed aside.

But . . . what . . . how . . . Singay scrubbed her arm across her face and stared.

It was another Rose. Another Driver. He knelt beside her Rose's crumpled body and carefully lifted his head.

BOOK THREE

Look to the Stars

North of the Jungle, they look to the mountains; south of the Jungle, they look to the sea; either way, they miss the point.

(Borang proverb)

CHAPTER THIRTY-SIX

The Tale of Trout

Soaked and battered and bewildered, Singay and Pema could only stare.

There were silver tears streaming down the strange Driver's face. 'What have they done to you ... what have they done to you ...' he murmured, his voice anguished. He produced his own silver bag and began to trickle irradiant again and again onto Rose's skin.

'Is he ... Will he be all right?' croaked Singay.

The new Driver turned on her abruptly, spreading his silver hands protectively. 'I won't let you kill him!' he snarled. 'I don't care what you do to me, but you won't kill him!'

Then a voice spoke, a voice Pema and Singay – and the new Driver too, perhaps – thought they'd never hear again.

'You found me. How did you ... ?'

It was Rose. He sounded infinitely frail and weary, but in some unidentifiable way more *himself* than he had in such a long time.

'You called me,' said the strange Driver. 'So I came.'

For a long moment, the two little silver men from beyond the stars stared into each other's eyes with a joy too huge for laughter or smiling. Pema felt tears welling up and Singay sniffed loudly, causing the strange Driver to leap away from her wildly.

Rose gave the ghost of a chuckle. 'Don't worry. It's just a breathing thing. You'll get used to it.' He closed his eyes again, as if even the effort of holding them open was too much for him.

The new Driver grabbed hold of his hands, looking stricken. 'Please, be strong – you mustn't let go now! You have every right to be angry with me. I know I did *everything* wrong. *Don't get noticed?* I couldn't have been more noticeable if I'd put a gigantic arrow in the sky saying, "Look, here's an alien, why don't you come and kill him while he's still young and stupid?" Just as stupid as I ever was, I'm afraid, dear friend, but not so young anymore. It's been so long . . . so long . . .'

'More?' Rose murmured. 'More irradiant?'

'Yes. Yes, of course,' the other Driver soothed. 'We have more than enough. But gently does it. A little at a time.' He leaned down and whispered in Rose's ear, 'Don't worry, I'll get you away from them the second you're strong enough.'

'It's all right,' said Rose. 'These two are my good friends. I'd never have got back to you without them.'

'But you're right to worry about the others,' put in Singay, nodding her head at the workers on the other side of the tank. They were milling about in shock. 'I don't think they're ready for anything more, not after what they've been through already today!' She pulled Pema over to stand beside her, to screen the two Drivers from sight as much as possible.

Rose nodded his head and then frowned. 'But where's Amelia?'

'What's an Amelia?' The younger Driver was concentrating on administering more irradiant.

Rose found the strength to look both modest and

proud at the same time. 'I named us,' he said. 'I'm Rose. You two are Trout and Amelia. Aren't they wonderful names? I've been longing to tell you!'

'Careful,' Pema interrupted. 'Someone's coming.'

It was one of the workers. He was cradling a broken arm, and he leaned against the railing beside them as if he needed the support to stay upright. He seemed to be very carefully not looking directly at them.

'It's strange,' he said, to no one in particular, 'how something huge like this can play tricks with you. I guess it's the fear and the stress that make you maybe see things you couldn't possibly have seen.'

Trout went utterly still, his body as tense as a pulled bow.

'What do you think you saw, sir?' asked Pema cautiously.

The man still kept his gaze focused on the middle distance. 'No need to call me that, boy. I'm just a Flatter. We all are. But I'll tell you. I'll tell you what I thought I saw. I thought I saw a silver man, riding the crest of the wave like he was riding a great green beast. He was searching for something, or maybe for someone, and for just a fraction of a second he looked at me, and I looked at him, and I thought, *He's coming to save us! We're not going to die.* And he did save us, because look, here we are, not dead! I thought I saw a silver god come out of the Sea to save a bunch of Flatters and oilmen. How likely is that? But it makes a good story.'

And he suddenly turned and looked straight at Trout.

'Thank you,' the man said.

Trout's eyes showed white all the way around the silver.

'I … you … I … you're …' he squeaked, ending with a strangled-sounding 'welcome?'

The man nodded and walked away.

'Nicely handled, lad!' said Rose. His voice was still weak but the smile on his face was the old Rose come back again.

Trout collapsed into a little heap. 'This is not what I was expecting,' he murmured.

'You're doing really well,' Pema reassured him. 'It's a lot to take in all at once.'

'And I don't imagine Amelia's going to find it any easier! But where *is* she?' Rose asked again, looking about eagerly.

There was a pause. There should have been something, some sudden chill, a hint to warn them of what was coming next. But there wasn't.

'She's dead,' said Trout. 'I found her body when I woke up.'

'Oh no,' breathed Pema, and Rose made a small sound of pain.

'Are you *sure*?' Singay couldn't believe her ears. *This can't be happening. We've come so far, been through so much.* 'How could she die?'

Trout looked at her with his not-Rose eyes.

'She lost hope,' he whispered. 'So she died.'

Singay shook her head. 'I don't understand.'

'Tell me,' said Rose. His voice was bleak, but calm.

Trout's words came out in a rush. 'You must understand, we had no way of knowing what had happened to you. The interference from all this' – he gestured at the metal devastation around them – 'meant we couldn't hear

238

you. We just went on nudging the tectonic plate, year after year, because we couldn't think what else *to* do.'

He reached out and touched Rose on the shoulder, as if he needed the contact to reassure him that his friend was finally, truly there.

'We were afraid something terrible had happened to you, some awful accident. Maybe the humans had discovered you and you were dead. I mean' – he looked embarrassed as he turned to Singay and Pema – 'maybe some *bad* humans had discovered him. And if he wasn't coming back to us, you see, we wouldn't be able to leave.'

'Because it takes three to drive a comet,' said Singay slowly.

Trout nodded. 'Without Rose, we'd never be able to go home. It was then we decided that I should go into longsleep.'

'But why?'

'It's a good way to conserve resources. Drivers can go on for a long time without needing irradiants when they're in longsleep.'

'But I thought you said it was really dangerous,' objected Pema. 'I thought it was something you can't easily wake up from.'

'That's right. You need to be called. But Amelia never called me. I think she must have decided it was all over for us, and it would be better not to wake me, just to let me go on, unconscious of our fate, until, eventually, I was dead too. She was always so kind.'

'Kind? To let you die in your sleep?' Pema was incredulous.

'I still don't understand,' said Singay. 'How did she die?'

'I told you,' said Trout. 'She lost hope.'

'Nobody dies of losing hope!'

'Drivers do.'

And then Singay suddenly remembered all the way back to the day they'd first met Rose, inside the Mountain. He'd said, 'I don't lose hope, of course. That *would* be fatal.' And she'd thought he was just being dramatic, just using a figure of speech.

I should have known better.

'How *did* you wake up, then?' she asked. 'If Amelia couldn't call you anymore?'

'I heard, er, Rose,' said the young Driver. It was obvious the name still felt unfamiliar.

'You *heard* him? But you said you *couldn't* hear him! I thought—' Pema stopped abruptly and shivered, remembering the intensity of Rose's silent cry, just before the world fell apart.

Trout was remembering too.

'I can't tell you how awful it was – waking up, thinking, "But that's *him*! He's not dead – we can leave!" and almost in the same instant seeing her, and realising that *she* was dead, and our chances with her.' He rubbed a silvery hand across his face. 'You must think I'm bad, to have such thoughts. It isn't that I don't grieve for her – I do! – but I so want to go home!'

Pema put a hand on Trout's thin shoulder. 'Of course we don't think you're bad – not for a second,' he said reassuringly. 'Do we, Singay?'

There was a peculiar, still expression on Singay's face, and for a moment she didn't say anything.

'Singay?' Pema prompted.

'What? Oh no, we don't think you're bad,' she said abruptly. 'Not at all.'

'If only she'd been able to hold on,' the young Driver whispered.

Another voice interrupted. 'If you'd all just gather round . . .' It was the man with the broken arm. He was standing in the centre of the tank. He must have been some sort of shift leader, for even though he was starting to look really ill with the pain, the habit of authority was clearly stronger.

'You go, Pema,' said Singay. 'I want to stay here with Rose and Trout.' There was an odd note in her voice.

As he joined the edge of the crowd, Zamin appeared suddenly at Pema's elbow. He looked down at her. *I should hate you*, he thought wearily, *for what you did. But somehow I can't find the energy.*

'Where's your brother?' he asked instead.

'Za's gone to tie up a little unfinished business with Impeccable.'

'What? Where?' But then Pema saw Impeccable, skulking amongst the oilmen. He'd been hit on the forehead by something sharp and had blood all over his face, but he was alive. He'd come through the horror. He'd turned the world inside out and it had cost him no more than a scratch. Pema felt a wave of fury so fierce it made him feel sick. He forced himself to look away.

Standing in the centre of the tank, the shift leader was speaking.

'... still some hope. We have to remember, the Flats are – were – near enough *built* on boats. It's my belief some Flatters will have survived. Some Flatter boats will have survived too. It's only a matter of time before they come looking for us. When that happens, those of us who are still fit will stay put and the injured will be taken ashore first. I think we're safe here. I think all we need at this moment is patience. Meantime, we have some medical supplies. If you need help, line up here, and we'll have a look at injuries ...'

Without appearing to have moved, Impeccable was suddenly at the front of the queue. Pema turned away in disgust and started back to Singay and the Drivers.

'The man said they're expecting boats to come out, looking for survivors,' he told them. 'So we just stick tight till that happens. We'll have to wait till the ones that are hurt get off, of course, but then it'll be our turn to go to shore. Right?'

When Singay just shook her head at him, he had no idea why.

CHAPTER THIRTY-SEVEN

Singay's Choice

'Pema,' she said. 'I'm not going back to the shore. I'm going to go with Rose and Trout.'

Pema could feel his face freeze in a silly smile. *What on earth is she talking about?*

'I'm going to be the third Driver.'

It was as if she'd suddenly kicked him in the stomach. Her words tapped straight into the fury he'd just suppressed against Impeccable and shoved it out of his mouth.

'DON'T BE STUPID!' he yelled. Heads turned on the other side of the tank, but he didn't care. 'YOU'RE HUMAN!'

Singay flinched, then reached out, putting her hand for a moment on his arm.

'I know,' she said. 'But I don't have to be. Look, we've known from the very beginning that to save the world there needs to be three Drivers. Three to stop the Mountain forever, three to keep all the land from getting dragged back into the Sea until there's nothing left but those things, you know, the fossils. So, if I can become a Driver, the third Driver, and we can make things safe again, for everybody, then I have to do it, don't I? But – I want to be honest – there's more. Pema, how can I make you understand?' She looked down, struggling to find the words. 'It sounds so pathetic – so wrong-headed! – saying it out loud, but all my life, I've wanted to do something special. *Be* something special. Have a great adventure.' Her laugh was sad. 'And getting here, getting Rose to the Sea, you'd think that was enough of an adventure for anybody! But now I know *that* journey was just the beginning. I want to be a Driver, Pema – I want to do this. It's as if everything has finally come together, as if everything has been leading up to this. Even those awful dreams I kept having – Trout and Rose think I may already have some sort of an affinity. To rocks, you know? Like the way you are with animals? I *know* this is the thing for me to do. I ... do you understand? At all?' There was pleading in her eyes, but also a strength, a sureness, that he didn't remember ever seeing before. It made his heart hurt.

'You never needed to do *anything* to be special, Singay. You always just were. I can't believe you didn't know that.'

Singay just looked at him. She didn't answer. Desperately, Pema turned to the two Drivers. 'This is crazy talk, isn't it? How could it even be physically *possible*?' Distress made his words a wail. Rose didn't meet his eyes.

'Um, yes, it's perfectly possible,' said Trout nervously. 'It's just a question of mineral manipulation.' He took a step back from the flare of anger in Pema's face, but floundered on. 'Perhaps I could explain the process in terms of organic and inorganic proportions. Human and Driver anatomy have some things in common – the organic bits are surprisingly similar. However the *inorganic* bits aren't, and the ratio of organic to inorganic is where we differ the most.' He went on talking, explaining about the relation between the organic components in humans which kept them alive, 'and the inorganic ones that do the fine-tuning. With Drivers, it's the other way around. So with Singay, all we would need to do is encourage the mineral side of things and discourage the non-mineral side.'

'I haven't a clue what you're talking about and I don't think you do either.' Pema didn't care how rude he sounded or how upset the young Driver looked. He turned on Rose and snapped, 'You're very quiet through all this – what do you have to say for yourself? Well?'

Rose looked up, his face still pale, his eyes sad.

'Pema, go to the railing. Look out. Tell us what you see.'

No, Pema thought. *No!* He'd been aware the wind had picked up, and the obscuring mist was dispersing. He'd been aware that he could see the damage, see what the wave had done, but it felt like there was no room left in his brain for any more pain. *I don't want to go*, he thought, *I don't want to see*, but he went anyway. He clutched the railing with his hands so tightly his knuckles showed white, and he looked out over the world the wave had left.

The City and the Flats and the Wall were gone. The mud and fine palaces and the barrier between had been smashed and swept away. Where they had been was now a great basin of sea water, oil-slicked and uneasy, pierced with jagged metal that seemed to move in the swell, like twisted creatures in a death throe.

Pema could see rubble strewn onto the shore and floating thick on the waves and, bobbing about with the other detritus, the thing he had feared most to see and feared he would see forever, to the end of his own life – hundreds of corpses.

They were alive – they were all alive. He covered his face with his hands.

Rose's voice was gentle and inescapable.

'Trout and I won't abandon your world. We'll do our best, for as long as we have the strength. But two Drivers are just not enough. He and I can hold the Mountain steady for a time, but we can't *ground* it. We can't make it so it will never walk again. As we weaken and lose control, there will be earthquakes and tsunamis and destruction far worse than this, and the life that depends on green things will die as the mountains return to the Sea. We need to be three to finish what we came here to do, to make good again. We *need* Singay.'

Singay put her hand on Pema's shoulder. 'They need me. *We* need me – and I want to do it.'

I don't care. I don't care! He was desperate to argue and kick and scream, do *anything* to make Singay change her mind.

He looked into her face, and he knew there was nothing that would do that.

'Will it hurt?' he found himself asking instead. 'When you change her?'

'We won't let it.' Trout spoke solemnly. He was about to continue when, suddenly, Zamin and Za popped up with a money sack and smug expressions.

'Impeccable owed us,' Zamin said, as she poured a pile of coins into her hand. 'The rest is yours.' And she handed the sack to Singay.

Singay looked confused. 'I don't . . . what's this for?'

Zamin tutted. 'What do you *think* it's for? It's Rose's fee for doing Impeccable's job. Minus our finder's fee.'

'That's right – for finding the money sack in his pocket when he wasn't looking,' Za grinned.

And with that, they walked away.

Singay stared after them, spluttering, 'I . . . they . . . they really are the most incorrigible, barefaced . . .' She shook her head and then she handed the sack over to Pema.

'Here. Use it to get home. And then, if there's any left, maybe you could send it to the Abbey.'

Pema nodded.

'It can be a replacement for my dowry. Or they could send it back to my family. Whatever they think is best.'

Pema nodded again. He was looking at the sack in his hands as if he would never look at anything else again.

'Pema, please, talk to me!' Her voice broke on the words.

'All right. And when I do that – give them the money – what do you think I should tell them about *you?*' He looked up then and his eyes were hot and angry. 'Do I tell them I just *lost* you, somewhere along the way? Terribly careless of me, so sorry? You think they're just going to *accept* that?'

'No, of course not. You must tell them the truth. All of it.'

'They won't believe me.' He sounded sulky and tired now, as if the fight had suddenly gone out of him.

'I think they might,' said Singay slowly. 'Rose and Trout have got things steady again, in the short term, and when I'm fully a Driver, the three of us will be able to ground the Mountain and make it be still at last. But there will have been damage. Every time Rose lost control . . . Now, they'll be busy repairing, rebuilding, but still afraid of what might be coming next. I think they'll be happy to be told that it's all over!'

Pema shrugged. 'All right,' he said, but silently he was repeating her words.

It's all over.

There was nothing more to say, but when she took his hand, he didn't pull away.

After a time, rescue boats began to appear, moving cautiously through the metal-laced water, looking for survivors among the floating bodies and on the wrecks of tanks and rigs still standing. The top of their tank gradually cleared. Impeccable (apparently not yet aware that he had been robbed) was one of the first to go, making sure up to the very end that he had at least three other people between him and the group he'd coerced here with him. Later they noticed Za and Zamin leaving, and saw that they'd teamed up with the Flatter man who'd originally urged them up onto the tank. And then the time came when the four looked around and found they were alone.

A single seagull had returned to the sky overhead, its desolate cry hanging in the air.

'Pema, you should go now,' said Singay. 'Please. I don't want you to watch.' Her eyes were enormous and solemn.

Pema started to protest, but then he realised he didn't want to be there either. He didn't want to watch Singay changed from the girl he knew into something else. *No, I mean SOMEONE else. I never thought of Rose as a thing. Why would it be any different with Singay? Am I becoming like those awful people at Cliffton, who hate anyone who isn't just like them?* He knew he didn't hate Singay. He just ... didn't want to watch.

She was looking at him as if she understood every twist and turn his mind was taking.

'Goodbye.' Her voice was husky. 'And don't worry, I'll mind my manners – I won't talk with my nose full!'

Pema tried to manage a grin, and failed.

There was so much unsaid between them. She was the first girl he'd ever loved and he'd only just admitted to himself that he did love her and he'd never even kissed her.

And then she stepped up and kissed him.

It was the sweetest, saddest thing that had ever happened to him.

'And I mean it, too,' she added. Then she and Trout, who looked as if he were about to cry and could only half lift a hand in farewell, walked away to the far side of the tank.

And then it was Rose's turn.

'I don't know what to say,' said the Driver plaintively. 'I'm so full of feelings I can barely feel a thing – do you know what I mean?'

Pema nodded, thinking, *That must be it. That must be what this numbness is about.* 'It's hard. Before all this, I'd lived my whole life knowing that everybody I'd ever met would, more or less, always be there. And then I met *you* and since then ...'

'It's been final farewells and goodbye forevers, right, left and centre!' Rose shook his head ruefully. 'I'm really sorry about that.'

'I'm not saying I'd have missed it,' Pema said, trying to

understand,' because I wouldn't have. Not for *anything*. I'm just saying . . .'

'It's hard. I know.'

There was an awkward pause.

'A handshake seems a bit formal. How about a hug?' Pema suggested.

'Yes. And some words. Just a few, but none of them should be goodbye or any variation of goodbye, agreed?' said Rose.

'No farewell or cheerio or anything like that.'

'No, just . . . *Travel well*. Yes, just that and no more.'

'All right. Shall we do it now?'

'Yes. Now.'

Solemnly they hugged. Earnestly they said, in unison, 'Travel well!' Manfully they turned on their heels and walked away, straight of back and firm of purpose.

Pema had started down the metal staircase when he heard Rose's voice, high-pitched with a new excitement.

'I know – I could make a *legend* out of us. Us and the journey. A Driver legend! I've never made a legend before!'

It sounded just so like the old Rose, so enthusiastic and childlike, before the irradiant sickness had made him strange and sad, that Pema had to smile.

He was still smiling when he reached the bottom of the stairs, and a passing rescue boat hailed him.

'Come on, lad! We've room for one more.'

He stepped into the laden boat and, for a moment, couldn't understand why one of the men offered him his handkerchief.

It was only then that he realised his face was wet with tears.

CHAPTER THIRTY-EIGHT

The Return

The journey north was slow, painfully slow, and weary. Pema carried a weight of loss that bowed his shoulders and made his legs heavy, but still he aimed himself at home.

Everywhere he looked, he saw people in flux, in the aftermath of the tremors and earthquakes. Some were rebuilding, mending, adapting. Some were on the road, looking for new beginnings. It was as if the world had been stirred up with a gigantic spoon.

So many people. So turbulent.

Now that the Mountain has stopped walking, there won't be any new land for them, yet they'll go on having children, becoming more and more, and using up more and more of what the green wedge has to offer. How long would it be before the pressure of numbers sent them onto the plateau, into the Jungle, into the High Lands, even into the desert beyond? Would they wait until they were desperate, and then act the way desperate people do? Sometimes his thoughts made him moan out loud. His fellow travellers gave him a wide berth.

He spoke to no one in all that press of people. He sometimes felt a jolt run through his body when he thought he saw someone he knew – someone like Bob from the *Aubergine* looming out of a crowd, or Dasu the dugg running past his feet – or thought he heard Lady Allum's neighing laugh or Ma Likpa's sharp shrilling. It was always an error, but he knew that if it had been true, he would have turned away without a word. And if a stranger or a place or a scent reminded him even for a second of Singay or of Rose, his chest tightened unbearably. He put all thoughts of them behind doors in his mind and turned the key.

He took boats when he could, and walked the rest. He ate when he remembered, though there was no savour in the food. At night his dreams were haunted with images of home and his grandparents and all the different ways they could have been hurt, harmed, obliterated. So many different ways. By day he did his best to push the images away and focus on the next step, the next league. But in his dreams they were always there.

One night, he woke from his restless sleep to a strange sight. He saw what seemed to be a shooting star in reverse, an arc of impossibly bright light angling up and away across the dark sky. It came from the direction of the Sea.

The last snow of winter was falling, soft and cold, as Pema climbed the final stretch to home.

The Mountain was safely grounded now, committed to the slow changes worked by wind and water and no other. Everywhere there were signs of the destruction Singay had seen in her dreams. Only Pema knew how much worse it could have been.

But what about his grandparents? Had Dawa and Wadipa survived the throes of the Mountain?

For so long he'd fought against the images in his mind, of them hurt or dead, of the farm swallowed up by a sudden chasm or buried under falling rock. The closer he got to home, the harder it became to push those thoughts away. Now, as he climbed the final path, he could barely breathe.

Snowflakes landed on his face like cold feathers.

They'll be there. They must be there. I'll be seeing them very soon.

But then what? What would he say to them? What *could* he say? They would never understand what had happened during all the months he'd been gone, and yet they deserved an explanation of his long absence. He'd sent them the letter, of course, right at the very start of it all, but that told so little – the journey had barely begun when he'd written that!

Time and again, he'd tried to put a story together in his mind, something that would satisfy them, reassure them, not upset them with its strangeness, but nothing he came up with rang true.

My chest hurts.

'Pema? *Pema?*'

It was his grandmother, coming round the corner of the house, her arms full of pine branches for the gows. She stumbled forward and for a heart-stopping moment just stood there, a few paces away. Then she dropped the branches with a strangled cry and wrapped him in a hug. For the rest of Pema's life, the resiny scent of pine would bring that moment back to him, in tiny flashes of its original warming intensity.

He hadn't cried for so many leagues. Not even when he'd watched the Driver comet rising up into the sky and known, all over again, that Rose was gone and Singay was lost to him. He'd had no tears to give. But in Dawa's hard, old arms, he cried like a child. And when she finally let him go, the doors in his mind were ajar, and the pain in his chest had started to ease.

Then Wadipa was there too. He'd heard Dawa call out from the garden. Pema couldn't help noticing he seemed smaller and more bent, but there was nothing wrong with the strength of his hug.

'Stop – you're crushing the boy!' Dawa scolded, laughing.

'Come in, come in, what are you thinking of, woman, he must be famished!' Wadipa's voice was husky. 'I'll wager he hasn't had a decent meal since he left. There's someone else inside who'll be happy to see you too. That is, if we can get him to wake up long enough to notice.'

'Who . . . ?' Pema couldn't think who it might be, until he was bustled indoors and saw the basket, set in the cosiest corner by the fire. A mound of soft brown fur was curled up in it, rising and falling gently with each breath.

'Jeffrey!'

His grandparents gazed fondly at the sleeping marmole.

'One of the Sisters brought him down to us from the Abbey,' explained Dawa. 'We wondered if he'd stay with us, when he didn't find you here.'

Wadipa snorted. 'Of course he stayed! Why should he go and sleep in a cold hole in the ground when he can nest in front of the fire wrapped up in the remains of my old best shirt, with as many meals a day as his greedy heart desires?'

'No, the marmole was waiting for you. He knew you'd be back.' There was only the slightest hint of a quaver in

Dawa's voice as she said this. 'You don't think he'd have got this fat if there'd be anything for him to worry about, now, do you?' She prodded Jeffrey with her toe and, eyes still tight shut, he wrapped himself around her ankle, as far as he *could* wrap himself, and pretended to savage it. It was obvious they adored each other, and Pema had a sudden pang of something that felt a lot like jealousy. Then the marmole disentangled himself and waddled over, chittering to be picked up, and Pema had him in his hands again, and felt the warmth of his fur, and smelled that sweet, fresh-grass smell.

'I've so much to tell you,' he said. As he began, the doors in his mind opened, one after another, and all the careful lies he'd been planning evaporated like so much mountain mist. He told them everything, rediscovering it all as he did so. The return journey had taken it away from him. Now he had it back again.

The story took the rest of the day to tell, and Pema knew he'd be answering questions for weeks to come. But for now, he was talked out. Dawa brought him another plate of food and watched him eat. He smiled at her.

'I want to hear everything that's happened *here*,' he said with his mouth full. 'But first, I think I'll just sleep for a year.'

'That's right,' said Dawa. 'Finish that and off to your bed. It's waiting for you. Just one thing, though. I know you said we mustn't speak of the things you wrote to us. But the Sister – I can't remember her name just at the minute, but she was the one who brought Jeffrey down to us – we showed her your letter, Pema. She was so worried about the girl, Singay, so worried and sad. We wanted to put her mind at rest.'

'And did it? Was she upset? About the Mountain? And Rose and the Drivers and the rest?'

'Now I asked her that myself. It seemed to me possible she might be distressed. But she wasn't at all. I remember exactly what she said to me. She laughed, and she said, "Dawa, do you take me for a fool? Why would I be upset at finding that the world is even more amazing than I already thought?"'

Dawa patted Pema on the shoulder and smiled.

'Off with you, now. Rest well.'

Wadipa and Dawa sat either side of the hearth, savouring the heat of the fire. Pema had gone away to his bed under the eaves. For the first time in many months, they were not alone in their house anymore. It felt strange.

'Good to have him back,' murmured Wadipa.

Dawa nodded, staring into the flames.

'Did you notice, he didn't once knock anything over? Or bang his head? Or drop a plate?' he added. 'Grown into himself, he has.' There was a pause and then, 'It was good to hear the rest of the story.'

Dawa nodded again.

'You didn't tell him about the Abbey. About it being destroyed in the quake.'

'No. Tomorrow, maybe. Or the next day.'

'Well, I'm away to bed. You'll bank the fire?' Wadipa got up stiffly. The cold seemed to be getting into his bones

lately in a way it'd never done before. He hadn't said anything to Dawa.

'The gows'll be pleased he's back,' he said.

Dawa gave him a look that suggested she knew exactly
what had gone on in his head. She usually did.

'I'll be up in a while,' was all she said, however. Then,
as he left the room, she called after him, 'It *is* good, to have
him back.'

She looked down at the ragged shirt in her lap, then up
towards Pema's room.

'For as long as it lasts . . .' she added softly, but only the
fire heard her words.

CHAPTER THIRTY-NINE

The Scent of Nutmeg

It was some years later, and far from the cold, white peace of a High Land home. The air was gritty and hot and harsh, and for hours now it had been whipping itself up into a frenzy of noise and fury. It would be hard to recognise the younger Pema in the thin, battered figure who staggered forward through the screaming storm. He was wrapped to the eyes in the clothes of a desert man, and still the biting sand got through to scour his skin and make each grating breath feel as if he would never draw another. He had been travelling for a long time, and the sandstorm had come out of nowhere. He was at the end of his strength. When he fell forward onto his face, he didn't get up.

Almost as suddenly as it had appeared, the storm blew itself out, and a spectacular sunset blazed up across half the sky. The hump of sand that was Pema didn't see its splendour, or the way the light gilded the southern mountains, or the swathed figure on a camel that came towards him from the north. He might have not seen *anything* ever again, if the camel hadn't sensed there was something still (just) alive under that particular mound and ambled over to investigate.

When Pema came to several hours later, it was dark night, he was lying on the ground wrapped in a stripy blanket, and the light from a fire revealed two faces peering down at him with keen interest. One was the camel's, and the other belonged to a young woman.

She was a stranger to him. *Of course she is,* he thought blearily. *I'm not likely to meet up with some old neighbour way out here.*

She was beautiful. She had fair skin that showed almost translucent in the firelight. She had pale eyes the colour of winter milk, except for a startlingly bright blue ring round the irises. He'd never seen eyes like that before. She had hair like a mantle of night flowing around her shoulders. She leaned closer to him.

'Who *are* you?' she said. She smelled of nutmeg.

Pema laughed, a hoarse, slightly hysterical sound, and then managed to whisper, 'I'm Pema. And I've been looking for you ...'

THE END

Notes from the Author

Bhutanese-based Names
(Sharchokpa-lo dialect)

It's strange, how ideas can lodge in your brain. Years ago I met a woman called Jamie Zeppa, who'd been living and working in Bhutan. She said that in the Sharchokpa-lo dialect, which she'd been learning, her name meant 'beetroot', and she showed me a ragged, randomly organised booklet that was the only Sharchokpa-lo–English dictionary available at that time. When it came to writing *Walking Mountain*, I knew that the names I needed for people and places were in that booklet. She lent it to me and I spent a long train journey reading it and taking notes and grinning with excitement as I discovered each perfect word.

And, just so you know, Zeppa from Jungle Head is not like Jamie at all – they just share a name.

Borang – Jungley forest
Dasu – Ker's dugg – his name means little
Dawa – Means moon, because the moon is made of cheese
Gata – Tea kettle
Geyma – Lost or thrown away – in other words, Granny
    Geyma is Granny Garbage

Jathang – Means the plains, which is where this people originally lived, before agriculture and the growth of settled populations drove them onto the plateau

Jopi – Pointed

Kerkerbabu (Ker for short) – Cricket

Klepsang Zale – To make a profit

Phophor – Puffed rice, so Madam Phophor is Mrs Puffed Rice

Ma Likpa – Cruel, not loving, not nice

Noksam – Sudden idea

Pema – Lotus

Shisha – Shepherd

Singay – Snow lion

Sister Grale – To like food

Sister Khalu – Bitter

Sister Loong – Stone

Sister Menpa – Doctor

Sister Shing – Wood

Sister Yi-mala – Means very roughly, 'Blood? No!'

Wadipa – Cow

Za and Zamin – Boy and girl

Zeppa – Beetroot

Other Names

Amelia – Named after Amelia Earhart, the pioneering aviatrix

Sister Hodges – The falconer, named after another famous falconer in another world

Trout – Named after the fish

Animals and Plants

Some of these animals and plants are unknown to us. Others are like, but also unlike, those we see around us. Some divergence is inevitable, because even when conditions are similar, evolution never produces exactly the same things twice.

Botatoes – An enormously versatile vegetable, like our potato, but without the pesky eyes

Celeriac – An odd vegetable in any world

Dentrice – A creature with no equivalent in our world. Not large, but with more teeth in proportion to its body size than any other animal in existence

Dugg – Pronounced as the Scots do – 'dug'

Eels – Many different types of eels thrive in the mud and muck of the Flats: the Cutthroat Eel, not to be confused with the Muddy Cutthroat Eel, the Sawtooth Eel, the Witch Eel and, of course, the Vomerine Eel that has teeth not only in the usual places but also in the roof of its mouth

Ferreck – Because it would be a sad world indeed that didn't have something like ferrets in it

Fur snake – Its pelt enables it to thrive in the cold temperatures at high altitude

Gow – Smaller than our cows and with a wider diet, but otherwise very similar. They are essentially mountain beasts, small and sure-footed like groats, but far prettier, with much nicer eyes, and none of the groat's more questionable personality traits. In summer, they are capable of clambering after patches of grass on the steepest cliff face, and are happiest grazing on the tiny jewel-like meadows scattered about the mountainside. Their winter fodder is a combination of hay and finely chopped pine branches, which they somehow manage to digest. What little milk they produce during the winter months has a wonderfully fresh pine scent to it. Wintercheese is a particular High Land delicacy

Groat – More or less goats, with all that that implies

Grunt – Unlike our pigs, which are difficult to drive over long distances, grunts have a highly developed herd hierarchy and are good travellers, with a strong homing instinct. The closest equivalent in terms of colour would be our red-coated Tamworth

Ice Eagle – A similar size to our Golden Eagle, with blood particularly rich in red blood cells, adapted for the thinner air of the High Lands

Killstrel – Delicate tabby-marked bird of prey, arch nemesis of mice, but will if desperate tackle a marmole

Lesser Spotted Trumpeting Butterfly – Feeding exclusively on the nectar of the rare Tarantella Orchid, it is the only known species whose voice is audible to humans. At full volume, this rare, pretty butterfly's voice is about as loud as the proverbial pin dropping

Marmole – A finely-furred rodent, larger than a marmoset, prettier than a prairie dog

Minkey Monkeys – Like our Spider Monkeys in appearance, but with added diarrhoea

Rabbid – A few similarities with rabbits in appearance and general size and shape but with important differences

– a red tail, for example, and a level of ferocity well beyond anything our bunnies aspire to

Rhinophant – Just the way it sounds

Salad Panda – One of the few mammals ever to have mas-
tered the art of being green

Scorplion – Creature of the plateau, a shaggy-maned lizard
with a sting in the tail

Shup – The differences between our sheep and a shup are
evident only on the genetic level

Strombomble – A raspberry-strawberry with a slight hint
of guava

Tarantellas – Large, black, hairy spiders which hypnotise
their prey by dancing

Tarantella Orchid – A rare orchid, black and hairy and
shaped, for reasons of its own, like a Tarantella Spider

Wulf – The Mountain Wulf is a small but very efficient
predator, with a luxuriant pelt to cope with the extreme
cold of the heights. The Plateau Wulf is only distantly
related, substantially larger and less furry, and is one of
the few mammals to have developed the ability to produce venom

Also available by Joan Lennon from BC Books

SILVER SKIN

Shortlisted for the
Scottish Teenage Book Prize 2017

ISBN: 978 1 78027 284 9
£6.99

Skara Brae, Orkney, the end of the Stone Age. The sun is dying, storms batter the coast and people fear the end of the world. When Rab crawls out of the sea wearing the remains of his Silver Skin, he throws the islanders into confusion. Who is he? Why has he come?

Voy, the village wise woman, is certain he's a selkie, a source of new power. Cait isn't so sure.

Rab, thousands of years from home, injured and desperate, must learn fast about this ancient world. What started as a high-tech study trip has turned into a struggle to survive.

Praise for Joan Lennon's *Silver Skin*

'A skilful mix of sci-fi, historical thriller and romance with interesting, believable characters. This is a book that will stay with readers for a long time'
Lovereading4kids

'A beautiful and mesmeric tale'
The Herald

'A brilliant blend of ancient and modern with characters who are perfectly of their time'
Parents in Touch

'Has all the ingredients of a prehistoric transcendental romance'
Scotland Magazine

'An imaginative and gripping tale ... very enjoyable and highly recommended'
Scottish Home and Country

'A weird but wonderful fantasy book'
The Guardian

'Joan Lennon writes with humour, clarity, sympathy'
The Times

An extract from *Silver Skin*

Rab: Age of the Alexander Decision, Tower Stack 367–74/ Level 56, Delta Grid, Northwest Europasia

'Oh, come on – not a storm as well!' moaned Rab, but his friends just laughed.

'You can do it, Rab!'

'Bet you're wishing you still had that knife, eh?'

Chillingly realistic rain was now drenching all the participants, but none of the others were having to wrestle with a wolf at the same time.

'Com? Com! I could do with some help here!' said Rab, desperately trying to keep the wolf from closing its jaws on him. It was growling continuously and its breath stank disconcertingly of half-digested meat.

'As your friend suggests, your options at this point are substantially fewer since you broke the knife at the last level,' said his Com. It was sounding smug, since it had advised strongly against using a knife on a rhinophant. It was also safe from the wind and the rain, lodged in Rab's wrist unit.

'Yeah, yeah. Get on with it.'

'So at this point you could either a) strangle the beast, which, given the average historical thickness of wolf neck fur and the digital reach and compressible strength of your hands, has only a zero point six per cent chance of success, or b) engage Vulcanski's Pack-Mind Manipulation Gaze. Since the Gaze is almost certainly fictional I have no statistics on the likelihood of its success, but it would certainly have the element of surprise.'

'That's all you've got?'

'Yes.'

Rab groaned as the wolf arched suddenly and almost wrenched itself free.

'Or . . .' said his Com.

'OR WHAT?!'

'Or you could just let go and see what happens.'

Thanks, thought Rab. He tried to remember what he knew about the Vulcanski Gaze. *I think there's no blinking.* He shifted himself round until he could see the wolf's eyes. The close quarters made it go squinty. *And then I pour all my innate superiority into its skull – no doubts, no uncertainty – I'm the Alpha male – that's me, not you – you are inferior – you are inferior – you are . . .*

The wolf burped, but showed no other sign of being intimidated.

'Hey, Rab! Your mum's here,' one of his friends called.

Rab risked a glance over to the observation booth. His mum was waving something – a package – at him. But while the simulation programme was running, she couldn't come in.

'Work with me here,' Rab whispered so only the wolf could hear. 'My mum's watching . . .'

There was a brief pause while the wolf thought about this. Rab had the distinct impression it was reliving moments of its own cubhood. A look passed between them, and Rab carefully loosened his grip . . .

In elaborate slow motion, the wolf lowered its head, tucked its tail between its legs, flattened its ears. Rab maintained his gaze. The wolf began to back away . . .

'Look at that!' said his Com. 'It's working!'

And the wolf disappeared.

Rab leapt into the air. 'Yay! Ha! Me – ONE. Canis lupus – NIL. Rab is OFF the menu!' And he pranced across the floor, doing a wild gangly victory dance. The others joined in, three young men who had momentarily forgotten their dignity.

From the observation room, Rab's mum smiled at her tall brown son. He'd been working so hard, for so long – she couldn't remember the last time he'd just taken the time out to be silly. His friends too, of course. They'd all been studying and researching and writing and analysing – whatever their chosen subjects, they were all desperate to acquire enough credits to move out of their parents' spaces. Ever square centimetre of living space in every tower stack in the world had to be earned.

She glanced down at the package she was carrying.

Rab deserved the best chance, the best equipment his mother could provide. And the *Retro-Dimensional Time Wender with Full Cloaking Capability* – the one they called the Silver Skin – was it. It was the future of historical research. It was what her Rab needed to move ahead. To move out.

She tried to imagine what it would be like to have her space to herself again, after all these years, but her mind shied away.

Her Com heard her sigh. 'I know,' it said. 'But it's time.'

And then Rab came in, freshly sanitized and glowing with excitement.

'It's *come?*' he yipped.

'It's come?' echoed his Com, going squeaky.

'It's come.' And she handed Rab the package.

He stared at it, his brown eyes wide. The reports

– *first-hand* reports, not just something from sources – he could produce with a cutting edge tool like the Silver Skin – it would be amazing . . . His studies in history so far had got him on the way to a tiny unit of his own, but with this, who knows – he might even manage a window!

'Mum – *thank* you!' And he enveloped her in a rare, rough hug. A tiny part of his mind wondered, *When did she get so small?* But the rest was too excited to do anything but repeat over and over, *My own place! I'm going to earn my own place!*

Rab's Com had downloaded the extended manual and kept trying to read it aloud to him. 'The suit will protect us from danger – weapons discharged, for example, even at close quarters, will not be able to penetrate our molecular structure because of the sideways displacement – projectiles will simply pass through the space we'll be occupying, or *not* occupying – would you like me to read you the bit with the quantum physics?'

Rab raised a hand. 'No, no. That's fine.'

His Com sighed.

Rab sighed too. He was passionate about history and ecstatic about his new bit of kit, but he couldn't care less about its innards. He knew enough about the new time travel to know that it was ridiculously technical, but the basic premise boiled down to this: a traveller's position remained constant and time passed by them, rather than the other way around. So instead of Rab moving back and forth in time, time moved back and forth around Rab. Which was all fine and good, but so far he was just moving *himself* back and forth, in the tiny bit of his mum's unit where he slept.

'Come ON!' he groaned. The Silver Skin was lying there on his bed, shimmering tantalizingly. His Com just clicked at him and went on with its calculations. So Rab went back to pacing – three up, three back, three up, three back.

Ever since they'd first heard rumours about the Silver Skin – first started fantasizing about getting hold of one – Rab and his Com and his friends and *their* Coms had been arguing about which period of history it could be best used on.

The others all liked the Catastrophe Ages best, when things fell apart and the world teetered on the brink of annihilation – and Rab was tempted too. The Nadir, the Flood, the time referred to as The Bulge, just before the Alexander Decision finally managed to put a cap on the world's runaway over-population – near-disasters were always exciting, especially now that everything was so safe.

But the time for idle speculating was over. It was time to make a choice.

'If we want this to get noticed, we'd need something that hasn't already been done to death.'

'Pre-Nadir, then, do you think? But that still leaves an awful lot of history.'

'Something that's far enough back in time that there isn't a lot of vid evidence already available. Something like . . . Com! I did that project – remember? – on the First Industrial Revolution? That was Victorian – and they didn't even *have* vids. Or wait, no, they were just inventing cameras and stuff, but they were rubbish. No sound, no temperature control, no colour, single point of view – nothing.'

They discussed it back and forth, getting more and more excited. There were so many aspects of the time period that would be utterly fascinating to study at first hand. How could they possibly choose just one?

It was his Com who came up with the idea of Victorian archaeology.

'It was pretty much the beginning of that, wasn't it? Properly, I mean, not just bashing in, looting the gold, making wild guesses?'

Rab was delighted. 'That's *it* – but we won't do the sites everybody's heard about already. Not Egypt or China or Atlantis. Someplace obscure . . .'

And then it hit them.

'Someplace like right here?'

It was a brilliant idea. Every bit of the world had history of some sort – and the location of Tower Stack 367-74 was no exception. Fifty-six floors down was the site of the Orcadian Islands from long, long ago.

'Right under our feet!' His Com began to download co-ordinates into the Silver Skin's arm panel. 'Time: 1850, the year of the discovery of a Stone Age village which became known as Skara Brae. Place: what was then called Orkney and is now called – *here*! Stack 367-74, Delta Grid, Northwest Europasia. We'll use the big storm that winter – the one that blew away the sand, uncovering the village for the first time in thousands of years – as the anchor point. Neap tide. Full moon. Factor in a test stop . . . mid Deluvian . . .'

Rab wasn't really listening to the details. 'This is going to be amazing – they didn't have Coms or scanners or infra-beige – nothing! Just shovels and little brushes!'

'And now, it's time to download me!'

As the Com's download into the arm panel proceeded, the suit began to change. It shimmered more quickly, in and out of focus, like a heat wave or a mist. It was there, but only just.

Rab frowned. 'Are you sure it's my size? It's starting to look small.'

'What? Oh, don't worry. It will individualise to you when you put it on. It'll fit you like a second skin.'

Exactly like a second skin.

'I have to be naked?'

'Of course,' said his Com. 'The suit needs to make a perfect seal with your skin in order to function properly. It draws energy from your specific electrical field, for one thing, and for another, the cloaking mechanism is extremely finely tuned – even a millimetre out of alignment and it starts to fluctuate.'

'But . . .'

'Look at it this way – would you rather have a suit which makes you invisible, or one that leaves a pair of underpants walking about in history? I'm not at all sure Queen Victoria would approve.'

Rab was tempted. 'Is that *possible*?'

'No, of course not. Don't be silly. The suit just wouldn't work.'

'Spoilsport.'

He put it on. It was perfectly comfortable, and when he checked in the mirror, it covered him in mistiness up to the neck, while his head remained perfectly in focus.

'You won't be properly invisible until the helmet is on. That comes out of the suit when you press the button on the arm panel, there. The only tricky bit is making sure you keep your eyes open, otherwise you'll be stuck with them shut. Since anything touching your eyes makes them blink automatically, you'll need to apply a short-term response paralyser to your eyelids . . .'

'But won't my eyes dry out?'

'No,' said his Com. 'The suit provides lubrication as required. I can explain how, if you'd like . . .'

'No! No, that's all right,' said Rab, reaching for the paralyser and applying it to the outer corners of his eyelids.

'Excellent, excellent,' muttered his Com. 'Now press the helmet initiator on your arm panel . . . Here it comes!'

Rab felt something cool, almost like liquid, rising from the neck of the suit, up under his chin and onto his face, but as it covered his mouth and nose he couldn't help struggling for breath.

'Calm down – just breathe normally.' He could hear his Com's voice through the helmet's earpiece. 'The helmet draws oxygen from the surroundings, cleans it, and expels carbon dioxide as you breathe out. There, the seal's complete . . . It's not bad now, is it?'

And, really, it wasn't. Rab found that once he stopped *thinking* about breathing, he could do it just as if he weren't wearing anything over his face at all. He moved his arms experimentally and walked up and down a little.

'This is great!' He could speak without difficulty.

'Right. Now, you'll be able to move about without being detected, as long as you're careful not to knock into anything – or anyone. Remember, the Non-Intervention Contract's no joke. You can observe but you cannot interact. The clause on fines – well, put it this way, you'll be living in your mother's clothes closet from now to eternity and still be in debt. Oh, and remember you won't be able to eat or drink anything while the suit's sealed, or, um, excrete anything either, but since the recommended first session is no more than two hours, that shouldn't be a problem.'

'I know, I know – are we ready?'

'There *are* more checks we really should do, this being our first go . . .' But the longing in his Com's voice was clear.

Rab grinned and with a big theatrical flourish, he brought his right arm up and over, finger heading for the control panel on his left forearm, and –

– a high-pitched whistling sounded in his ears – his vision blurred – he felt his stomach drop –

The blurring before his eyes cleared abruptly and Rab found he was squinting into bright sunlight – and the floor had disappeared! He was suspended high in the air over an enormous expanse of sparkling sea. He yelped and reached for something to catch hold of, but there was nothing there to grab.

His Com sighed in his earpiece. 'What did I say? Test stop, mid Deluvian, remember? Time moves around you, not the other way around, so if you start out 56 floors up in a tower stack and you go back to a time before the stack was built . . .?'

'Yeah, all right. I forgot. This is – this is *amazing* . . .'

The Deluvian Period had taken place during the height of the ocean rise, when the part of the Northwest Europasian continent that he lived in – *would* live in! – had been completely submerged.

'Look!'

Floating settlements undulated on the silvery winter swell below him like vast mats of seaweed, anchored to the mountains lying out of sight under the surface.

'Can't we go in closer?'

But his Com was already humming to itself in the way it did when it was happily engaged in calculations.

'Not today, not today. Here we go again . . . 19th century . . . 1850 . . .'

The blurring returned. Rab thought, *And next there'll be the I–just–lost–my–stomach thing and the whistling and then . . .*

He swore. 'SCUT! Com? *WHAT—?!*'

This was different – this was worse – much, *much* worse – the whistling was rising higher and higher, louder, a shriek that clawed at his ears – there was a blinding flash – a jolt that made his teeth rattle in his head – the shriek became a roar – Rab tried to shield himself but his arms wouldn't move. Just at the edge of hearing, he could make out his Com crying, '*This isn't right – this isn't supposed to—*' From nowhere something grabbed Rab in an enormous fist and squeezed, hard, so hard he felt his bones grind on one another and his eyes bulged and all the air rushed out of his lungs. His mouth opened and closed uselessly, like a stranded fish – darkness began to swallow him up – then, as if from far away, he heard his Com screaming into the black,

'WE'RE GOING DOWN – 19TH CENTURY – MAYDAY – MAYDAY—'